Red Alert

Elise Noble

Published by Undercover Publishing Limited

Copyright © 2017 Elise Noble

v1

ISBN: 978-1-910954-59-1

Edited by Amanda Ann Larson

Cover art by Abigail Sins

www.undercover-publishing.com

www.elise-noble.com

Music is what feelings sound like.

CHAPTER 1

I'D DIED AND gone to hell. Okay, maybe hell was a bit of an exaggeration, but I'd landed in limbo at least. Where else would a small man in a sparkly red waistcoat with devil horns perched on top of his afro be playing ping pong across his desk? Each horn had a butterfly perched on the end, and two more were clipped to his lapels.

I hesitated in the doorway, about to back away when a ball flew past, missing my ear by a whisper.

The ball was swiftly followed by a paddle, and by some miracle, I caught it.

"Come on, join in!" the man shouted. "Myrna needs all the help she can get."

The blonde's pigtails smacked her in the face as she whipped her head around to look at me, her expression half surprise, half grimace.

The man—Ishmael, my new boss—snapped his fingers. "Myrna! Concentrate."

She frantically tried to return his shots as I stepped forward, fast regretting my choice of footwear. What with my new job being in fashion and all, I'd worn four-inch LK Bennetts and a Calvin Klein pencil skirt, neither of which lent themselves to exercise. I glanced enviously at Myrna's ballet flats. If only—

The ping pong ball zipped in my direction, and I

shielded my face with the bat. *Pop.* The ball bounced off it and landed in a glass of water.

Nice one, Tia.

Ishmael didn't miss a beat. He simply fished a spare ball out of his desk drawer and whacked it straight at me. At least this time I managed to hit it back in his direction. All those tennis lessons Mother insisted I take as a kid had paid off at last.

"Move faster," Myrna muttered under her breath.

After a minute or two, I kicked off my heels, which at least saved me from breaking an ankle. Ishmael bounced around like a monkey on speed, and at one point, he had a paddle in each hand and three balls in play while I puffed worse than an out-of-shape nicotine addict.

Then a cuckoo popped out of a clock on the wall, and Ishmael stopped mid-stride.

"Half past eight," he announced. "Time to start the day."

My stay of execution had ended.

He walked towards me, hand extended and fingers down. Was I supposed to shake it or kiss it?

"Don't worry. I won't bite," he said. "Not at work, anyway. My lawyers tell me off."

I gripped his hand and shook, and despite his exertions, I was the one sweating.

"Hi." One word and my voice still managed to tremble.

"So, you're Tia?"

"That's right."

"Bradley said you'd be coming today. And not a moment too soon, I must add. Since J'Nae left, I haven't had anyone to throw things at."

I swayed a little as the blood drained out of my face, but he just laughed. What the hell had Bradley got me into?

"Well, I need my power nap," Ishmael said, dropping his paddles onto the desk. "Myrna will find you something to do."

He flounced off, leaving me with Miss Pigtails, who peered at me over her glasses. Nice to meet you too, lady.

"Take a seat," she said, motioning at the pristine white leather sofa behind us.

I sank back, sucking in a ragged breath now Ishmael had disappeared and I didn't need to pretend to be fitter than a potato. Hell, I was so out of shape Internet Explorer could run faster than me.

Was it too late to go home?

My chest seized the instant I had that thought, because where was home now? Not England where I'd spent my childhood or Virginia where I'd been so happy until recently. The rather vague employment contract the receptionist downstairs had made me fill out said I lived in Tribeca, but that was just where I ate and slept.

Home isn't a place; it's the people in it, my sort-of-sister, Emmy, always used to tell me. Which meant I was homeless, because the man I'd once shared my life with was gone.

Remember, remember the fifth of November,
Gunpowder, treason and plot.

We see no reason
Why gunpowder treason
Should ever be forgot!

My descent into Satan's playground officially began on the fifth of November last year, with the gunpowder, the treason, and the plot, even if I wasn't there to see the fireworks.

And I'd certainly never forget the aftermath.

First came fury. I'd lashed out at everyone close to me with jagged words and clenched fists, but that initial burst of fire was soon followed by a crippling numbness. I didn't get out of bed for a week.

Then came the funeral, swiftly followed by the guilt. Guilt that my last words to Ryan had been angry ones. Guilt that I hadn't given him the support he needed and deserved. And as time passed, guilt when I stopped thinking of him every minute of every hour of every day.

And what drowned out the guilt? That's right—alcohol.

In only a month, I'd been arrested five times for drunk and disorderly. A record, possibly, but not one I was particularly proud of breaking.

Before the fifth of November, my brother would have yelled long and loud at me for that behaviour, but after Ryan died? Luke spoke quiet, measured words through gritted teeth, his eyes filled with pity. That was the worst part. The pity.

I went through the motions at Christmas and slunk away before the ball dropped on New Year's Eve. Every smile drove nails through my heart, and to me, my friends' laughter sounded like the *clank, clank, clank* of chains tightening around my chest.

I didn't want to be at the Riverley estate that night, but I was too tipsy to drive back to the apartment Luke shared with his wife, Mack.

"Aren't you staying up to see in the new year?" my best friend, Lottie, asked as she passed me in the hallway, glass in hand.

"I don't feel like celebrating."

She pulled me into a drunken hug. "Aw, I'm so sorry. You want me to come sit with you?"

And miss out on the party? She'd dealt with her own nightmare over the past few years, and she deserved to have some fun, not to mention a midnight kiss with her new boyfriend, Nigel.

"I'll be fine. I'm just gonna go to bed."

"As long as you're sure?"

Stop with the pity. I knew she meant well, but I just wanted to be treated like a normal person rather than Tia-whose-boyfriend-died, or I'd never be able to get on with my life.

"I'm sure."

My old room in Little Riverley felt icy tonight. It was the first time I'd slept in there since Ryan died, and in truth, I'd been avoiding it because we'd shared the bed whenever he stayed in Virginia with me. Luke hadn't been at all happy about that idea to start with, but Emmy had convinced him that I was a grown-up and should be treated like one, even if I still felt ten years old half of the time.

Little reminders of Ryan lay everywhere inside. His comb on the dressing table, his jumper tossed over the back of a chair, a pair of shoes underneath. When I flopped down onto the bed, the pillow still smelled of him, just a little. I hugged it to me, crying into its softness.

And something crinkled.

I rummaged around in the pillowcase and found an envelope, one that made my tears fall harder.

Tia

(Open if I don't come back)

I traced Ryan's untidy scrawl with one finger, and the ink smudged as it dampened. Dammit. I grabbed a tissue and wiped my eyes, unsure whether I truly wanted to read his letter but knowing that I had to.

One page. His final words didn't amount to much, and I wondered if it hurt him as much to write them as it hurt me to read them.

Tia,

If you're reading this letter, it means I didn't make it back. I fucked up, and babe, I'm so sorry for that.

The Russian trip was always going to be a challenge, and I know you didn't want me to go. Kind of wish I'd listened to you now. But I died doing what I loved, and my only regret is hurting you in the process. You told me once that if I kept going with the special ops team, I'd have to decide between you or work, and I hung onto you as long as I could because I was a selfish bastard. The job was in my blood. Hard to explain, but the more operations I went on, the more addictive it got. The thrill of it, I guess.

But now we're both free, and I don't want you to waste your life. Travel the world and spend a month on the beach. Move to New York and take that painting course you always wanted to do. Meet a man who puts you first every time.

Just promise you won't spend too much time thinking of the one who let you down.

I love you, always,

Ryan

I wanted to read those words a hundred times and I wanted to rip his letter to shreds. I wanted to sit in a corner and rock and I wanted to scream and throw things. Why? *Why?* Why had that damn job been so important to him? If he'd turned it down, we could have had a future and as much as I loved Ryan, I hated him too. The ball of grief that had been sitting in my stomach swelled and enveloped me, first with agony, then with an empty nothingness as I stumbled out of the room and into the library.

Emmy's husband kept his Scotch hidden inside an antique globe, and even though I didn't like whisky, I flipped the top back and grabbed the bottle. Who needed a glass? The amber liquid seared my throat, cutting through my deadened senses and burning all the way to my stomach. I relished the pain.

Another mouthful, then another, until half the bottle was gone and I couldn't see straight. I barely noticed when my knees hit the floor, the bottle slipping from my hand and spilling what was left of its contents over the Persian rug.

Then nothing. The blessed darkness came.

CHAPTER 2

FRIDAY DAWNED COLD and clear. A week had passed since my New Year's Eve meltdown, everyone was tiptoeing on eggshells around me, and as I'd done every Friday for the last two months, I walked slowly down the winding path, carrying a bunch of flowers.

Roses. White ones. The same as Ryan had given me on our first proper date, and the same as he'd sent me on the anniversary of that date every month since.

Never again.

It seemed fitting to come to the cemetery on a Friday. Friday had been the day he died. I took a right turn and walked along a row of headstones. The early January sun hung low in the sky as if it too couldn't see a reason to get out of bed in the morning. The rays hadn't even been warm enough to melt the frost today, and the wings of a stone angel sparkled as I passed by.

All too soon, I came to the grave second from the end and dropped to my knees. The black marble gleamed, so shiny I could see the blurred outline of my face as I wept. He hadn't been there long enough for the stone to weather.

Two months, though it seemed like forever. Forever since I'd seen him, forever since I'd breathed his musky scent, forever since I'd felt his arms around me. Forever since I'd heard his voice whispering, "I love you."

Forever since I'd said those last angry words to him.

I swept away a few leaves that had gathered in front of his headstone and lifted the flowers I'd left last week aside, replacing them with the fresh ones. As if by removing the dying blooms, I could somehow keep my life with him alive.

There was one other tribute besides mine. A single black rose. I knew who had left it.

Emmy.

My relationship with Ryan wasn't the only thing that had shattered that terrible day. My bond with my sister had also been broken.

Okay, so she wasn't really my sister, but for the last two years, she may as well have been.

She'd been there for me through everything, from angst at my mother to nerves over my first time with Ryan. I'd told her my hopes and my dreams, my fears and my secrets.

But now I could barely look at her.

When she'd crouched down in front of me and told me Ryan wasn't coming back, I'd screamed at her. Told her that I wished it had been her who'd lost her life in that barren wasteland on the edge of Siberia. Then I'd slapped her as hard as I could. She'd just rocked back on her heels and taken it.

By the time I found out the truth about what had happened that day, it was too late. The trust between us had been lost. The connection severed. I'd tried to fix it, but it was like trying to tie two slippery strands of silk together in a raging hurricane.

I reached out to the cold marble in front of me, trailing a fingertip over the engraved words.

Ryan Young
To live on in the hearts of others is not to die

In the last nine weeks, the ache in my chest had barely dulled. My brother, Luke, had done his best to help, letting me stay with him and his wife after I'd moved out of Emmy's place, but I was still adrift.

If this was what happened when you loved and lost, I never wanted to love again. It wasn't worth the risk. I pulled off my gloves and laid both palms on the icy slab.

"Why, Ryan? Why did that damn job mean so much?"

There was no answer, of course, save for the whistling of the wind through naked branches.

There never would be.

I rose to my feet, and my knees cracked. I'd aged a lifetime in two short months, from a teenager to an old crone. Who would have believed I was just eighteen?

Emmy always said that each person had a soul mate. Some people never found theirs. Some people met theirs too late and were left to enjoy what precious little time remained. Some people, those lucky few, got a lifetime together. I'd once thought Ryan was my soul mate, but in the months before he died, we hadn't always seen eye to eye. Now, I felt terrified in case I'd lost the man meant for me and guilty for wondering whether he was still out there somewhere.

A man who didn't put work first.

Ryan had been employed at Emmy's company, Blackwood Security, since he turned eighteen, and that job had been his life.

I pulled my coat tightly around me as I made my way back along the path. Unseen hands caressed my face, clawing at my cheeks and tugging my hair. Winter was in full bloom, bitter as my soul and merciless as my thoughts.

I hastened to the safety of the car.

Emmy's car.

Well, it was her who'd bought it for me. A birthday gift. Most girls my age got a couple of DVDs and a pair of concert tickets. I'd got a BMW from my crazy, outrageous, generous sister.

And now I felt guilty every time I climbed behind the wheel.

Where to go... Where to go?

Not to Luke's apartment, that was for sure. Or Riverley, in case Emmy was in residence. And I couldn't bring myself to go to the flat Lottie shared with her boyfriend, Nigel, because they were just so damn happy together.

So I drove. I just drove. Drove halfway across Virginia, according to the fancy SatNav Emmy had included when she specced the car. Miles of countryside flew past as I blanked out my wayward thoughts and concentrated on the road ahead. Nothing else mattered.

Including the amount of petrol left in the tank.

I'd just passed Blacksburg when the car sputtered, lurched, and ground to a halt in the middle of nowhere.

Shit.

Okay, Tia, it's not the end of the world. That already happened two months ago.

I reached behind my seat for my handbag and found empty air. Panic gripped me as I scrambled around to check properly, and sure enough, the footwell was empty. Where the hell was my bag? I visualised it sitting on the kitchen counter at Luke's where I'd put it as I grabbed one last mouthful of coffee. Aaaaand...it was still sitting there.

Double shit.

Okay, three months ago, I'd have called Emmy. She'd have sent a crew of commandos and a helicopter or something, and I'd have been home before it got dark. But with the awkward chasm still stretching between us, that wasn't an option. And my brother would kill me for being so dumb.

Who else?

Lottie couldn't drive, and Nigel was at a seminar on reflexology today. That left one person. Thank goodness I carried my phone in my pocket and not in my handbag.

"Bradley?"

"The one and only, doll. What's up?"

Emmy's assistant was perpetually cheerful, fearsomely efficient, and the only person who hadn't treated me like a porcelain doll since Ryan died.

"Uh, I have a slight problem." I gave him a quick rundown of the situation, and he didn't yell or anything. "So you see, I'm sort of stuck."

"Don't you worry, chicky. I'll fix it."

"Thanks." The word came out as a gulping sob.

"Hey, hey, it's okay. When have I ever let you down?"

"Never."

"There you go. Sit tight, and leave it with me."

Half an hour later, about the time I'd decided to revoke my own driver's licence and only take chauffeur-driven transport from now on because I was shivering and perhaps a tiny bit scared, a guy not much older than me hopped out of a tow truck. He wiped his hands on his overalls before holding one out for me to shake.

"Robbie Morton, Morton's Autos. The gentleman on the phone said you'd run out of gas?"

"That's right. I don't know how I didn't notice. I mean, I know there's a warning light and everything..."

"Happens more often than you might think, ma'am. You're English?"

The accent was a bit of a giveaway. "Yes."

"Always wanted to go there myself. See Buckingham Palace."

Buck-ing-ham, not Bucking-um like us Brits pronounced it.

"Then why don't you? England's small compared to America, but the countryside's pretty and London's got lots of other places to visit as well."

He unscrewed a jerry can of petrol and tilted it through a funnel into the tank. "Wish I could, but I work with my old man, and I don't get much time off."

"Can't you ask him for a holiday?"

Robbie shook his head. His cap slipped, and he righted it again. "Ever since he got sick, he's needed me around to do the heavy lifting."

"I'm so sorry. That can't be much fun."

"Life's what you make of it. I've got a roof over my head and food on the table. And today I get to talk to a pretty girl."

I couldn't help smiling at his sentiment, conveyed matter-of-factly, nothing flirtatious in his manner. Wise words. He'd made the best of what he had.

But had I? At school, I'd scored mediocre grades, and I'd never held a proper job despite the amount Luke had invested in my education. I might have money, but I'd never earned it. In terms of achievement, Robbie in his grubby clothes and twenty-year-old truck was one step ahead of me.

"Thank you for coming out to help."

He gave a salute before screwing the cap back onto the can. "That's what I'm here for. Besides, your buddy on the phone paid a handsome tip."

Trust Bradley. "That doesn't surprise me."

"You got much further to travel tonight?"

"Back to Richmond."

Robbie gave a low whistle. "Well, you drive safe, ma'am."

Too many times I'd thought of jerking the wheel to the side and ending it all, but I nodded back. "I will."

As I drove off slowly, Robbie's words replayed in my head. *Life's what you make of it.* What had I made of mine?

Nothing. Ryan had been the one with the job, the career he loved. I'd never actually buckled down and done anything.

Once I finished school, I'd moved to the States, living with Emmy as my brother still split his time between London and Virginia. Luke had provided the essentials, Emmy bought me all the things Luke said I couldn't have, and apart from a few favours for Emmy, I'd never done a day's work in my life.

Even Lottie had a job as a receptionist, and while I secretly thought it must get kind of boring stuck behind the same desk the whole time, at least she wasn't spending her days at home, pining over her mistakes.

Where would I be in a year's time? Five years? Still sitting in my bedroom crying? Or could I make my mark on the world like Emmy had?

Ryan and Robbie were both right. I shouldn't waste my life, and it would only ever be what I made of it.

CHAPTER 3

WHAT COULD I do with my life?

The question preyed on my mind for the whole drive home, and by the time Mack served up dinner, I was still none the wiser.

"Where's Luke?" I asked her.

"Still at the office. Black hat hackers aren't considerate enough to stick to business hours." She adopted *that* face. Pity disguised as polite interest. "How was your day?"

Mack had two sides to her—tough and businesslike at work, sweet Southern charm the rest of the time. I adored her, don't get me wrong, even if I'd once hoped Emmy would marry Luke instead, but right now, I kind of wished she wasn't so flipping *nice*.

Nice hurt more than indifference.

"My day was okay."

"You went to visit Ryan again?"

Sure, like I'd popped out for coffee with him. "Yes, I went to the cemetery again."

"Oh, honey. Things'll ease in time, even though it might not feel that way at the moment."

I knew they would. I'd already dealt with grief once, when my father died. But I'd been younger then and bounced back faster, or maybe I just hadn't been as close to the man who'd donated half my DNA as I had to the man I'd chosen to spend my life with, harsh though that may sound.

Yes, time healed. But the seconds ticked by much slower than before.

"How's Emmy?" I asked.

"I haven't seen her much this week. She's been spending time with Ana."

I sucked in a breath then held it as Mack looked up. Ana. If it hadn't been for Ana's drama, Ryan would still be alive, and to cap it all, she'd walked right into Riverley and become Emmy's new best friend. I tried to like her, really I did, but it was...difficult. And despite what Emmy said, Ana's cold demeanour suggested she wasn't too keen on me either.

But I forced a smile. "That's great. Emmy works so hard, and she needs a break."

"You've got that right. And Ana's daughter is just so cute! Two years old, and you can see so many similarities to her mom."

Fantastic. Next thing we knew, Tabitha would be toddling around with an automatic weapon in her hands.

"I'm glad Tabitha's back." My voice sounded flat to my own ears, and I hated that. Hated that I couldn't sound happier for them.

"It was so great Emmy and Ana found each other, right? Talk about lucky. I mean, if Emmy hadn't gone to Russia at the right moment, then none..." Mack stopped mid-sentence as she realised what she'd said. "Oh, honey. I'm so sorry. Of course, the part about Ryan wasn't lucky. It's just... Well..."

"It's fine, really. You know what? I think I'll go to bed."

"But you've hardly eaten anything."

"I've lost my appetite."

"Tia..."

The sound of Für Elise echoed through the apartment, and I leapt up. Saved by the bell. As long as it wasn't Emmy. *Please don't let it be Emmy.* Of course, Emmy rarely bothered to knock. She simply picked the lock and let herself in anywhere she pleased.

I squinted through the peephole. Bradley. Thank goodness.

"I thought you had a key?"

"Yes, I do, but the last time I used it... Mack and your brother..." He covered his eyes with his hands. "I can't un-see."

"Euewwww!"

"Precisely. Did I interrupt dinner?"

"I lost my appetite."

"You need to eat."

"I do, most of the time." Okay, so I was living on chocolate, but it still had calories.

Bradley's pursed lips said he didn't believe me, but after a few seconds, he shrugged. "Anyhow, I thought I'd stop by and check you were okay after earlier."

Mack was staring in our direction, and I hadn't mentioned my small error in judgement with the petrol, so I nudged Bradley backwards out of sight.

"I'm fine."

"You forget I'm gay, doll. I know exactly what 'fine' means. Now, tell me what's wrong apart from the obvious."

"I want to get a job."

Mack's voice drifted through from the dining area. "Is everything okay?"

"Uh..."

"All good," Bradley called. "Just talking shoes." Then to me he continued, "A job? Where did that come from?"

Everything spilled out. Ryan's letter, my lack of direction, Robbie's words about life being what I made of it.

"So it's obvious, isn't it? Everyone else works, and all I do is sit around all day. I should do something constructive. You know...a fresh start...a career."

"Are you sure you're ready for that?"

"No, but I need to do it anyway."

"I'll have a chat with Emmy."

"No! I mean, I'm grateful for everything she's done for me, but I don't want her to just give me a job out of pity."

Bradley tilted his head to one side. "I thought you two made up after...you know."

"We did, sort of. I guess things are just awkward, what with Ana being around too." I dropped my voice to a whisper. "She scares me."

"You and me both, doll. You and me both. So, what job do you have in mind?"

I'd never really thought about it before.

The career advisor I saw in year thirteen had been useless. Not that their advice was truly necessary for the kids who attended the Marsden Academy. Mother had sent me to the most exclusive private school in the area, and earning a basic wage upon graduation simply hadn't been an issue for most of my fellow pupils.

I still recalled the day we'd been forced to take one of those automated job questionnaires that suggested a career based on our likes and dislikes. An hour of my life, wasted.

"What did yours say?" Arabella asked. She'd been my best friend all through school, but I didn't see her nearly often enough now.

"Landscape gardener or fish farmer. How about yours?"

"A seamstress!" She'd hooted with laughter. "Can you believe that? Mother would *die!*"

Another of our classmates wandered over. "It's a pointless exercise. I'm joining father's company as soon as I've done my master's degree."

"A lady doesn't need to work," one of the other girls put in. "She just needs to marry well."

"Yes, I wouldn't want my wife to work," the boy standing next to her said. "That would look terrible." He practised swinging an invisible golf club. "I'm going to be a golf pro. After all, I've been playing since I was eight."

What were they doing now? Sitting around, spending daddy's millions most likely. Or preparing for a life in politics. Arabella was at Cambridge University, studying biology, but I'd lost touch with everyone else.

My A-level passes had been in art, textiles, English literature, and classics. Unless I fancied writing historical fiction and illustrating my own book jackets, I couldn't see how those would help in the real world.

No, I was stumped.

"I don't have any job in mind," I told Bradley.

"Tell you what, let's go out for dinner, just you and me. We can talk it over then."

"I'm not sure I—"

"What else are you planning to do? Sit in your room on your own?"

Yes, that was exactly what I'd been planning to do. "No, but—"

"Mack, I'm taking Tia out for dinner. Don't wait up."

"Bradley, I—"

"Sparkly top, good shoes, don't forget your ID. Go."

I went. When Bradley was in one of these moods, arguing with him was pointless. If I flat out refused to go, he'd just bring the party to me, and that would be even worse. Think I was kidding? When Carmen said she was too tired to go out for her birthday last year, Bradley turned up at her house with caterers, a mariachi band, and sixty guests.

I dug out a black sequinned top and teamed it up with black trousers and black heels. He said sparkly, but he didn't say anything about colourful. Where was my ID? I last used it before Christmas when I got arrested for the fifth time.

That ID had been an eighteenth birthday gift from Emmy, along with my car. A driver's licence and passport, both proclaiming me to be three years older than I actually was.

She'd held them out of reach for a second before handing them over.

"I figure that as you're legally old enough to drink in England now, it's only fair that you can buy alcohol in the US too. I'm trusting you. If you fuck up, I'll take these back, and you can be eighteen again. Got it?"

"Got it."

And in the last two months, I'd screwed up badly, but she still hadn't stepped in. She'd given me leeway because of Ryan—something else to feel guilty over.

When I first met Emmy, she'd been grieving

herself, but she'd hidden it well and soldiered on, with my brother of all people. Looking back, I could see she hadn't been happy, exactly, but she'd coped a hell of a lot better than me. I needed to take a leaf out of her book and move on, difficult though that seemed right now.

And I started by taking Bradley's arm and following him out to a waiting town car.

"Where are we going?" I asked.

"Rhodium. We can have a quiet dinner, a few cocktails, and plan your future."

At least if I was being forced to dine out, I'd be doing it at the best restaurant in town. One that served my favourite baked brie as an appetiser and perfectly gooey chocolate fondant. Oh, and did I mention the margaritas?

Bradley had the waiter well trained, and the drinks kept coming, one after the other. Suddenly, a night out didn't seem like such a bad idea after all, and when Bradley began asking me questions after the main course, my tongue had loosened enough to answer them.

"So, this fresh start... Emmy can find you a job if you want one."

"No!" I half shouted, and people several tables over turned to stare. "I already said no," I repeated more quietly.

"I suppose I can understand that. She's a nightmare to work for."

She couldn't be that bad. Bradley had been working for her for over ten years now.

"Mack already made that suggestion, but I want a job that's mine, you know?"

"How about something arty? You like to draw."

I hoped to sell my work some day, but I wasn't good enough yet. Emmy had a friend who'd been a professional artist and I just wasn't in the same league. His paintings drew you in, spoke to your soul, then dropped you back into reality as a changed person. He'd given me painting lessons, and I could see the improvement in myself, but the one time I'd picked up a brush since Ryan died, the colours came out flat. One-dimensional. I'd lost the fire inside me that I needed to create a work of art.

"Not right now. My heart wouldn't be in it."

"Something musical?"

Not when I'd been booted out of the school choir aged twelve. "I'm tone deaf."

"Finance?"

"I got an E grade in GCSE maths."

"What about food? You could go to chef school?"

I liked eating food, yes, but cooking it? I shuddered as I remembered helping Emmy in her first and only attempt at making Christmas dinner. It hadn't gone well.

"I'd probably burn the place down."

The waiter brought a fresh cocktail, and I downed half of it as Bradley's lips twitched. They always did that when he was deep in thought.

"Landscape gardening? I hear it can be relaxing."

I burst out laughing, much to his bemusement. "No way. Not gardening."

"There must be something. How about fashion?"

Fashion? I did like clothes, although I was more of an end user. Did customising a few T-shirts qualify me for even an entry-level position?

"Maybe."

"Maybe? Well, that's better than an outright no. Leave it with me."

I didn't like that gleam in his eye. "Bradley, what are you planning?"

"Don't you fret about that, doll. Drink your margarita."

"But—"

"And here comes dessert. Eat up before it gets cold."

"But—"

"Trust me. I'm a genius when it comes to these things."

Chapter 4

I SHOULD HAVE put my foot down and stopped Bradley, but thanks to the deliciousness of a chocolate fondant, a crème brûlée, and one too many margaritas, I'd more or less forgotten all about his plan when I stumbled out of Rhodium sometime around midnight. My headache the next day precluded rational thought, and he didn't say another word about our little discussion until a week later.

Mack had mentioned Emmy was out of the country, so I snuck over to Riverley to tidy up my old bedroom. I needed more clothes, and although I hated to move Ryan's things, I couldn't leave the room in some sort of bizarre time warp. Otherwise where would it end? Would I still be tiptoeing around his discarded boots in a year? Two years? Better to rip the Band-Aid off and deal with it now.

Luckily, Ryan had never been a hoarder. That was me, with my wardrobes full of clothes and drawers full of make-up. In three hours, I'd reduced his life to two suitcases, and I shed a tear as I zipped the lid on the second.

"You okay?" Bradley asked from the doorway, and I jumped so violently I fell on my ass.

"Not now. Could you give me some warning next time?"

"Sorry, doll. Do you want me to find a home for those?"

I nodded, the lump in my throat blocking my words.

"How about the apartment in London?"

Ryan's flat, the one I'd shared with him. "I can't face that at the moment."

"Shall I have a tidy up there the next time I'm over?"

"Would you mind?"

"I wouldn't have offered otherwise. Besides, it's time for your fresh start. I've organised everything, and you need to be in New York tomorrow."

"Ha ha. Very funny."

"No joke, doll. I said I'd fix everything up, and I have." Bradley rocked back on the heels of his silver cowboy boots, his grin stretching from ear to ear. "You can thank me later."

I scrambled to my feet. "What. Have. You. Done?"

"You wanted a fresh start and a job in fashion. Now you've got them."

"Bradley, I was drunk when we had that conversation, and I only said 'maybe.' *Maybe* I'd like a job in fashion. And I didn't say anything about moving to a whole other state!"

"I've seen you moping around this place. It's full of memories, and you need a break from them. Emmy would never have suggested New York because she likes you close, but I know I'm right."

Had he lost his damn mind?

"I can't live in New York by myself."

"Nonsense. I did when I was your age."

"Luke will never let me go."

"I'll admit it took a few days to convince him, and Emmy too, but they've both come around to my way of thinking."

"I can't—"

"Stop being so negative. One month. Give it one month, and if you hate it, I'll pick you up myself. But I really think this internship will be just what you need to take your mind off everything that's happened."

"What internship?"

He got that worrying grin again. "It's a surprise. But you'll love it—trust me."

Trust him, Bradley said.

I could have acted like a brat and refused to leave Virginia, but how would that have helped with my fresh start? And for the two years I'd known Bradley, he'd only ever done good things for me. Ryan's words echoed in my head and heart: *Move to New York... Don't waste your life.*

Which was why, twenty-four hours later, I found myself standing in the middle of a loft-style apartment in New York City, my new digs as cold and empty as my soul.

But not for long, if Bradley had his way.

"Let's put the sofas here," he said. "Right by the window so you get the light."

"I'm not sure about this."

"Well, where would *you* put the sofas?"

"I mean the whole moving-to-New-York thing."

"One month, Tia. Here, hold the end of this tape measure."

I dutifully obliged, and he jotted suspicious notes in his little pink notepad. He'd even brought a pink pen, sparkly with a feather stuck on the end.

"And you still won't tell me where I'll be working?"

"Patience, doll. You'll find out at eight o'clock tomorrow morning. I'm taking you there myself. Now, do you want any gym equipment? We could put it in that far corner."

"Is it really worth it for a month?"

"Tsk tsk tsk. I have complete confidence you'll love it here."

At least one of us did.

Bradley paused long enough to glance out at the twinkling lights of Tribeca beyond the balcony. "And isn't it a great apartment?" he said.

It was, and that worried me. This place was costing somebody a fortune, and Bradley refused to tell me who. So had Luke before he flew back to England yesterday evening. Which meant it was probably Emmy, and my new apartment was yet another thing I'd be in her debt over.

A knock sounded at the door, and Bradley dropped his tape measure and rushed over to answer it. Eight men in overalls traipsed in with various boxes and stacked them in the centre of the cavernous space.

"Leave the door open, buddy," the tallest guy said. "Reckon we've got another ten loads to come."

How many strings had Bradley pulled to get furniture delivered at seven o'clock on a Sunday evening?

More than I wanted to think about.

But Bradley merely tossed the keys to the man and linked his arm through mine. "We'll head out for dinner while you put the furniture together. I've left a sketch of where to put it over on the kitchen counter."

"Shouldn't we stay and help?" I asked.

"No offence, ma'am, but we've got a system." His unspoken words: *And you'll get in the way.*

I let Bradley lead me out to the elevator, and a minute later, we'd descended the six floors to street level.

"Follow me," he said. "I know a fabulous little place right around the corner."

Of course he did. Bradley knew fabulous little places in every city around the world, as well as the best hotels, the hottest bars, and the people who could get him into all of them. Everyone raved about how well-connected Emmy was, but Bradley wasn't far off.

And in Cariba, the maître d' spread both arms the instant we walked through the door.

"Bradley! So wonderful to see you again. A new lady friend this time? You break my heart."

See?

The maître d' air-kissed both of us then led the way to a prime table by the window. I sat, and he draped a dark red napkin over my lap. The colour of blood. Oh, how I hated these constant reminders of Ryan's death. The pain I'd hoped to leave behind prodded at my ribcage.

Distraction. I needed a distraction.

"This is an interesting place."

From the name of the restaurant, I'd expected Caribbean food, but the menu was Italian, our waiter hailed from Mexico, and the music in the background was a strange mix of rap and show tunes.

"The owner's a little eccentric," Bradley said. "But

the food's to die for." As soon as the words left his
mouth, he clapped his hand right over it. "Shit. Sorry, I
didn't mean that."

Was this what my whole life would be like? "It
doesn't matter. Let's stick with eccentric. A little
eccentric is good."

"I'm glad you said that."

"What? Why?"

Before I could quiz him further, our food began
arriving. Melt-in-your-mouth tapas dishes made for
sharing—one of everything on the menu, it seemed,
together with a bottle of red wine. Before long, the
waistband of my jeans bit into my stomach, and I had
to loosen my belt a notch. How did Bradley stay so slim
when he ate as much as me? He never visited the gym
apart from to put flowers on the water cooler. Probably
all the rushing around he did for Emmy kept the weight
off.

"Room for dessert?" he asked.

"Um..."

"The answer's yes, by the way." He waved the
waiter over. "Two portions of the tiramisu, please."

"I won't be able to move."

"That's fine. I'll just call the furniture guys over
from your apartment, and they can wheel you home on
one of their dollies. You can't leave before you try it—
it's the best I've tasted outside Italy."

Home. He'd called the Tribeca apartment home,
but to me, it was just a space to sleep. When Bradley
had worked his magic, I had no doubt it would be a
very beautiful space to sleep, but a home?

I couldn't see it.

But Bradley was right about the tiramisu. I scoffed

the lot, popped open my top button, and pulled my jumper over my poochy stomach while he handed over his credit card.

"Feeling better?" he asked as he guided me out of the door.

"Sort of." And sort of sick, if I was honest, but that was my own fault for eating so much.

"Amazing what a bottle of wine can do, isn't it? In moderation, of course."

"Don't worry. I'm not planning to go off the rails again."

"Glad to hear it. Emmy's running out of favours."

Never. She'd been banking them for years. But I appreciated the sentiment, and that was another reason I was determined not to screw up my time in New York. I didn't want to let everybody down.

We ambled along the street, and I took a few minutes to drink in the atmosphere. I'd been to New York once or twice, but always with an event to attend or for the occasional shopping trip. This was the first time I hadn't had an expiration date on my visit, no hurry to be somewhere. Even late in the evening, the pavements—sorry, sidewalks—were full of people, mainly young professionals judging by their attire.

"I'm glad you picked Tribeca," I said to Bradley.

"It suits you. The artist community, plenty of cafés and restaurants. And it's got low crime rates. Emmy insisted on that particular bit."

"Did she choose the apartment?"

"Don't you worry about that."

Dammit. Years of working for Emmy had taught him how to stay tight-lipped.

"I want to visit the art museums while I'm here.

And Times Square. And the Statue of Liberty, and the Empire State Building."

"You'll have plenty of time on the weekends."

"So I'll only be working Monday to Friday?"

"The next few weeks might be busy."

The next few weeks? What was happening at this time of year? Fashion. Bradley said I'd be working in fashion... "I'm interning for fashion week?"

He put a finger to his lips then pointed at a shop across the road. "That store often has interesting trinkets. It's well worth a visit."

Gah! Why couldn't he put me out of my misery? Eight o'clock in the morning might be less than half a day away, but that seemed like forever. I itched with impatience. My insides felt as if they'd been filled with ants.

When we got back up to my apartment, the men had disappeared, leaving a coffee table, sideboards, a huge TV, a pair of white leather sofas, plus a dining table that seated six. Who on earth did Bradley expect me to invite for dinner? I didn't know a soul in New York, and even if I did, I couldn't cook to save my life.

But somebody thought otherwise. The fridge had been stocked with the basics—milk, bread, butter, cheese, orange juice—and I also recognised the influence of Toby, Emmy's nutritionist. Green stuff sprouted from every shelf, and I had three kinds of organic yogurt and enough quinoa to open my own health food store.

Perhaps I could eat at Cariba every night?

Black stools sat beside the breakfast bar in my monochrome kitchen, which was separated from the remainder of the space by a half-wall behind the counter. Flowers. It needed flowers.

I took a quick tour of the rest of the apartment. A California king bed had appeared on the mezzanine next to a roll-top bath. A bath in the bedroom? Okay then. The shower, toilet, and two basins were hidden behind a wall of glass bricks. Quirky, but I liked it.

"I can't believe you got the apartment finished so fast," I said to Bradley.

"Finished? Oh, doll, I'm just getting started."

Should I be thrilled or worried by that? After a few seconds of thought, I shoved it to the back of my mind —Bradley no doubt had a vision, and he wouldn't quit until it had been achieved.

"Are you staying here tonight?" I asked instead. "There's only one bed, but it's big enough to share."

"No can do, doll. I have to stay at Black's apartment instead. The plumber's fitting new taps at 6:00 a.m. tomorrow, and I need to chivvy him up so I can get back here early."

"Oh."

Of course, Emmy's husband had an apartment in New York. He had homes everywhere from Australia to Zambia. Okay, so the place in Zambia was more of a safari lodge he'd invested in, but it still counted.

I'd visited his New York apartment in the Upper East Side once with Emmy, and the place couldn't have reeked more of money if he'd wallpapered it with hundred-dollar bills.

And last year, he'd started a project, taking photos of Emmy in each of their favourite places to hang on their bedroom wall at Riverley. Upper East Side Emmy wore nothing but black five-inch heels, dark red lipstick, and an obscenely expensive diamond necklace as she reclined on a chaise longue in front of the city skyline. Her position left everything to the imagination, and apart from the lipstick, the final picture was in black and white.

Mesmerising.

I only wished I could be that beautiful.

"Do you want to stay there with me?" Bradley asked.

I quickly shook my head. I'd promised to pose like that for Ryan at Christmas, and I didn't need a reminder of what would never be.

"My new bed looks really comfy."

"We leave at seven thirty tomorrow. Don't be late."

"What should I wear?"

"You'll be working in an office."

"Office. Got it."

When Bradley left, I picked out suitable attire and hung the rest of my clothes in my new wardrobe. I'd brought four suitcases with me, but there was so much unfilled space. Perhaps it was time to start shopping again?

I flopped down on the bed, turning my head to the side so I could look out the windows. Even with the double glazing, I could hear the low hum of traffic outside, busy despite the late hour.

Odd.

Foreign.

I'd never lived in the city before. In England, home had been Lower Foxford, a quaint village with as many tractors and horses as cars. And in Richmond, Emmy lived in splendid isolation, deliberately so. She always joked that she didn't want people to find out where the bodies were buried, but sometimes I worried she wasn't entirely kidding.

In Tribeca, with the noise and flickering lights, sleep didn't come easily. If only Ryan were here beside me, sharing in this new adventure. This should have been our place, not just mine.

But it wasn't to be.

Instead, the vast apartment was as empty as my heart.

CHAPTER 5

"IT'S SEVEN THIRTY. Are you going to tell me where we're going yet?" I asked Bradley.

"Just around the corner from the Lincoln Center."

Grrr. That didn't narrow things down much.

"And my new job?"

"Okay, okay." He beamed at me. "Next month, Ishmael will be putting on his show at New York Fashion Week, and he needs an extra assistant. Voilà!" Bradley did jazz hands. "You're his extra assistant."

"Hold on...Ishmael? *The* Ishmael? Ishmael who dressed Velvet Jones in a dress made from orange peel for the Oscars last year?"

"That's him. I wanted to buy that dress for Emmy as a joke, but Ishmael said it had already started to go crispy by the time Velvet stepped off the red carpet."

I swayed a little and clutched at the breakfast bar. *Ishmael?* Girls would crawl their way through a pile of burning stilettos to breathe the same air as him.

"So you just called Ishmael up and got me a job? How many favours did Emmy have to call in for that?"

Bradley pursed his lips. "None at all. Ishmael's my old college roommate. It was me he owed the favour to, not Emmy."

"Sorry."

"So you should be. You can apologise with a smile."

I tried, but inside my nerves began jangling. Ishmael may have been hot property as a designer, but he also had a reputation for being demanding. And eccentric. Definitely eccentric. I realised now why Bradley had made that comment at Cariba.

"So as Ishmael's assistant, what will I be expected to do?"

I had visions of ending up like Anne Hathaway in *The Devil Wears Prada*, spending my days and nights fetching coffee for some male incarnation of Meryl Streep.

"We didn't go into that, exactly. But Ishmael's a darling. He'll look after you. Don't worry."

All very well for Bradley to say. He wasn't the one standing in a cavernous room in a city he didn't know, armed with only an 8:00 a.m. appointment to meet an eccentric stranger.

And that was how I'd ended up playing table tennis over Ishmael's desk before I'd even had my first cup of coffee, cursing my decision to wear a pair of high heels.

"What am I doing here?" I muttered, sinking into the pristine white cushions as I tried to get my breath back.

"You're here because you want to work for a premier fashion designer in the most prestigious city in the world," Myrna informed me.

Of course. My life's ambition. I almost rolled my eyes, but I had a feeling it wouldn't go down so well with Little Miss Haughty.

"Apart from playing ping pong, what do I actually

need to do?"

Myrna glanced at my feet, now firmly tucked back into black patent heels.

"Well to start off, you need to bring more practical footwear with you in the mornings. Ishmael exercises from eight to eight thirty every day. And when Ishmael exercises, we all exercise." She tapped away at her phone. "Tomorrow, we're going power walking."

"So I need to wear sports gear?"

"Make sure it's snazzy. And you'll need something suitably current to change into afterwards."

Had I brought workout clothes? A mental inventory of my meagre wardrobe told me no. Was Bradley still in New York? If not, I'd have to buy something this evening. Unless, of course, Ishmael expected me to work late. My employment contract said hours "as required," and all I had was Bradley's assurance that Ishmael wasn't a slave driver.

"Okay. Snazzy. Got it. So, apart from exercising, what do we do?"

Myrna plopped down onto the sofa beside me.

"Tia, have you ever worked in this industry before?"

"Not exactly. I've read a lot of fashion magazines, though."

She began choking, and I tried to recall how to do the Heimlich manoeuvre Emmy had shown me once. Then I looked at Myrna's face and realised she wasn't choking, she was laughing. Oh, dear.

"I see. A sacrificial lamb. Let me tell you, Tia, nothing in those magazines can possibly prepare you for the realities. I've been working in fashion for five years, and every day, I still have to pinch myself."

Pinch myself? I was kicking myself. And after I'd

kicked myself, I'd be aiming my foot at Bradley. But first I needed to get this glorious Tuesday over with.

"Have you lived in New York the whole time?"

"Of course. I grew up here, which positioned me perfectly to make that first step onto the ladder. And, let me tell you, it's not an easy climb. Ishmael's very demanding."

Demanding. Just as I suspected. Great.

"So, what's on our to-do list for today?"

She looked at her watch. "In precisely seventeen minutes, I have to fetch Ishmael's triple venti, sugar-free, non-fat, no foam, macchiato with one pump of caramel and two scoops of vanilla bean powder. You can stay here and do the paperclips."

She'd lost me at "non-fat." Somehow, "doing the paperclips" sounded like the lesser of two evils. Did I dare to ask what that entailed?

"Paperclips?"

"Every morning, Ishmael needs his paperclips laid out exactly right on his desk. In pairs, one pair in each colour of the rainbow. And next to those, he needs his pens. Purple, pink, orange, and green, in that order. Plus a fresh notepad so he can express himself creatively."

And Bradley thought Emmy was a handful?

After Myrna left, I set to work, squaring the stationery up with the edges of the desk. At nine, another alarm sounded, this time from Ishmael's computer, and two seconds later, he swept back into the room with Myrna hurrying to catch up.

"Your coffee," she announced, setting the concoction down on his desk, complete with a sparkly pink swizzle stick.

She'd brought herself a cup too, and she peered at me over the rim as she sipped. How kind of her to offer me a drink.

Ishmael perched on the edge of his seat, bawdily upholstered in pink fur. "What does my schedule say?"

Myrna hurried to produce her iPad. "At ten, you've got an interview with *Hot Banana* magazine over at the Lincoln Center. Then you have models to look at." She squinted at the screen. "Then... I'm not sure what this last one is. It says 'Tito?'"

"Ah, yes, I added that one myself." Ishmael looked extraordinarily pleased with himself. "T Ito. Professor Takashi Ito. I'm meeting with him because I've decided to change the theme for the show."

Myrna turned white and swayed a bit. I leapt forward and grabbed the coffee out of her hand before it ended up as a Rorschach on the shiny, white-tiled floor.

"Ch-ch-change the show?"

"Yes. Butterflies are so last year, don't you think?" He pulled the sparkly clips off his devil horns and threw them into the waste bin, followed by the pair from his lapels.

"But we've been organising it for months! A hundred people have been working on it. Everything's almost finished."

Myrna went from white to green, and I picked up the bin, just in case she needed to vomit. Because guess who would get stuck cleaning up the mess?

"Yes, I know," Ishmael said. "But it's just not 'wow' enough, don't you think?"

Her mouth opened and shut but no words came out, so I decided to lend a hand.

"What are you changing the theme to?"

He grinned, and his rings clinked as he clapped his hands in glee. "Death! Models and corpses. Not that anyone can usually tell the difference."

Now it was my turn to feel queasy. I hugged the bin tighter against my chest, ready to run out of the room if I had to. Visions of Ryan swam before my eyes as I tried, and failed, to stay on my feet. My knees gave way, and I fought back tears as I collapsed onto the sofa. Myrna was right beside me.

Models and corpses? This guy was certifiable.

And from the way Myrna was hyperventilating, she was going to fall into one of those categories. To give you a clue which one, she wouldn't fit into the sample size.

A minute passed before she got her breathing under control. "But Ishmael, there are only two weeks until the show. It took us six months to arrange everything for the butterflies."

"Yes, I know, but there's nothing like a challenge, is there? I can announce it in my interview this morning. Really get the ball rolling." He clapped his hands again, like a child given a favourite toy. "Come on, Myrna. Finish your coffee and let's get going."

Ishmael walked towards the door. Was I expected to go too? Or could I get away with heading to the airport and hopping on the next plane?

"Uh, I've done the paperclips. What should I do next?"

He backed up and peered over the array of colours. "The blue ones should be at the end."

Really? I frantically recited the old rhyme over in my head. Richard Of York Gave Battle In Vain. Nope, blue was definitely somewhere in the middle.

"But in the rainbow..."

He silenced me with a hand. "I know, I know. But the blue ones look much nicer after the violets. Remember that for next time."

I took a step towards the desk. "I'll just fix it."

"Stop! We don't have time. Myrna, come *on*."

I guess that meant I *was* supposed to go. We piled into the lift, but Ishmael pressed the button for the third floor rather than the first.

"Why are we getting off here?" I whispered to Myrna.

"So we can switch to the stairs."

"Er, what?"

"Ishmael believes it's unlucky to take the elevator for the last two floors," Myrna whispered. "Apparently, he heard that in an old Chinese proverb."

Seriously? No question about it, the guy was whacked.

Not to mention fast.

I could barely keep up as Ishmael marched along the street. Myrna and her ballet flats weren't having such a hard time of it, which was just as well because she was required to hold a Power Rangers umbrella over him as he walked.

Why? I had no idea. There was no rain or even any sun.

The Lincoln Center was a five-minute walk away, and I only twisted my ankle once before we got there. A doorman scrambled to open the door for Ishmael and then led us to a cavernous space where two chairs waited under a spotlight.

Myrna produced a packet of cleansing wipes and

scrubbed down the left-hand one while Ishmael greeted a skinny man who was hovering next to the other chair.

"Mike Walters, *Hot Banana,*" he said with a display of too-white teeth.

Ishmael ignored his proffered hand. "Ishmael. Survivor, warrior, inspiration."

Nothing like tooting his own horn, was there?

Myrna turned to the doorman, who seemed kind of starstruck.

"Where's the cushion?" she hissed.

"Uh...the cushion!" He dashed off, tripping over his own feet as he ran.

"Ishmael can't sit on hard surfaces," Myrna whispered to me.

The diva designer stood around, looking disgusted, until a harried-looking teenager sprinted across the floor holding a butterfly-decorated cushion in front of her like a shield.

He took one look at it and sighed dramatically. "I said no butterflies."

What were we supposed to do? Click our fingers and produce one covered in death?

Ishmael looked at Banana-man. Banana-man looked at Myrna. Myrna looked at Ishmael.

A full minute passed.

Finally, Ishmael let out the shuddering breath of a dying man. "I'll stand."

Banana-man wasn't sure what to do with himself, so he settled for perching awkwardly on the back of a chair, going for the casual look. He produced a digital recorder from his pocket and clicked it on.

"No recordings," Ishmael shrieked. "Modern technology is taking over the world. We need to rediscover tradition."

This coming from a man who had a MacBook on his desk, with an iPad, iPod, and iPhone lined up next to it.

Banana-man hurried to switch the offending item off, but I sensed he was struggling not to roll his eyes. After he'd found a crumpled notepad, he tapped a sleek silver pen on it and asked the question Myrna and I had both been dreading.

"So, Ishmael, can you tell me about the inspiration for your upcoming show?"

"We constantly analyse the clothes on the outside of our bodies, but what do we look like on the inside? We rarely think about that. So, my next show will blend the two concepts. A parade of the world's most stunning models will mix with an artful arrangement of corpses in a spectacle called 'The beauty of death.'"

Myrna excused herself and dashed in the direction of the bathroom.

Banana-man's eyes went wide. "Uh, corpses? Like, fake ones, right?"

"Of course not! Nothing about Ishmael is fake. Did you see me using fake diamonds last year in my 'All that glitters' show? No, you did not."

I recalled that one. Emmy's company had done the security. Much to their horror, Ishmael had made all the guards dress in sparkly ties so they wouldn't stand out. And Dan, predictably, had brought three of the models home with her.

"I didn't mean to suggest..."

"Good. You're not here to suggest. You're here to create a lasting memorial to my creative vision."

"Right. Okaaaay. So, these corpses... Where are they coming from?"

I had visions of Myrna and me having to rob a mortuary, but thankfully even Ishmael wasn't that nuts.

"I'll be teaming up with Professor Ito. My clothing, my models, stepping among his plastified works of art. It will be beautiful."

Beautiful. A display of elegant skeletons carefully arranged into eye-catching poses. And then there would be the corpses.

If this guy hadn't lost his marbles, there was certainly a hole in the bag.

Myrna returned, looking fragile, as Ishmael continued to outline the show to Banana-man. The show that was, so far, only arranged in his head. I had to admit that I shared Myrna's sentiments on this one.

And I tuned back in again just as Ishmael said, "...and I've also decided to include a menswear line in the show for the first time."

Myrna sat down with a bump, cushion or no cushion. Since when did Ishmael have a menswear line? He didn't, did he?

The next two weeks were going to be hell.

A car was idling at the kerb as we walked out of the Lincoln Center, waiting to take us to the model casting. I stayed silent during the ten-minute ride, trying to tamp down my rising panic. I'd come to New York to get away from death, not be thrust right into the middle of it.

I wanted to go home. More than anything, I just wanted to go home.

Or at least back to Luke's.

But then I thought about the effort people had put in to get me here. Bradley had organised a job for me. Emmy, I suspected, had rushed out and rented me a kick-ass apartment. Even Ishmael was trying to help in his own, special way. I couldn't just leave. It would be a kick in the teeth to all of them.

No, I'd have to steel myself and deal with whatever Ishmael threw at me. Literally.

The car stopped, and as I stepped onto the pavement behind Ishmael and Myrna, I squared my shoulders.

I could do this.

I *would* do this.

Inside, stunning women lined up in front of us as a booker ran back and forth primping them. Ishmael simply walked along, pointing at each in turn.

"No, no, no, no, yes, no, no, yes, no, no, no, no, yes, no, no."

Three. He'd selected three.

Two blondes, one brunette, with nothing in common as far as I could see.

"How many do we need?" I asked Myrna.

"Thirty," she whispered back.

We'd have to do this nine more times? In two weeks? As well as organising an entirely new fashion show?

I'd have put my head in my hands but there was no time to stop. Ishmael was already on his way out of the door. I followed him, Myrna in a trance beside me. Maybe she was hoping this was all just a bad dream.

Back in the car, Ishmael fired orders at her.

"Cancel the live butterflies and the butterfly

costumes. We won't need the butterfly cakes, either. See if they can change them to something death related instead. Brains, maybe? Or skulls? Yes, skulls. I like skulls. And the giant light up butterfly, I'm not sure there's much we can do with that. See if there's a children's home that wants it. We need to change the lighting, too. No more twinkles. Something eerie..."

The list went on, and I could practically see the smoke coming from Myrna's fingers as they danced across the surface of her iPad. It matched the steam coming from her ears.

Finally, Ishmael stopped talking and produced a packet of flying saucers from his pocket. I didn't even realise you could buy those in America. Did he import them from the UK specially?

"Candy? It helps me to think."

Oh, how I longed to snatch the bag off him. He'd done quite enough thinking for the day already, thank you very much.

Myrna looked up, dazed and struggling to focus. "Uh, Tia, I'll need to give you some of this. The cakes, the—"

"No, no, no," Ishmael interrupted. "Tia's coming with me." He leaned over and patted Myrna on the hand. "I'm sure you'll do a fandabidozi job, as usual."

She glared at me, hate in her eyes. I wasn't surprised. Not only was I getting to hang out with the boss, she was stuck with the scut work.

"I could stay and help Myrna instead," I suggested. "There *is* a lot for one person to do."

Plus, it seemed safer hanging out with Myrna than with the wannabe Prince of Darkness.

"But, Tia, I need you to help me pick out the

corpses."

A small smile of triumph lit up Myrna's face, fighting with animosity. Maybe she hadn't got the short straw after all.

I, on the other hand, felt a little bit sick.

CHAPTER 6

I GAZED OUT of the window as we drew further away from the model agency, the Lincoln Center, and my apartment. Into the unknown.

Or, as it turned out, into a vast, loft-like space filled with dead things.

Professor Ito met us at the door wearing a set of surgical scrubs and greeted Ishmael as if he were an old friend. Perhaps he was.

"Come now, Ishmael. I have a good selection for you to choose from at the moment. I'm sure we can find something you like."

Dread clawed its way up my throat as we followed Professor Ito along a corridor and through a plain white door. I only hoped we had more luck with the dead models than the live ones. At least the corpses weren't going to be upset if they got rejected.

"Behold! My treasures."

The cavernous room in front of us was an avalanche of white. The floor, the ceiling, the walls, every piece of furniture—all white. Not off-white, apple-white, rose-white, or any of those other fancy colours you get in paint tins. Just stark, clinical white.

The only splashes of colour came from the corpses. Tens of them dotted around, maybe even hundreds. I'd thought they'd be gruesome, grisly statements of bad taste. I mean, they were *corpses*. But somehow, they weren't hideous. Horror gave way to fascination as the professor led us around his exhibits, explaining a few facts about them as he went.

"I call the process plastification. They'll never rot, smell, or deteriorate." He rapped on the chest of one with his knuckles as we walked past. "See? Solid."

The sound sent a shudder through me. These things were human. But they weren't...beings. Each was arranged into a pose, everything from graceful to dramatic.

A ballet dancer, impossibly balanced on one toe, forever extended one arm towards the ceiling. Her skin had been removed to show how each muscle worked in tandem to hold her there. Next to her, a sprinter ran for the finish line, head tipped forward to gain that vital extra inch.

"How do you make them stand up like that?" I asked Professor Ito.

Somehow, I'd got past the initial shock and my horror had turned to...interest? Fascination?

"They have hidden supports built in as part of the preparation process. They're very strong."

We continued through the huge room filled with unearthly delights. Even Ishmael stayed silent as I learned more about anatomy than I had in four years of biology at school. Muscles, bone, tendons, blood vessels... The only model with any skin was holding his entire body's-worth aloft in triumph, as if proud that his mortal covering could contain him no more.

I reached a finger out and touched him. His sinewy chest felt cool and smooth, but still, I snatched my hand away.

"He won't bite," the Professor said, caressing the spot I'd just felt.

I knew that, but even so...

It wasn't just humans on display, either. A panther stalked past, reminding me of Emmy's adopted cat, Kitty, although slightly smaller. Next to a sofa, a young girl stood hand in hand with a monkey, each gazing at the other with unseeing eyes.

"Why do you do this?" I whispered.

"A living being is the most beautiful, fascinating thing on earth. Flesh and soul come together to create something magical. Every body is different, but underneath, we're remarkably similar. I want to show the world that beauty isn't just skin-deep."

Didn't that make Professor Ito the antithesis to the fashion industry? And Ishmael wanted to join forces with him?

Did the man even know what he was doing?

I glanced across at my boss, who was staring at a woman tiptoeing on a tightrope made from her intestines. He felt my gaze on him and turned around.

"Beauty is more than just pretty clothes, Tia. It has to come from within."

He *did* know what he was doing, didn't he?

Yes, he may still have been batshit crazy, but my admiration for him went up a notch.

Ishmael was less animated than usual as he walked through the display for the second time, selecting the figures he wanted for his show. In true Ishmael fashion, he picked out the ones most likely to cause a stir, including tightrope girl and a couple in a passionate embrace.

"What time is it?" Ishmael asked as we climbed

back into the car. According to Myrna, he didn't wear a watch in case he got tan lines. In New York. In winter.

"Seven o'clock."

And I still had to buy sportswear because when I'd messaged Bradley earlier, his plane had just touched down in Los Angeles.

We'd been in Professor Ito's loft for hours. Hours, and I'd barely noticed because I'd been lost in the whole exhibition. The colour... The clarity... The poses... The amount of work that had gone into creating every detail astounded me, and although I'd felt utterly sick when we arrived, the icy fingers squeezing my throat eased with each macabre work of art I studied. Professor Ito had achieved something I'd never thought possible.

He'd found the beauty in death. The elegance.

And he'd given me something I hadn't had since Ryan left me.

Hope.

Hope that one day, even if I couldn't embrace death as the professor did, I could learn to accept it.

But today wasn't that day, and as we drove through Manhattan, a wave of grief crashed over me as old feelings rushed back. I turned my head to the window, watching the streets go past in a blur of lights as I tried to hide my tears from Ishmael.

But I couldn't keep my sobs quiet.

"Tia, what's wrong?"

I shook my head and held up my hand.

"Is it the show? We still have two weeks, and we'll do it. I have the utmost faith in you and Myrna. Bradley recommended you very highly."

I barely heard his words. Instead, I covered my face

with my hands and tried to wipe away my tears with a sleeve, but it was made of some weird shiny stuff and all it did was smear the wetness about a bit. Ishmael pressed something into my hand, and I looked down to find a handkerchief decorated with tiny hummingbirds. The cheerful pattern didn't match my mood, but I swiped at my face with it anyway.

Ishmael wrapped an arm around my shoulders and turned me towards him, tilting up my chin with his other hand.

"Tia, what's wrong? You're worrying me."

I couldn't speak, and his kindness only made me cry harder. Ishmael let go of my chin and hugged me. I buried my face against his chest, the smell of his perfume burrowing into my consciousness.

He spoke again, and it took a few seconds to register that his words weren't aimed at me.

"Bradley? She just keeps crying, and I'm not sure what I've done to upset her."

A pause.

"Well, I had an interview then we viewed some models. Oh, and the new theme for the show is death, so we went to look at some corpses."

Bradley's shriek pierced clear through my wall of pain. I couldn't make out his exact words, but it was clear from his tone that he was giving Ishmael an earful.

"But they weren't ugly corpses. They were very tasteful."

More Bradley.

"Well, how was I meant to know? You didn't tell me. Am I supposed to be psychic?"

Bradley's voice dropped an octave, but I still

couldn't make out what he was saying.

"Okay, I'll deal with it," Ishmael replied. "No, you stay put. I'll call you later."

He tossed the phone back one seat and turned my chin once again.

"Tia, you should have told me what happened to your boyfriend. I'd never have asked you to go with me this evening."

I gave another shuddering sniff. "How? I barely know you."

"I do appreciate the difficulty." He hit a button and the privacy screen between us and the driver wound down. "Take us to my place," he instructed the man behind the wheel.

His place. "What? I just want to go home."

"That's probably not the best idea. According to Bradley, your apartment's full of workmen. Something about the new chandeliers taking longer to install than they anticipated. And besides, I can't leave you on your own like this."

I didn't want to be alone with Ishmael, not least because he was my boss, but I didn't fancy being stuck in a half-built branch of IKEA either.

What to do? What to do?

IKEA lost. Even if I didn't know Ishmael, Bradley did, and I trusted Bradley's judgement. And weirdly, it was almost easier to break down and talk to a semi-stranger than somebody I knew.

No way did I want Emmy, or Mack, or my brother to see how weak I really was.

When the car stopped, Ishmael took my hand and led me into a swanky apartment building, and we caught the lift all the way up to the penthouse. None of that two-floors-worth-of-stairs malarkey he'd pulled earlier. Maybe he only did that in daylight hours?

 And although I didn't want to be there, I couldn't deny that a small part of me was fascinated to see where Ishmael lived. If his office and reputation were anything to go by, it would be a cave of eccentricities.

When we walked through the small hallway, complete with four different coloured walls, a ceiling covered in tinfoil, and a floor made from stainless steel, I wasn't disappointed. And that was nothing compared to the main room. I'd walked into a modern art gallery.

The sofa cut into the side of a life-sized hippopotamus in front of the turtle-shaped coffee table didn't surprise me. Nor did the model of the Terminator proffering the remote controls or the fish tank where a miniature shark swam around a model of Christ the Redeemer.

What did surprise me was when Ishmael led me all the way through the gallery and into a smaller room on the other side. Why? Because it was...normal.

A squashy leather sofa faced a flat screen TV. A plain wooden coffee table sat in front, home to a couple of copies of Vogue and Michael Anderle's latest offering. The lighting was subdued and tasteful, and the whole place felt homey. Comfortable.

I stopped short.

Ishmael looked over his shoulder and chuckled.

"Come on, girl, I'm showing you all my secrets. Bradley said I could trust you. Take a seat." He waved at the sofa.

I slowly sank down as instructed and found it as comfy as it looked.

"Do you want a drink? Afraid I'm out of bat's blood

but I make a mean margarita."

I nodded. Still speechless.

What was Ishmael playing at?

Five minutes later he came back, and he wasn't wrong about his mixing skills.

"This is amazing."

"I worked in a bar while I was at design college. It's where I met Bradley, actually." He took a sip of his own drink, not a swizzle stick in sight. "I've ordered pizza."

"Pizza?"

He kicked off his purple, sparkly cowboy boots and propped his feet up on the table. "I suppose you're wondering what's going on, aren't you? What all this is?" He waved at the room.

"It had crossed my mind."

"Well, this is me. The real me. Everything out there..." He pointed towards the hippo-room. "Is just for show."

"Come again?"

"Let me start from the beginning. I first met Bradley in my second year of college. I was designing clothes; he was designing the people that went inside them. The hair and the make-up. He's a genius at that, but I'm sure you don't need me to tell you."

He didn't. Not only had Bradley worked his magic on me, but I'd seen him transform Emmy from assault-course chic to red carpet ready in only an hour.

"We bonded over after-hours cocktails and a shared love of all things sparkly. At the time, my last roommate had just emigrated to Vietnam, and Bradley was sharing a place with a guy who liked to clip his toenails at the dining table. It worked out best for both of us when he moved into my spare room."

"How does one even clip toenails at a dining table?"

"The way Bradley described it, he was into yoga and he just used to prop his feet up—"

"Enough. It was a rhetorical question. Yeuch!"

Ishmael wrinkled his nose. "Exactly, dear girl. Anyhow, I always wanted to design beautiful clothes. Elegant dresses, well-cut suits. Outfits that women would love, and more importantly, pieces that would make them love themselves while they were wearing them. But the problem was, they didn't sell."

"Why not? It's always hard to find elegant clothes."

"I know, but elegant isn't always exciting. Anyway, it started with these." He held his drink aloft. "One evening, a few weeks before the end-of-year show, I was trying to work out how to improve my grades. My creations just weren't eye-catching enough to get the teachers' attention."

"I can't imagine that." Right now, Ishmael had the world's attention.

He gave a practised flick of his wrist. "Then my work here is done. Well, not quite. There's always somebody trying to imitate me, but nobody's managed it yet."

"So, how did a drink lead to all that?" I pointed out at the great room and its shark tank.

"Well, over too many margaritas, Bradley and I devised an experiment. We'd redesign the clothes for my show and see what happened. My grades sucked anyway, so I didn't have much to lose."

Okay, I understood the too-many-margaritas part. I could drink a whole bucketful of Ishmael's magical concoction.

"What happened? Did you seriously redesign

everything?"

"Too damn right I did. *We* did. Bradley helped a lot. We basically thought of every wacky idea we could then worked day and night right up until the show began to make them all."

"And what happened?"

"They loved it. Every single piece! The dress shaped like a candy wrapper, the giraffe boots, the hat made out of a tiny solar system. All I had to do was act like a buffoon and the critics lapped it up. Jon died, and Ishmael was born."

I choked on a piece of ice and Ishmael thumped me on the back.

"Your name's Jon?"

He chuckled. "Jon's my first name. Ishmael's my middle name. Or, now, my only name. Although I'm thinking of changing it into a symbol like Prince did."

"So you just carried on acting the way you do for the publicity?"

"Exactly, my dear girl. The fashion world loves a character, so we gave them Ishmael. The good thing about it is that the attention I get for designing what amounts to crap allows me to sell the beautiful clothes I always wanted to, albeit in a separate line." He grinned over the rim of his glass. "That's where the money is."

I took everything back. Ishmael wasn't crackers at all. He was a shrewd businessman.

"That's the most brilliant thing I've ever heard."

"Just don't tell anyone. Sometimes it's fun being Ishmael. Did you see the look on Myrna's face when I told her I was cancelling the butterflies? One day, I'm determined to get her to lose that stick she keeps up her ass."

Our giggles turned into full blown laughter, and I was clutching my sides when the sound of Britney Spears' "Crazy" filled the place. Ishmael pushed himself to his feet.

"Pizza's here, back in a few."

When he deposited the boxes onto the table in front of me, my mouth started to water. I hadn't felt hungry all day, but suddenly I was ravenous.

"Don't let the food get cold," Ishmael said over his shoulder as he headed for a door on the far side of the room. "I'm just going to change."

It was a very different Ishmael who came back. Gone were the skintight jeans and the sparkly waistcoat, and with his face devoid of make-up, he looked several years younger. An average, everyday guy in jeans and a T-shirt, albeit with the fantastic hair of a young Michael Jackson.

He saw my eyes widen and put a finger to his lips. "Ssh! Don't tell. You know, sometimes I put on a cap and sensible shoes and go out like this. Nobody ever recognises me. I just have to remember not to snap my fingers at anyone or tiptoe daintily around the cracks in the sidewalk."

"Perhaps I should start calling you Jon."

Three hours, two pizzas, a bottle of wine, and a rom-com later, both of us lolled on the sofa, barely able to move.

"You want to stay here tonight? Or shall I have someone drop you home?" Ishmael asked.

I hesitated. I didn't have any clothes or anything with me.

He misread my silence. "Rest assured, that's not what I'm thinking of. If you must know, my tastes extend more in Bradley's direction than yours."

"No, that's not it. It's just I'd have to go home anyway to get clothes for tomorrow."

"I have six bedrooms here, and four of them are stuffed to the ceiling with free stuff that people give me. Everything from clothes to shoes to skincare to jewellery to homeware. Help yourself. Don't forget that at work we're going for outrageous, yes?"

I stifled a yawn. "In that case, I'd love to stay. Thank you."

"I'll find you a T-shirt to sleep in."

The shirt he gave me was still in the plastic, advertising "Chateau Miel's ChaCha cream," whatever that was. I dreaded to imagine.

The room was nice, though. More of Jon showing through. Clean lines, decorated in muted pastels. No fake fur or disco balls in sight.

As I lay in bed, I felt more relaxed than I had in weeks. Despite the dramas and dead people, I'd coped, and maybe, just maybe, I could see a tiny chink of light at the end of the tunnel.

CHAPTER 7

"HOW ABOUT THIS one?" I held up a shiny pink top decorated with pineapples.

"Perfect," Ishmael said. "You need to make sure the skirt clashes, though. I love how you're getting into the spirit of things."

"What do you think?" I fished an orange mini with giant white spots off one of the seemingly endless racks in front of me. This was utterly ridiculous but somehow quite fun.

Ishmael gave me a thumbs up. "That absolutely doesn't match. Well done! But don't forget we're going walking this morning. Sportswear's in a closet in the next room."

Ah yes, the power walking. How could I possibly forget?

Half an hour later, Ishmael and I were in the car riding to the office. He'd gone for a blue velour tracksuit covered in glitter while I'd found yoga pants with a cat pattern and a matching jacket. Apparently, matching was okay if it was completely over the top. I'd topped it off with a set of neon-green sweatbands.

"This okay?" I'd asked, giving Ishmael a twirl.

He applauded before spinning around himself and glancing over his shoulder. "Does my ass look big in this?"

Anything but, and he knew it. He had one of those slim figures all girls envied.

"Oh, enormous."

The journey to the office only took ten minutes, most of it at a snail's pace.

"Why do we have to drive? Why didn't we just walk from your apartment?" I asked.

"Ah, young grasshopper. You have so much left to learn. The paparazzi know to wait outside the building on a Wednesday morning to get photos as I climb out the car."

Oh hell, and there I was, looking like a Walmartian.

He chuckled at the look of horror on my face. "Don't worry. They'll be taking pictures of me, not you. Just put your hood up if you want to be on the safe side."

Myrna was waiting for us by the kerb, wearing a black jacket and jogging bottoms with pink stripes down the sides. Plain. Too plain. Her eyes bugged out of her head when she saw me.

"Where did you get that outfit?"

"Just a little something I found lying around in the wardrobe."

She narrowed her eyes. "Well, we can't all be blessed with an endless budget for designer outfits, can we? And how come you're riding with Ishmael?"

He answered for me. "I saw Tia walking, and walking doesn't start until half past eight today."

At least she didn't know the truth. She'd been grumpy enough yesterday when I went to Professor Ito's with Ishmael, without her finding out I'd popped over to the boss's house for dinner afterwards.

"Time to go, girls," Ishmael announced.

He strode out in front of us, butt wiggling, while we tried to keep up. Eleven photographers scurried around him, all trying to get the best shot. A total circus. I'd never put much thought into how intrusive the media could be, but seeing this, it really hit home. At least Ishmael had worked out how to use them to his advantage.

We walked for exactly half an hour, finishing back where we started. Then it was time for the same routine as yesterday. Ishmael went for his power nap while I arranged his paperclips and Myrna headed out for coffee.

Did Ishmael really nap? Or was he checking stock prices and adding up the profits from his business empire?

Once again, Myrna didn't bother to get me a drink, and that didn't go unnoticed by Ishmael when he came back.

"Tia, didn't you want coffee?"

"Er, I didn't know I could have one."

"Myrna didn't ask you?"

No, she hadn't, and I could see that now she realised that possibly hadn't been the smartest idea.

She cut in, trying to save her own skin. "I didn't think Tia looked like a coffee person. She's quite perky enough already."

"Well, she might have wanted a smoothie. Or a bubble tea. Next time, ask her. It would be the rainbows and sunshine thing to do."

He smiled and waved his wand in the air. Yes, his wand. It was sparkly with pink feathers on the end. Goodness knows where he got it from. Probably the same place Bradley bought his pens.

"I'll be sure to do that," Myrna replied through gritted teeth.

"So what's the plan for today?" I asked, trying to lighten the atmosphere in the room. Myrna clearly wasn't feeling the rainbows and sunshine. She was more black clouds and thunder.

"Well, I have clothes to design," Ishmael said. "Which leaves you girls with a show to organise. We have corpses. Now we need the rest. Let's start a mood board!"

A stack of magazines was produced, Google was fired up, and Pinterest was consulted. The printer sitting in the corner of the office on a giant My Little Pony was soon working overtime.

And Ishmael? Ishmael got out a pad of paper and started drawing. And holy moly, the man had talent. I'd never seen anything like it. His pen flashed over the page, and soon we had pictures of dresses, tops, skirts, hats, shoes, and trousers.

If I'd had any doubts about his abilities as a designer before, they evaporated into a tiny puff of multicoloured glitter.

I picked up a rough outline of a pretty, floaty, slightly whimsical dress. At least it would have been whimsical if not for the pattern Ishmael had sketched in a panel at the side. Skulls, skulls, and more skulls.

"What do you think?" Ishmael asked.

"The design's pretty. I'm not sure I'd wear that pattern, though."

"I'll put the pattern on for the show then release the dress in different prints, so it's the design I'm most worried about."

Which made sense now I knew about Ishmael's

hidden business brain. I flipped through his other drawings, seeing as he didn't seem to mind. A top covered in a muscle print. A leather jacket with a giant skull stitched on the back. High-heeled boots with jewelled bones. All beautiful yet suitably outrageous—Ishmael would certainly maintain his reputation with that little lot.

And while I looked at his drawings, he'd been rifling through my printouts. He held up one of the sheets with a shriek.

"Would you look at this? I love it! We have to get these."

I peered at the photo he'd picked out and my eyes rolled all of their own accord. A squirrel had got its head stuck in a Halloween decoration and looked like a zombie.

"This'll be amazing! Where do we get trained squirrels from? We can have them give out the goody bags."

"I-I-I don't know, Ishmael," Myrna stuttered. "I'll get right onto it, though."

"Hang on a minute," I said. "I'm not sure you can train a squirrel. And could they carry a bag? I mean, they're really tiny."

Ishmael put the picture down and screwed his face up. "You're right. Of course, you're right."

Myrna breathed a sigh of relief behind me.

"We want our goody bags to be the best. Stuffed full. Let's go for monkeys instead."

I heard a thump, and Ishmael peered over my shoulder. I turned to find Myrna sprawled out on the floor, her lime green, peep-toe ballet pumps pointing up at the helicopter-shaped light fitting.

"Do you think her blood sugar's dropped or something?" Ishmael asked.

Good grief. "Or something. It was your sodding monkeys that did it. Help me get her onto the sofa."

I grabbed her arms and Ishmael lifted her feet, and between us we got her propped up on the orange stripy cushions that had appeared overnight. Ishmael fanned her with his sketchpad, and after a few seconds, her eyes flickered open.

"What happened?"

"You had an allergic reaction to monkeys," I told her.

She sank back into the cushions and put her hand over her eyes. "Oh no, not monkeys."

"Okay, okay," Ishmael huffed. "Ditch the monkey idea. We'll just have to find some hunky men to give out the swag instead. They can wear masks."

Myrna brightened at the sound of hunky men, and Ishmael didn't seem too unhappy at the prospect, either.

But Myrna's face took on a black look when Ishmael continued, "Tia, you handle the male models. Myrna can give you the details of the agencies. Try for twelve, ten minimum. Myrna, you sort out the revised catalogues and something appropriate for the seating."

"No problem," I said. "You go back to your drawings." *And stop interfering.*

"I need to go down to the workshop instead. Sprinkle some magic pixie dust around."

I thought he was speaking metaphorically, but he rummaged around in his desk drawer and came up with a small jar of something sparkly.

"Got it!" he announced before bounding out of the

room.

Well, he certainly had this acting bonkers lark down to a fine art.

As soon as he left, Myrna turned on me. "How come you get the models while I get catalogues and chairs?"

"Uh, I don't really know?"

"How did you land this job, anyway? You've never even worked in fashion, yet somehow you just walked into a job with Ishmael? I don't get it."

What was I supposed to say? Should I confess that I hadn't had so much as an interview?

"A friend of mine knows Ishmael, and he arranged it. It wasn't like I asked him to."

"So, let me get this straight. You got this job, and you didn't even want it?"

"Well, yes. I mean, no. Now I'm here, I do want it." And I found I really did. Ishmael was lovely, and I could learn so much from him about fashion.

Myrna's eyes darkened with fury. I took a step back, but she closed the distance, reaching out to prod me in the chest with one black painted fingernail. Wow. She fitted right in with the "death" theme, and she wasn't even trying.

"Listen up, Tia. I was here first. That makes me the first assistant and you the second assistant, which means Ishmael tells me what to do and I tell you what to do. And I'm telling you right now, I'm booking the models and you're doing the catalogue."

My mouth went dry. Then it stopped working, along with most of my brain cells. What should I say to her?

I tried to channel my inner Emmy. How would she deal with this? Okay, she'd probably shut Myrna's pointy finger in a drawer and call the first model agency on the list.

But I wasn't Emmy, and my emotions had been all over the place since Ryan's death. Any confidence I had left withered under Myrna's evil glare.

"Okay, no problem. I'll get started on the catalogue straight away," I said, then cursed myself silently for being so weak.

Worse, I hated the triumphant grin that spread across Myrna's face as she stalked off to stir her cauldron.

I spent the rest of the morning rearranging layouts for the new catalogue. Lucky Luke was such a techno-geek because I'd spent so much time around his computers I was well versed in the program I had to use. The pages looked kind of gappy, though, seeing as I didn't have the right pictures to use yet.

Meanwhile, Myrna yacked on the phone in the background, organising model castings for tomorrow. Her smug tone made me want to grab her throat and squeeze.

Think sunshine and rainbows, Tia.

I rarely felt angry like this, but dealing with Myrna was worse than chewing cotton wool. Eventually, she rolled Ishmael's chair back. Yes, she'd even taken to sitting at his desk.

"I'm going for lunch. Don't forget to sort out the seating, will you?"

"Yes, Myrna."

The seating took another hour and a half, and I decided on light grey covers, each with a rib cage stencilled on the back. Kind of raw, Banksy-style. Simple yet effective.

Myrna still hadn't come back, and my stomach grumbled like a cargo plane taking off. A sign in reception told me there was a staff restaurant in the building, so it seemed like a good time to investigate. Would it serve normal food? Or Ishmael's fare of magic mushrooms and stardust?

I never found out.

When I poked my head around the door of the Hoohah Café, Myrna's nasal tones greeted me. She faced the window, holding court with a bunch of other girls hanging onto her every word as she spread her nastiness.

"That new intern's got no talent, you know. She only got the job because of narcissism. She wouldn't have stood a chance if she'd had to interview for it like everyone else."

Narcissism? Surely she meant nepotism? I wasn't narcissistic, was I? A few years ago, perhaps, but I tried so hard not to be that person anymore.

"Don't worry, Myrna. We all know how hard you work."

"And she wanted to book the models instead of arranging the seating plan. Can you imagine her nerve?"

Now what? Should I confront the bitch? Emmy would push me to do exactly that, but Emmy wasn't here. Instead, I skulked behind a potted palm as Myrna carried on trashing me.

"She's dressing all fancy to impress Ishmael too, the snooty sneak."

"It was his suggestion," I wanted to yell. "He helped me to pick the damn clothes out."

But I stayed silent. Better to do that than dig my

grave deeper. Probably nobody would have believed me, anyway.

But I couldn't listen to another word, and my appetite had deserted me. I fled upstairs, skipping the elevator and taking the stairs two at a time, which meant I sounded like Darth Vader by the time I got back to my tiny desk in the corner of Ishmael's office. Honestly, this was worse than being at school with all the back-biting and snide comments. At the Marsden Academy, I'd adopted an "if you can't beat them, join them" ethos, but with my insides still so raw, the last thing I wanted was to get sucked into that world again.

When Myrna sauntered in half an hour later, my anger was simmering away nicely. I wanted to come out on top of this mess, but how?

Another of Emmy's gems sprang to mind: Never lower your standards to accommodate those who won't raise theirs.

She was right. I couldn't stoop to Myrna's level. The only way I'd win and be able to live with myself afterwards was to do a great job with whatever shit she dished out to me. Straight-up sabotage was out.

Instead, I turned back to my laptop and started double-checking everything I'd done so far.

Well done, Tia. Adulting like a pro.

CHAPTER 8

IT WAS PAST eight o'clock when I got back to my apartment, and I felt like a corpse myself. Myrna had swanned off at five, citing a date.

"Hot men don't wait, Tia," she'd said.

I'd almost offered her a packet of batteries, but I managed to refrain just in time.

When I walked in the door, I almost turned around and walked straight out again. How did I get tired enough to pick the wrong apartment?

Then I realised my key had fitted the lock and took a better look at the stunning vista of cream and blue in front of me.

Holy shit.

Rugs. I had rugs. My dining table sported a candelabra and six place settings, and artwork covered the walls. I recognised a few of my paltry efforts and one of Xav's masterpieces above a funky stainless steel fireplace. Tall white speakers, a desk, half a dozen ornate lamps. And flowers. Bradley must have shared my vision because there they were in a huge vase on the kitchen counter.

"Oh, Bradley, what have you done?" I whispered as I walked over.

A bottle of champagne waited in an ice bucket next to the peonies, the cubes long since melted. I felt the temperature. It had been here since yesterday.

A note was propped up against it.

Sorry I couldn't wait, darling girl. The bitch has sent me to her West Coast lair. Enjoy your new space, and I expect an invite for the housewarming party. B

The bitch was Emmy, of course, and no, she didn't mind being called that. Indeed, she referred to herself as one most of the time.

I carefully folded the note up and put it into a drawer—a drawer now filled with cutlery and a variety of other shiny kitchen gadgets, none of which I had a clue how to use.

Bits of label peeled off the champagne bottle as I lifted it out of the water, and I put it in the fridge. I'd got past drinking alone. The Veuve Clicquot could wait for a special occasion.

I had a feeling it would be waiting a long time.

Bradley's idea of a housewarming party was a bust too. Parties were for celebration, and there was nothing to celebrate about the circumstances that led me to New York. Instead, I found a loaf of bread and a block of cheese in the fridge, cursed as I grated off part of a fingernail, made myself a sandwich, then crawled into bed.

I'd been dreading work the next day, but when I arrived at eight, dressed in a pair of shorts and ready for my pogo stick session with Ishmael, I got a reprieve.

"Myrna emailed me," he said. "She said she was going straight to an agency to look at models. I thought I asked you to organise the models? I hoped you'd like that?"

Yes, I would have liked it.

"Myrna and I decided to swap. We, er, realised I was better with the catalogue software."

If I told him I'd had no choice, he'd have intervened for sure, but that would only have made things more awkward between me and the self-proclaimed number one assistant. Luckily, he was already off on another tangent. How he managed to talk and pogo at the same time, I had no idea. I struggled to do more than three hops.

"Speaking of catalogues, the first pieces are ready, and they need to be photographed. Jenna's going to do that. I'll send her up when she arrives, and you can work together. Bend your knees more, Tia."

I tried that and managed four hops as I considered today's tasks. *Please, don't let Jenna be another Myrna.*

She wasn't. As it turned out, she didn't like Myrna any more than I did.

"She's so big on herself," Jenna said, flicking her red hair over her shoulder as I followed her downstairs. She couldn't have been much older than me, but she exuded a confidence I could only dream of. "And she tells everyone she's been working in fashion for five years and that she used to work at Vogue, but what she doesn't say is that she spent two years working on the checkout at Bloomingdale's, and her year at Vogue was in the mail room."

I couldn't help but snigger. "She was supposed to be doing the catalogue, but she decided she was doing the models instead."

"Doing the models? Yeah, she wishes. She's been

single since she got here. Any guy with half a brain runs a mile."

"She told me she had a date last night."

"Meh, with her computer. She spends most of her life in internet chat rooms. Her 'date' was probably some fifty-year-old pervert." Jenna used little finger quotes around the word "date."

"Seriously?" I started laughing.

"For sure. She let it slip one evening when she'd had too much to drink. Mostly, she goes on this old-school chat room called SpeedChat, and her username's MissMyrna. Sometimes we go on there just to wind her up, but don't tell her that, whatever you do."

"My lips are sealed. I can't believe she skipped off work to message strangers on the internet."

"Believe it, sister. Now, let's sort out these photos."

If Ishmael was a design genius, then Jenna was his photography counterpart. She picked exactly the right angles, selected the perfect lighting, and knew how to show each piece at its absolute best.

"These are amazing," I told her as I peered at the tiny screen on the back of her camera.

"Thanks! Do you have what you need?"

"Absolutely. My biggest problem will be narrowing down which to use."

Jenna grinned and blushed at the same time. "Can't help you there, I'm afraid. Same time tomorrow?"

"I think so, if Ishmael's finished more pieces."

"Oh, he will have. He works like a demon. He'll barely sleep for a week, and at the end of it, he'll have a collection that any other designer would have taken months over."

"He's done this before, then? This last-minute

thing?"

"Every season. He does it every season."

You know, it was actually a relief to hear that. I'd assumed all this panic, all this rushing around, was something unusual. But once again, it was just Ishmael.

"Things'll work out okay then, I hope."

"This is Ishmael. Things will work out spectacular."

I spent the rest of the day sorting out the catalogue and organising the set changes, seeing as Myrna had managed to make the model viewings last eight flipping hours. Ishmael brought me lunch, and we ate together while I showed him the photos from the morning.

"Fantastic, Tia. This show is going to be the bomb. I know it."

"I'm so nervous in case it goes wrong."

"Don't be. If shit happens, we'll throw glitter on it. Are you coming over for pizza again this evening?"

Aw, Bradley definitely found me a gem of a boss. "I'd—"

A knock at the door interrupted me, and Jenna poked her head around the edge.

"A group of us are going out for drinks. Wanna come?"

Ishmael beamed at her. "Tia would *love* to come."

"I, uh..."

"She'll be ready in ten minutes."

"Fab! We'll be downstairs in the atrium."

The door swung closed, and I bit my lip. "Ishmael, I'm not sure I'm ready to start going out again."

"It's only a few drinks."

"But I barely know any of the girls here, and what if we don't get on?"

What if they were all like Myrna?

"Jenna will look after you, and her friends are darlings. Now, sit down and I'll sort out your make-up."

"I'm not sure—"

He pointed at his chair. "Sit."

Nine and a half minutes later, Ishmael had given me smokey eyes and adorned me with a jewelled necklace. Just a sample, he said, but it looked expensive. Before I could protest further, he'd shoved me out of the door and into the lift.

"Have fun, sweetie."

Fun? I didn't have fun anymore. I existed.

When I got downstairs, I found Jenna standing with a brunette while three more girls fidgeted on a grey leather sofa. I suspected the main reason they looked uncomfortable was the metal spikes studding the cushions.

Jenna saw me staring at it.

"Ishmael calls it the 'bed of nails.' He doesn't want people hanging in the atrium for ages. We only sit on it when our shoes hurt too much."

I checked their feet and sure enough, each of the seated girls was a slave to fashion. Their heels ranged between four and five inches. Thank goodness I'd worn kitten heels today even if I did feel kind of short.

The Wild Heart cocktail bar was only a block from the office, and I suspected the girls had made it their regular haunt because they physically couldn't walk any further. A neon heart lit up the outside, while inside had dim, multicoloured lighting and a drinks menu nobody without a PhD in bartending could understand.

Jenna's confidence didn't waver as she ordered a Cloud Surfer.

"What is it?" I asked.

She shrugged. "That's part of the fun. You never quite know how drunk you're gonna get." A click of her fingers, and the barman raised an eyebrow. "Make that two," she told him.

After my fifth mystery cocktail, I'd stopped worrying about what might be in them. I was, however, a little concerned that the room wouldn't keep still.

"Why do thingsh keep moving?" I asked Jenna.

She giggled, slightly lopsided in only one shoe. She'd tossed the other into the crowd at the bar, convinced that her Prince Charming would find it and bring it back. So far, there was no sign of it, but the night was still young.

"Don't know. But I can see sounds. Ish that normal?"

"No idea." But I did have a brainwave. "Hold on, and I'll find out."

I took out my phone and dialled. Two rings later, Emmy answered, and I pressed the phone against my ear so I could hear her over the thumping music.

"Ish it normal to shee shounds?" I asked her.

Emmy would know. Emmy knew everything.

"Tia?"

"Yes! That's my name."

"Have you been drinking?"

"I don't know. Guysh, have I been drinking?"

A chorus of yeses and a hiccup gave me my answer.

"Yesh, apparently I have."

"Stay put; I'll send someone."

"I'm fine. Just a little...confused?"

Oh, oops. I dropped my phone into my Original Orchid. The barman fished it out and blotted it with a napkin, and Jenna slid something blue and frothy in my direction.

"Try this. It's...uh..."

"A Cayman Cruise," the barman said. "Blue Curaçao, vodka, and lemonade with a dash of coconut cream."

Fantastic. Who needed a phone, anyway?

Two drinks later, maybe three, a pair of strong arms picked me up and carried me towards the door. What the...?

"Wait! Am I being kidnapped again?"

The face that belonged to the arms swam into view, and boy, the guy was pretty. In fact, both of him were. Okay, yeah, I didn't mind being abducted this time.

"I'm Cade, from Blackwood's New York office. The boss said to get you home."

"Oh, like a taxshi?"

"Yeah, like a very expensive fucking taxi," he muttered under his breath.

"Hey, can you kidnap me too?" one of Jenna's friends asked. She held both wrists out. "You can even tie me up."

"I'll pass."

"How about staying for a drink?" Jenna asked.

Cade didn't bother to answer, and outside, he slid me into the back of a black town car waiting at the kerb.

"Are you gonna puke?" he asked.

I pondered that while he did up my seatbelt.

"No, I don't think so."

Cade didn't say anything, just tapped on the partition between us and the driver, and the car glided into the night.

Ooh, look at all the sparkly lights. So pretty...

My head throbbed as I turned over and buried my face in the pillow. What had I done to deserve this?

Last night came back in flashes, stills from a movie reel. The bar... The drinks... Jenna's shoe.

Shit.

I held my breath as I peered under the covers. Phew. Fully clothed. Hmm, maybe I could just go to work like this again?

Speaking of work, when did I need to leave? I glanced over at my alarm clock. Oh, that's right. Thirty minutes ago.

Wait. What?

Five minutes to freaking eight! I leapt up and took the world's fastest shower, cold to wake myself up a bit. Nope, didn't work. I still felt like the undead as I sat down at my desk, having missed the morning's Zumba session.

Myrna gave me a filthy glare and looked pointedly at Ishmael's cuckoo clock, but Ishmael hooted with laughter.

"Girl, you look like you had the night I wanted to have."

"If I'm honest, I don't exactly remember what kind of night I had."

"Well, you should have them more often."

I didn't know about that. At the moment, Myrna's version of a good night had a lot to be said for it. At least she wasn't running on aspirin.

My partner in crime didn't appear too perky either when she arrived to do the next batch of photographs.

Jenna had a decidedly green tinge to her face, and when Ishmael offered her one of his organic, low-cal beef and lettuce wraps, she quickly shook her head.

"You look like you need to Photoshop yourself," I told her on our way downstairs.

"I'll be fine by this evening. Are you joining us? Friday nights at the Wild Heart are always, well, wild."

"What? For more drinks? No! I'm never drinking again."

"Nonsense. Practice, that's what you need. Practice makes perfect. And speaking of perfect, tell me more about that fine specimen who picked you up."

More hazy memories flitted back—the bar, the cocktails, the phone call. Oh, hell. I'd called Emmy. Should I apologise to her for drunk-dialling? Or simply pretend it never happened? Yes, that was a better option. Then there was Cade, the car ride, being carried up to my apartment. At least I knew why my phone was sticky. Amazing that it still worked at all.

"He's nobody special. Just a friend of a friend."

When I said I was never drinking again, it turned out I was lying. Oops.

That evening, I channelled the nineties and serenaded Cade with "Wannabe" by the Spice Girls as he carried me up the stairs.

"If you wannabe my luuuuuuva, you gotta get with my friennnnnnds."

He didn't crack a smile as he laid me down gently on the bed. "Heaven help me. When I retired from the Navy SEALs, I thought I was signing up for an easier life. How much did you drink?"

"Not sure." I'd lost count when I ran out of fingers, although my queasiness was partially due to the platter of cheese-stuffed jalapeños I'd eaten too.

I closed my eyes as Cade's footsteps jogged down the stairs, but a few minutes later, he came back.

"Here. Drink this."

"What is it?"

"Water."

Kind of boring, but he'd saved me from walking home so I gave him a thumbs up. "Thanks, Caaaaaaaade."

He sighed, saluted, and disappeared.

Tonight, I'd been knocking back Mellow Yellows. Small and sweet, a vivid daffodil colour that could only have been achieved with liberal amounts of artificial crap. Each came with a Skittle at the bottom of the shot glass, and Jenna had choked on a red one until the bartender walloped her on the back.

I drifted off for an hour, maybe two, but come midnight, I was wide awake, vaguely sober, and anything but mellow. All those E-numbers had finally hit the spot. Music. I needed music. And food. I ran down the stairs, well, tripped down the last three, and snatched up the remote control from the coffee table. How did my new stereo work? Hmm... Trickier than I thought, but then again, I never had been good with electronics. Too many buttons and a lack of instruction manual. Not to be deterred, I soon had cheesy pop blaring from my still-slightly-sticky phone as I danced around the kitchen. What could I make to eat that didn't require perfect hand-to-eye coordination?

Somebody—Cade?—had left a bottle of mineral

water on the counter with a post-it note stuck to the side. *Drink me.* I rolled my eyes, even though he wasn't there, and poured myself a glass to go with my incredibly artistic peanut-butter-and-potato-chip sandwich.

This was what single girls in New York did, wasn't it? Had fun? I sure knew how to have fun.

At least, more fun than Myrna.

Right? *Right?*

What was she up to tonight? Another "date?"

Hey, I could find out, couldn't I?

I slid my MacBook out of its case, proud of myself for entering the password correctly on only my second attempt. What had Jenna said that website was called? SpeedTalk? Nope. SpeedChat. That was it, all purple and orange and flashy.

Join a room!

Start chatting!

When the bell rings, decide whether to skip or save! If your partner saves you too, you can chat again.

Ah, so it was basically online speed dating, but without the dating part. Lame. So much for Myrna's hot man. Hadn't she heard of Tinder?

I typed her username into the search box: Miss Myrna.

Search functions are restricted to registered users only.

Dammit.

A box popped up: *Registration is free!*

Well, I'd got this far...

I needed a username, and I could hardly call myself Tia Cain, could I? Even Myrna wasn't stupid enough to miss that one. My full name, Portia? Too posh. My middle name, Victoria? Too British. No, I needed something completely different.

Got it!

Ashlyn Hale. I'd be Ashlyn Hale. That was the name Emmy had been using when I first met her, but now she'd gone back to being Mrs. Black, she didn't need it anymore. It was mine now. Hah!

I typed it in: *Ashylyn Hale*.

Usernames cannot contain spaces.

Fine. *AshlynHale*.

Username accepted. Registration complete.

Perfect. I tried the search box again. Each chat room was named after a place, and MissMyrna was in Tahiti. She wished. Bitch.

Visit Tahiti. Click.

Aw, how cheesy. Pairs of sun loungers sat beside a digital pool, each with a user icon attached. I'd chosen a generic cat as mine, and there it was, floating around in the water as a timer counted down from a poolside cabana.

Kind of ghastly.

Still, I'd got this far. I poured myself a glass of wine —just a small one—and waited for the clock to hit zero.

CHAPTER 9

DING DING!

MY cat ended up on a sun lounger next to an icon of a quill with a blue ring around it. So, a guy.

You are now chatting with BrilliantBanquo.

Who picked a username as pretentious as that? Well, when he started typing, I got my answer.

A complete dick.

AshlynHale: Hi.

BrilliantBanquo: Good evening. Delighted to meet you.

Formal. Okaaaay.

AshlynHale: So, what do you want to talk about?

BrilliantBanquo: Shall we discuss English Literature?

Literature? Like actual literature? Not some euphemism for crack or something? Because that was certainly what he'd been smoking if he thought I'd come to a chat room wanting to talk about ye olde English books. I'd had enough of that at school.

Still, this was my first go, and I didn't want to start off with an argument. I should be channelling those Yellow Mellows. Hic. Mellow Yellows.

AshlynHale: Is your name really Banquo?

BrilliantBanquo: No, my name is Bryce. Banquo is a character in Macbeth. I'm a Shakespearian actor.

AshlynHale: I think I saw Macbeth once.

Think? I remembered that day well. I'd watched the DVD in desperation the evening before my English literature exam when I realised I hadn't actually got around to reading the final act of the play.

BrilliantBanquo: Ah, Macbeth. One of the Bard's darkest and most powerful works. Written in 1606, did you know? A true tragedy in the most powerful sense of the word. I thought the characterisation of the Thane himself...

He was off. Line after line after line. Who did he think he was? Bloody Wikipedia?

I went to the kitchen and uncorked another bottle of rosé. Thank goodness Bradley had his priorities right when it came to the catering. The bell dinged as I sat back down, and I erased all of Banquo/Bryce's crap off my screen as I waited for my next potential playmate.

A pop-up appeared.

BrilliantBanquo has added you as a friend. Do you want to skip or save?

BrilliantBanquo could sod off back to the 1600s where he belonged. I clicked the *skip* button.

The icons shuffled around the screen, and I found myself lounging next to...I squinted closer...a rather famous pop star, microphone in hand.

ZaynMalik1234: Hello!

AshlynHale: Hi.

ZaynMalik1234: Hello!

I may have had a couple of drinks, but didn't he already say that?

AshlynHale: You're not actually Zayn Malik, are you?

ZaynMalik1234: lol, no! but I really really want to

be. my mom bought me the wig for christmas and I've got my own microphone and everything.

Someone shoot me now. I peered into my wine glass. Nope, there wasn't enough in there.

AshlynHale: So, can you sing?

ZaynMalik1234: not yet, but I'm going to learn.

AshlynHale: That's great. How old are you, then?

There was a long pause. Long enough for me to count to "twelve" many times over.

ZaynMalik1234: nineteen.

Okaaaay then. That would make me about thirty-seven. But who was I to shatter some young boy's dream?

AshlynHale: That's great! I'm sure you'll have your own boy band in no time.

ZaynMalik1234: yeh, my friend kevins gonna be in it wiv me. hes got his own drums.

AshlynHale: Awesome. Drums.

ZaynMalik1234: yeh, and i write the songs. I'll sing you one. i saw a girl, she was relly pretty, she gave me a twirl, when she walked down the streety...

No, Zayn, "streety" does not count as a word. It seemed like an excellent moment for a chocolate break. I got up and shuffled over to the kitchen. Tofu, spinach, kale, more green stuff. Aha! Jackpot—a family-size box of Belgian truffles. Thanks, Bradley. I truly loved that man.

I popped one into my mouth then picked up the box and took it back to the computer with me. Chocolate came from cocoa, which was a plant. That made it a vegetable. Therefore, by eating more of these delicious gems, I was getting my five a day. Not to mention the wine. Grapes were fruit, after all. Go me!

Rubbish filled my screen again, and I groaned around a mouthful of truffle. Delete, delete, delete. Oh, look. Brad from San Francisco wanted to talk to me. He had a little icon of the Golden Gate Bridge.

Please, let him be normal.

Brad-SanFran: Hi, Ashlyn.

AshlynHale: Hi, Brad. How are you?

Brad-SanFran: Great, thanks. So, where are you from?

AshlynHale: England.

Brad-SanFran: So you're an English Rose?

AshlynHale: I guess you could say that.

Brad-SanFran: I'm from West Coast USA myself. San Francisco.

AshlynHale: Your weather is probably better than ours.

Brad-SanFran: You English, always wanting to talk about the weather.

AshlynHale: Yes, we do tend to, don't we? What would you suggest?

Brad-SanFran: Tell me about you.

A good sign. So many men only liked to talk about themselves.

AshlynHale: What is there to tell? I'm nineteen, I'm working in my first job, and I like horses.

Brad-SanFran: Horses? So you enjoy riding, huh?

AshlynHale: Yes, I love it.

Brad-SanFran: Nothing like the feel of a big piece of meat between your thighs, is there? I do like a dirty girl.

I spluttered wine, narrowly missing the screen. That sure escalated quickly.

AshlynHale: That wasn't what I meant, you

pervert!

Brad-SanFran: Don't play coy. All girls like it hard. They're lying if they say they don't.

AshlynHale: You're sick in the head.

Brad-SanFran: Do you have a webcam???

The bell rang, and not soon enough. I had just enough time to copy and paste the chat transcript into a separate document and save it before the next weirdo arrived. If I sent it to Mack later, she could track Brad down and put him on a watch list or something. Of course, that would involve admitting I'd been hanging out in an internet chat room, so perhaps not.

The icons rotated again, and my pussy parked itself next to a steaming cup of black coffee. At least the guy had his priorities straight. I kept my fingers crossed for fourth time lucky.

AshlynHale: Hello.

WellRed: Hi. Nice cat. Yours?

To lie or not to lie, that was the question.

AshlynHale: Nope. I'm not sure my landlord allows pets. Nice coffee.

WellRed: Can't live without it. If you have a landlord, that makes you an adult?

AshlynHale: According to my birth certificate.

WellRed: Hallelujah. I keep getting twelve-year-old boys. Some kid just typed out an entire screenful of terrible song lyrics.

AshlynHale: Zayn Malik?

WellRed: That's the one. The only other girl I talked to tonight was kind of uppity. Kept on about how she worked in fashion.

At least it wasn't just me who found her obnoxious.

AshlynHale: MissMyrna?

WellRed: Yeah, that's her. She'd make any guy run a mile. You've had the pleasure too?

AshlynHale: Unfortunately, yes. It's probably not a good moment to mention that I work in fashion too.

WellRed: I've got nothing against fashion. It was more the attitude.

AshlynHale: I can understand that. So, what do you do?

WellRed: I work on my family's ranch.

AshlynHale: That sounds cool. What do you have there? Cattle? Horses?

WellRed: Both of those. And sheep, geese, and a couple goats. Plus the cats and dogs.

AshlynHale: Wow! A real menagerie. I just have horses.

WellRed: You ride? English or Western?

Well, what a pleasant change from Brad. Dare I assume that WellRed was reasonably normal?

AshlynHale: English. I'm English.

WellRed: England's a beautiful country. Kinda small. I went there a few years ago, but I didn't get a chance to look around much.

AshlynHale: Yes, it's small, but there's still a lot to see. Maybe you could take another trip there someday?

WellRed: I don't really travel anymore. But hey, I have the world at my fingertips with the internet, right?

AshlynHale: Too right. I mean, tonight I've managed to speak to a popstar-wannabe, a Shakespeare-obsessed weirdo, and a pervert all in twenty minutes.

WellRed: Which of those am I?

AshlynHale: Lol, none of them, thank goodness!

WellRed: Happy to hear that. Who was the pervert? I'm only on here to keep an eye on my little sister, and men like that need reporting.

AshlynHale: Brad-SanFran. He wanted to know if I had a webcam.

WellRed: I'll send in a report ticket. Can you do the same? There's a button on the support page.

AshlynHale: Sure. Which user is your sister?

At least if I reported Brad to the site, I could avoid the discussion with Mack. Because she'd tell my brother, and he was still in denial over me even knowing about the birds and the bees.

I was more than happy for him to stay that way.

WellRed: She's in another room at the moment, but I've already checked on the folks in there. Anyway, enough serious talk. Ice cream or fries?

AshlynHale: Sorry?

WellRed: Ice cream or fries? You can tell a lot about a person from their choice of junk food.

AshlynHale: Oh, in that case, I'm more of a chocolate girl myself. How about you?

Just as I looked down at the box of truffles going squidgy in my lap, trying to decide which one I wanted next, the bell rang. Chat over.

Why did I feel hollow inside?

How had I felt so relaxed having a five-minute conversation with a stranger sitting at the other end of an internet connection? I mean, I didn't even know how old he was. Or that he really had a ranch. He could have been a fifty-year-old man hunched over a laptop in a bedsit in Poland or a fifteen-year-old with a bad complexion and a good command of English.

I didn't even know whether he liked ice cream or fries.

So why did my finger hover over the *Save* button?

I had ten seconds left to decide. Did I click it? Did I?

The timer reached zero.

I hadn't clicked, and now I couldn't. The hollow feeling turned into a full-on pang of regret. What if? What if? What if? What if WellRed was a genuinely nice guy? What if I'd missed out on the chance to talk to somebody who didn't judge me by my history? Or worse, what if there was only one person out there for everyone and I'd be alone for the sorry remains of my life?

But then a small box popped up on the screen.

WellRed has added you as a friend. Do you want to skip or save?

My mouse clicked on the smiley face, seemingly of its own accord. What had I just done?

Whatever it was, I had no time to dwell on it because MissMyrna was up next.

Now, here's the great thing about the internet. You can be whoever or whatever you choose. Too many people chose to be stupid, but I chose to be devious. Emmy had taught me well.

MissMyrna: Hi.

AshlynHale: Hi, how are you?

MissMyrna: I'm exhausted. I work in fashion and I've had an extremely tiring day.

AshlynHale: Fashion, huh? I bet that's awesome.

MissMyrna: Usually it is, but my assistant hasn't been doing her job properly.

That little witch! She was talking about me, wasn't

she? How dare she say that when she'd done next to nothing all day? She couldn't even be bothered to organise Ishmael's paperclips. Oh, I was so going to enjoy this.

AshlynHale: That sucks. What do you do? Design? Modelling?

MissMyrna: I'm the right-hand woman of a top fashion designer. He keeps telling me he can't live without me.

Yeah, sure. Sort of like how a foot can't live without a verruca.

AshlynHale: Wow, that's such a coincidence. I'm a model myself. Will you be at NY Fashion Week?

MissMyrna: Of course. Will you be working there?

AshlynHale: Sure, I'm an old hand at it now. It'll be my fourth year. Such a magical event. The best of all the fashion weeks.

MissMyrna: Of course, I barely get time to enjoy it because I'm so busy working.

AshlynHale: I bet! I'm sure you'll be rushed off your feet—you sound like you're so conscientious. Say, if ever you're looking for a new job, you should give my dear friend Ishmael a call. You know, the orange peel dress?

MissMyrna: Yes, of course I know who he is. Why should I call him?

AshlynHale: He was telling me just a week or two ago how disappointed he was with his assistant. Apparently, she struggles with the most basic tasks. So he's on the lookout for a new one. You sound like you could be perfect for the job!

There was a ridiculously long pause, and I began drumming my fingernails on my fancy glass desk.

Come on, take the bait. Had she gone?

MissMyrna: Really?

AshlynHale: Yes! You should look him up. What he needs is someone efficient like you. Your boss is so lucky.

The bell dinged, and I punched the air. *My work here was done.*

Suddenly, I felt super tired, and it was all I could do to roll my chair back and drag myself upstairs.

Where was Cade when I needed him?

CHAPTER 10

WITH GOD AND the bird sitting outside on my balcony railing as my witnesses, I was never drinking again.

I rolled over in bed and groaned when I saw that once more I was late for work. Eight flipping thirty. I'd made it halfway to the shower before I realised it was Saturday.

Thank goodness.

Yesterday, I'd offered to help Ishmael out over the weekend, but he'd declined, saying, "Sometimes, darling, I just work better in peace."

I knew the feeling. I worked better without Myrna in the room. Or, in fact, anywhere in the building. Simply imagining she might be nearby cast a black cloud over my mood.

But with a whole weekend to do as I pleased, I blocked her out and focused on the positive. Or at least, I tried to. New York was a place I'd longed to spend time in, but I'd always planned to do it with Ryan. To be here without him, contemplating all the things we never got to do, visiting the places we never got to see, felt like a betrayal.

I pulled my bathrobe around me and crawled back into bed. Did I really want to be out and about in New York alone? Ryan's words came back to me, and I leaned over to pluck his letter from the drawer in my bedside table.

I don't want you to waste your life.

An involuntary sniffle escaped, and I wiped a lone tear away before others followed it. I *would* go out, dammit, and Ryan would be with me, if only in my heart.

MoMA. I'd go to the Museum of Modern Art. It had long been at the top of our list, although I suspected that was only because Ryan had known how much I wanted to visit.

Rather than dress up, I went with a pair of jeans and Converse, old and well-worn. Much as I loved fashion, I'd had enough of Ishmael's wackiness in the week to tide me over Saturday and Sunday, and if I got lost in the art for hours as I hoped, I wanted to be comfortable.

But first I had to avoid getting lost on the way to the museum.

Rather than head for the subway, I decided to stay above ground and see the city from a cab. But how the hell did I get one to stop? I stepped to the edge of the pavement and stuck an arm out, then leapt back when a car almost hit my outstretched hand. Shit!

A piercing whistle blasted my eardrums, and a cab screeched to a halt right in front of me.

"After you."

What the...? I turned to find Cade standing there, nonchalant in jeans and a battered leather jacket.

"What are you doing here?"

He shrugged one shoulder. "Boss's orders."

Emmy.

"Why? Doesn't she think I'm capable of looking

after myself?"

"I guess after the drinking episode she figured you needed help."

"But that was a one-off."

"Two-off."

"Whatever. It's never happening again. Can't you go back to the office, or the gym, or wherever it is you live?"

"She warned me you might be difficult."

"I'm not difficult. I just don't need a babysitter."

"If you've got a problem, you'll have to take it up with the Queen Bee directly."

Call Emmy? Er, no.

"You can't keep following me. If you try to get in my cab, I'll scream."

"*My* cab. If I recall correctly, you almost got run over and I was the one who stopped it."

"That's not the point."

"Whatever." He mimicked me, and I wanted to slap him. "I'll just follow in another cab, but it's not so great for the environment."

He made an exaggerated sad face, which I ignored.

"What if you get stuck in traffic?"

"I'll find you. Don't worry about that."

He meant he'd track my phone. Emmy had done that plenty of times, like the other night at the bar, and I'll admit it had been quite useful on occasion. But now? Blackwood's abundance of technology was just annoying.

"Are you getting in or aren't you?" the cabbie yelled. "I haven't got all day."

"Fine," I told Cade as I yanked open the door. "Get in. I hope you like art."

He raised his eyes to the sky and muttered something I didn't quite catch under his breath. I suspected it was none too polite.

"We're going to MoMA, please," I told the driver.

As the cab pulled away, I pretended to stare the other way as I studied Cade's reflection in the window. I put him at twenty-four or twenty-five, brown hair, brown eyes, with the hot, ripped look that abounded among the men Emmy gathered up like trinkets. Except his face was marred by a frown, and even though he relaxed when I turned to look at him properly, the faint lines between his eyebrows suggested it was an expression he wore all too often.

And one I'd seen before, not on Cade, but on Ryan.

"I take it you're not an art fan, then?" I said.

"No."

"Have you ever been to MoMA before?"

"No."

"Any other art museums?"

"No."

Fine, if that was the way he was going to be, he could ride in silence. I ignored him the rest of the way and let him pay for his own damn ticket to get in too.

Then I tried to put him out of my mind.

Tried and failed, at least for the first hour.

Cade hovered on the periphery of my vision like a bluebottle at a picnic—you know, that bloody fly you long to swat but it's so damn smart that any attempt would be a wasted effort. In the end, it was the paintings that banished him from my thoughts. And the sculptures. I'd been to the Tate Modern many times while I was in London, but it didn't have a patch on MoMA. MoMA blew my mind.

I flitted from Monet to Matisse, from Pollock to Picasso. By the time I stopped in front of Andy Warhol's Gold Marilyn, Cade had taken on the look of a condemned man on his walk to the gallows.

"Enjoying yourself?" I asked brightly.

I got a grunt in return.

"So, tomorrow... Would you prefer to go to The Met or The Guggenheim?"

I hadn't intended to go to another museum that weekend, but since Cade seemed to be enjoying himself so much, it seemed a shame not to.

He muttered something that sounded suspiciously like, "Kill me now."

"Well, you don't need to come, you know. I can manage perfectly well without a shadow."

"I'm coming."

"Suit yourself."

When I got home, I did feel a little guilty about making Cade look at art all day. It obviously wasn't his thing. But I was frustrated. Here I was, an adult, out on my own in the big wide world, and I wasn't allowed to do anything by myself.

Okay, so I'd made a teensy miscalculation with my alcohol consumption, but I wasn't going to sneak a bottle of vodka into a bloody gallery, was I? Not anymore. I hadn't done that since school, when Arabella and I poured her father's gin into an empty mineral water bottle and made a class Latin trip to the Verulamium Museum a whole lot more fun.

Still, the only way I could get rid of Cade would be to speak to Emmy, and I wasn't ready to have that conversation yet. No, I'd have to put up with him. Being honest, he had his uses. Hailing cabs, carrying me to bed... I bet he'd be handy in a gunfight too.

So, where to go tomorrow? The internet would help me out, but I needed food first. I'd been so engrossed by exhibits all day, I'd forgotten to eat. That peanut butter and crisp sandwich I ate last night hadn't exactly been filling, and my growling stomach demanded sustenance.

I went for the sensible options today—a cheese salad sandwich and water instead of grape juice. The fridge fairy had visited again, but I had no idea what to do with his/her offerings. Salmon fillets, kale, minced beef, buttermilk. Nope, nope, nope, and nope.

If only I knew how to cook.

Really, I needed to expand my culinary repertoire if I planned to keep living on my own. I couldn't survive on sandwiches for the rest of my life. Or could I? I was pretty sure my biology teacher said that bread contained everything necessary for life, in the right quantities, save for a few amino acids. So as long as I topped up with vitamin pills, I'd be fine.

Apart from being sick of bread, I'd be fine.

Okay, museums and recipes. I had two things to look up. But before I could consult Google, a message flashed on the screen.

WellRed: Fries.

Sorry, what?

I peered closer. Oh, it was from that dodgy chat site. I delved into the recesses of my brain, past the empty shot glasses, past the freak, a popstar-wannabe, a pervert, and...WellRed. Who liked fries. Better than ice cream, if I recalled correctly.

AshlynHale: Fries? Too healthy. Potatoes are a vegetable.

Nothing. Perhaps he was offline? Or maybe he'd decided I just wasn't worth talking to anymore.

Hang on, what was I doing? There was every chance WellRed was some weird old freak sitting at home in his momma's basement with a computer mouse in one hand and his cock in the other. Yes, he'd said he was looking out for his sister, but how many people told the truth online?

About none. Not even me.

Met or Guggenheim? *Met or Guggenheim?* As I weighed up the pros and cons of each museum, I found myself wondering which one Cade would prefer. Oh, dear. It was a bad sign indeed when any sense I had left could be so easily overridden by a pair of taut buttocks in well-fitted jeans.

I closed my eyes briefly. *Taut buttocks.* Wasn't that what first attracted me to Ryan?

Art. Think of the art and forget those errant thoughts, Tia. Logic dictated that I should pick the museum Cade would hate the most because then he might leave me alone. So, which would that be? Hmm, maybe he'd prefer the Met with its historical slant? Their Egyptian collection was supposed to be fantastic.

Tia! Stop thinking of Cade.

The Guggenheim it was. Definitely the Guggenheim. Decision made.

Now I needed to think about cooking. I typed *recipes* into the search bar and got 56,400,000 hits. Okay, I needed to narrow this down. I tried *recipes easy* and got 172,000,000 hits. How could there be more? How did anybody ever learn to cook?

I tried the link for salmon kedgeree, because I had fish in the fridge. Twenty ingredients and forty minutes of preparation time. In what world did that count as easy?

Meh, what did it matter? I had sandwiches, chocolate, and take away menus. I'd survive.

Ping.

WellRed: I'm not sure potatoes count as healthy when they're deep fried. What about strawberry ice cream? That's a fruit.

Basement dweller or not, I had to concede he made good points.

AshlynHale: Using your thought process, that doesn't count when it's covered in sugar and cream. I may be about to have it for dinner anyway, though.

WellRed: Cupboard bare?

AshlynHale: On the contrary—it's full of ingredients. I just don't know what do with them. Google is no help.

WellRed: LOL. What have you got?

AshlynHale: Healthy things. Like, actually healthy. Vegetables, bread, fruit, rice, tins of chickpeas. Real fun.

WellRed: If you don't know how to cook, how did that stuff get into your kitchen?

AshlynHale: A friend brought them.

Or at least, he'd arranged for them to be brought.

WellRed: Can't your friend cook dinner?

AshlynHale: He's not here right now.

A pause. Enough time for me find a packet of biscuits and make a mug of coffee. Black coffee.

WellRed: Is he coming back tonight?

AshlynHale: I don't know when he'll be back. He's my sister's PA, and she's sent him on an errand to California.

A lump came into my throat when I read back over my message. I'd called Emmy my sister out of habit, something I'd been doing since the day she told me I could pick my own family if I didn't like the one genetics gave me. Was she still doing the same with me? Or had I been relegated to her friend's husband's little sister by now?

WellRed: In that case, do you want help?
AshlynHale: Help with what?
WellRed: Cooking...
AshlynHale: You can cook?
WellRed: My grandmomma taught me.
AshlynHale: And you're definitely a guy?
WellRed: I was last time I checked.

Wonders would never cease. I knew a lot of guys, mainly because Emmy always seemed to have a houseful. They had many talents, but being handy in the kitchen wasn't among them, unless you counted the time Nate built a bomb out of a microwave, a few batteries, several cans of hairspray, and a Brillo pad. My ears had rung for several hours afterwards.

And Ryan had been no exception—he could manage to heat up pizza in an emergency, but mostly we ate at Emmy's or we ate out.

In fact, the only man I knew who cooked was Toby. If you needed a protein-packed vegan power bar that tasted like sawdust, Toby was your man.

But actual food? No.

AshlynHale: Okay, I've just picked myself up off the floor. I'd love some help.
WellRed: Do you have any food preferences? Allergies?
AshlynHale: Please, no tofu burgers.

WellRed: You're safe there. You said you have rice. Do you have any seafood?

AshlynHale: You mean fish? I have salmon.

WellRed: No, not salmon. Prawns?

Who knows? I hurried over to the freezer and rummaged around. Sure enough, there was a bag of lobster tails wedged in between a packet of organic peas and a tub of frozen yogurt. Lobster would do, right?

AshlynHale: Affirmative on the seafood :)

WellRed: Then we're making paella. You're gonna need a frying pan.

AshlynHale: Paella?

WellRed: I might live in one of the southern states, but we don't always eat chicken fried steak and biscuits.

Oh, gosh, had I just offended him? It was hard to tell over an internet connection.

AshlynHale: Sorry, I didn't mean to upset you.

WellRed: You didn't. We only eat that stuff every other day.

Okay, he'd been kidding. Thank goodness. Sandwiches really weren't all that great. I carried my MacBook through to the kitchen, and my mysterious mentor talked, or rather, typed me through how to make a delicious meal. The first proper dinner I'd cooked by myself, and there were hardly any burnt bits.

When he deemed it ready, I spooned the food into a bowl and carried it through to my ridiculously large dining table, sitting the MacBook opposite me so I had company.

Did the paella taste as good as it looked? I took a small spoonful.

AshlynHale: OMG, it's edible!

WellRed: Sure glad to hear that.

AshlynHale: Aren't you hungry?

WellRed: So hungry I could eat the north end of a south-bound polecat. You weren't the only one making paella, you know. I'm eating right along with you.

My heart did a little skip when I realised I was sharing a meal with a man other than my brother or Bradley or my boss for the first time since Ryan died, even if WellRed wasn't physically present. Come to think of it, I didn't even know where he was.

AshlynHale: I'm curious. Where are you from?

WellRed: West Virginia. Whereabouts in England do you live?

AshlynHale: Near London, except I'm not there at the moment. I'm in New York.

New York was a big place. It couldn't hurt to tell him that much, right?

WellRed: We're practically neighbours, then.

Okay, so that was a slight exaggeration. But the thought of him sitting four or five hundred miles away eating paella with me was...kind of nice. Odd, but nice. He'd cared enough to spend a virtual evening with me, even though we were strangers.

Did he feel a connection too? Something more than impulses down a wire?

AshlynHale: I guess—so, neighbour, are we having dessert? I have ice cream. Well, frozen yogurt. The healthier alternative.

A minute passed, then another.

WellRed: Wish I could, but my daddy's just come in. He's busier than a moth in a mitten today, so I need to lend a hand with a sick horse in the barn.

Why did I feel so disappointed? I was only typing, and with a guy I met in a chat room, for goodness' sake.

AshlynHale: Okay, I understand. I hope the horse is okay.

WellRed: Me too. Will you be around tomorrow?

A pulse of warmth rushed through my veins. *Stupid, Tia.*

AshlynHale: I'm out in the day, but I'll be here in the evening.

WellRed: Got to run, talk tomorrow. Type.

AshlynHale: Bye.

No answer. He must have already gone.

As I cleared up the mess I'd made in the kitchen, I realised why I didn't cook more often. Perhaps I could just throw this pan away and buy a new one? What was in this rice, anyway? They could patent it as superglue. Twenty minutes and two fingernails later, I was done. Exhausted.

I briefly contemplated eating the frozen yogurt anyway, but I'd lost my appetite now I had no one to share it with, so I went to bed.

Sleep came quickly, and for the first blessed night since the fifth of November, I didn't dream about Ryan. Instead of running from blood and pain, I walked around an art museum with Cade, both of us sipping from steaming cups of black coffee. A harried curator followed us, warning us not to spill a drop. Cade was even smiling.

What did it all mean?

My waking mind had no idea, and my subconscious wasn't sharing. Sleep also meant I missed my final message from WellRed, but it was there in the morning when I woke up.

WellRed: Good night. Sweet dreams x

CHAPTER 11

SWEET DREAMS? WAS WellRed just being friendly? And if so, why the little "x" at the end?

I didn't have time to think about it because Cade was waiting outside my door, sitting in the corridor, back to the wall and legs outstretched. He wore the same leather jacket and the same cheesed off expression as yesterday. How long had he been there? Had Emmy told him I never got up early at the weekend?

I gave him a small smile as I locked the door, and one corner of his lips quirked up. Progress.

"Can you hail a cab again?"

If I was stuck with him, I might as well make use of his talents.

"I've got a car waiting today."

Of course he did. A black town car was parked at the kerb, much to the annoyance of all the drivers having to swerve around it.

"Where are we going?" he asked, holding the door open for me. At least Emmy had trained him to have manners. "More art?"

I wanted to go to the Guggenheim, so why did I find myself saying, "The Met?"

"The Met it is. Don't forget to put your seatbelt on. It's my head on the block if anything happens to you."

Two art museums in two days—I got more excited the closer we got. And what a pair! But funnily enough, Cade didn't share my enthusiasm. He spent the trip fiddling with his phone, only sparing me the occasional glance, but even his indifference mixed with the odd scowl couldn't dampen my enthusiasm.

I paid for us to get in today, seeing as Cade had arranged the car and got up early on a Sunday. I figured I owed him. Inside, he became my shadow as we trailed around the exhibits, sticking a little closer than yesterday. And perhaps, I thought as I snuck the occasional glance at him, Cade didn't look quite so pissed off.

By the time we got to the Egyptian display, he'd graduated to reading the notes next to each exhibit. Maybe we could try the opera next? The idea of him sitting next to me holding those little glasses made me snort.

"What's so funny?" he asked.

"Nothing. I knew you were a secret art lover."

His scowl returned. "I'm just bored."

He made a point of checking his emails, but two minutes later, he was reading the cards again while I got immersed in the art. Totally immersed. I was as surprised as anyone when I took a step backwards and trod on somebody's foot.

"Hey! Watch it," a peroxide blonde screeched.

"I'm so sorry."

"Be careful where you're going, you clumsy bitch."

"I said I was sorry."

And if she hadn't worn four-inch stilettos to a flipping museum, perhaps her feet wouldn't have hurt so much.

A man stomped up beside her, wider than he was high. Steroid Stan. "What did you do to my girlfriend?"

"She trod on my foot, the stupid bitch."

"Look, I've already apologised. I can't un-tread on it, can I?"

An arm snaked around my waist, pulling me back against a hard body, and I began to realise the advantages of having a fairly grumpy Blackwood bodyguard on my heels at all times.

"What did you call her?" Cade growled.

Steroid Stan looked up. And up. He may have been wide, but he wasn't tall. Cade had six inches on him, and when he flexed the arm holding onto me, muscles bulged.

"Uh, nothing. We're sorry, aren't we babe?" Stan grabbed peroxide-woman and pulled her backwards.

"I'm not hearing an apology," Cade said to the woman.

"S-s-sorry."

They turned and fled. Okay, I concede Cade did have his plus points.

"You okay?" he asked.

"I'm fine. Thanks."

He nodded, and I saw him smile properly for the first time. Oh, shit. My stomach flipped, sparks shot downwards to somewhere they shouldn't, and I resisted the urge to start fanning myself.

"Er, you can take your arm away now."

"Oh. Yeah."

He removed it slowly. Too slowly. Had he felt my heart racing?

For the rest of the afternoon, Cade's eyes stayed on me rather than his phone, and I was careful not to tread on any more toes. I'd seen the way Cade's eyes glittered earlier, and I didn't want to cause a fight in one of the world's greatest institutions.

Not only that, I didn't want Cade's arm around me again. Not because it felt uncomfortable—quite the opposite, in fact—and that worried me. I shouldn't crave anybody's touch but Ryan's.

Room after room, treasure after treasure—we explored most of the museum, and the parts that were left would have to wait for another day as I'd begun to feel slightly lightheaded.

"Can we sit down for a minute?" I asked Cade.

"Are you feeling all right?"

"Just a little fuzzy."

He checked his watch. "I'm not surprised. It's five o'clock, and you haven't eaten anything. What did you have for breakfast?"

Two cups of coffee. Black coffee. And dammit, the message I'd found on my computer screen this morning kept preying on my mind. What did that "x" mean?

"Not a lot," I admitted.

Cade led me over to a bench. "Stay here. I'm going to get you a snack. Then we'll get some proper food."

"You can just take me back to the apartment. I've got food there."

"No chance. I'm not dropping you home until you're in tip top condition. The boss would kill me."

What was I, a show pony? And for a second I'd thought Cade cared.

He walked off, turning heads as he went—all female, of course—and came back minutes later with a cup of tea and a packet of biscuits.

"I thought these would do, what with you being

English and all," he said, holding them out to me.

"Thanks." I was tempted to tell him I ate American food too, but he was only being kind so I held my tongue.

When I felt my strength returning, he helped me up and guided me out to the car which had magically appeared in front of the museum. His arm was back. And worse, I found I didn't mind as much as I thought I would.

In the backseat, Cade strapped me in then sat on the other side watching me as the car pulled out into the busy traffic on 5th Avenue. My eyes kept closing, and I barely had the energy to look at all the exclusive, high-end shops that lined our route.

Once, I'd have been out of the car and into the nearest boutique before you could blink, but in the last couple of months, I'd learned a lot about what was important and what wasn't.

The only precious things in life breathed. Everything else was just window dressing. It could be replaced.

Ten minutes later, the car pulled over again, and Cade half carried me into a restaurant.

"I thought we'd go for Chinese. Are you okay with that?"

It was food. Anything with calories was fine by me. I nodded.

"Where's the menu?" I asked.

"We don't need one. Mr. Lu will just bring us whatever's good. Is there any food you don't like?"

I'd gone through a brief phase of being a vegetarian a few years back, but I'd soon changed my mind when I realised how much I missed bacon.

"I'll try pretty much anything. As long as it's not something weird like chicken beaks or bulls' scrotums."

A rare chuckle left Cade's lips. "I'm pretty sure they don't serve those here. In fact, I'm not sure they serve chicken beaks anywhere. They'd be too crunchy."

I giggled. "I guess. In that case, Mr. Lu can bring it on.

And he did.

Dish after dish of deliciousness, not the usual egg fried rice with crispy shredded beef that appeared in every Chinese restaurant in England.

"These are delicious. I didn't know the Chinese even ate sausages."

"They eat all sorts of things that don't appear on takeaway menus," Cade told me.

"What's this stuff?" I asked, poking at a brown and green thing arranged in a flower pattern and covered in shredded ginger and soy sauce on my side plate. It tasted good, but I couldn't work it out, even after eating several pieces.

"It's called century egg. They take an egg then preserve it in a mixture of rice husk, clay, lime, salt, and ash for weeks or sometimes months."

I paused with a piece halfway to my mouth.

"You're telling me this is months-old egg?"

He nodded, chewing a mouthful of something that wasn't potentially going to kill him. I dropped my fork and leapt up, searching furiously for the nearest bathroom.

"You shit! How could you let me eat that?"

He got up and caught me, wrapping his arms around my waist so I couldn't run anywhere.

"Let me go! I'm gonna puke."

"No, you're not."

"I am if you keep squeezing me like that."

He loosened his hold a little. "Are you done now?"

"No! I should get to a hospital. What if I catch salmonella? Or worse?"

He laughed. "Calm down, Tia. Century eggs are a delicacy. Thousands of Chinese people eat them every day, and they don't all drop dead. You'll be fine."

I wasn't convinced, but the initial waves of nausea had passed. I sat back down, pushing the plate of yuckiness over to Cade's side of the table. The asshole picked up a slice and popped it in his mouth.

A shudder ran through me. "You're disgusting."

"You should be more adventurous. I think I liked you better drunk."

Bull's-eye. My balled-up napkin hit him square in the chest.

"I told you, I'm not drinking tonight. Or ever, in fact. No matter how much I might want to after those."

I pointed at what was left of the eggs of evil.

"Suit yourself. I've eaten far worse things."

"When you were in the Navy?"

"Yeah."

"Like what?"

"Locusts in Israel. Muktuk in Greenland."

"What's muktuk? Sounds like some sort of footwear."

"That's Mukluks. Muktuk is a delicious lump of frozen whale blubber with the skin left on."

"Yeuch! You seriously put that in your mouth?"

He made a face. "Believe me, when you've just spent a couple of hours swimming in a near-frozen sea, you'll eat anything."

I'd rather starve, thank you very much.

"What else have you tried?"

"Gaeng kai mot daeng in Laos. That's ant egg soup to you."

"Sounds disgusting."

This conversation should have been marketed as a slimming aid. If Satan's eggs hadn't made me lose my appetite already, I certainly would have skipped the rest of my dinner.

"It wasn't as bad as the tacos filled with ant larvae I tried in Mexico. They're called escamoles. Somehow, they didn't sound nearly as bad as they tasted."

"How could you eat that stuff?"

"When you're out with a team of your buddies and you've all been drinking beer, bets get made."

"What's the most horrible thing you've ever eaten?"

"That would be a duck embryo in the Philippines. I needed a lot of chilli powder for that one."

I shuddered. An embryo? Was it slimy? Or crunchy? I couldn't bring myself to ask. It actually made the egg horror sitting on the table in front of me look quite appealing.

"Do you miss it?" I asked Cade.

"What? The world of culinary delights?"

"No, the teams. Being with your friends."

"Yes and no. It's not a job you can do forever. And when the opportunity to work at Blackwood came up, I couldn't afford to say no."

But Blackwood wasn't forever either, was it? It sure hadn't worked out that way for Ryan. A sob threatened to escape, but I swallowed it down and pasted on a smile.

"What would you have done if you didn't get the job

at Blackwood?"

"Truthfully? I have no idea. As a long-term career move, it was perfect. I mean, Emmy's a legend."

So I'd heard, but I never really saw that side of her. To me, she was just the big sister who took me shopping even though she hated it and rescued me when I did stupid things. And unfortunately, the rescuing had happened more times than I wanted to remember.

"In what way is she a legend?"

"Smart, fearless, and she's got this instinct, this sixth sense. I've only been out on one job with her so far, but she's inspirational."

"Except now you're stuck here with me."

"I can think of worse things to be doing than eating dinner with a pretty girl."

I stared at him, and colour crept up his cheeks. Should I be pleased by the compliment or worried by the flutter in my belly? *Quick, Tia—change the subject.*

"Uh, do you want dessert?"

"Not unless you do?" He didn't meet my eyes.

"No, thank you." Even the idea of something sweet couldn't fight off the queasiness from those damned eggs. "Can we just get the bill?

Mr. Lu arrived the instant Cade waved his hand, placing a small cat-shaped box on the table with a bow. A lucky cat. And boy did I need that.

Cade reached into his pocket for his wallet, but I held up a hand.

"I'll get it," I said.

"You're not paying for dinner."

"Why not? You're just working."

"If I was just working, I'd have taken you home and

made you a sandwich."

Oh.

He'd gone red again. "Forget it. I shouldn't have said that."

"Uh, okay."

So, what exactly was this, if it wasn't work? Dinner between friends?

A date?

Oh, hell. What about Ryan? How could I have laid those memories aside so easily? Cade slid his credit card into the machine as dread added to the weight in my stomach. I shouldn't be here, not with him. Ryan should be the man sitting opposite me, nobody else.

My arms didn't feel like my own as Cade held up my coat for me to put on. I'd drifted back to another world. A world where it was Ryan who opened the restaurant door for me. Where Ryan's hand pressed on the small of my back, making my thighs clench as he guided me to the car. Where Ryan helped me inside and brushed his fingers over my stomach as he did up my seatbelt.

I stared out of the window, unseeing, as the driver fought through traffic. The noise, the lights, the bustle of city life, none of it penetrated my brain.

All I felt was Ryan's haunting presence and the very real aura of Cade, watching me from the other side of the squashy leather backseat.

CHAPTER 12

MY COMPUTER PINGED the second I walked through the door of my apartment. Why? What did it want? Couldn't it understand I was busy being emotionally confused?

Tempting though it was to crawl into bed and wallow in pity, I bent to peer at the screen.

WellRed: If you're ignoring me, I hope it's because you're out having fun :)

Above that, there was another message from an hour before.

WellRed: Hey, Ashlyn, are you there?

Ashlyn? Oops, I hadn't even told him my real name. Awkward, especially after all he'd done for me yesterday. But the thought that I barely knew him still lurked at the back of my mind. I was sure even a pervert could cook paella if the mood took him. What if WellRed was a Spanish freak?

Oh, what the hell... I plonked my ass in the chair and typed.

AshlynHale: I'm here. At least, I am now. I just walked in the door.

WellRed: Have you been out somewhere nice?

AshlynHale: I went to the Met. It was AMAZING!

WellRed: But big, huh? Did you get around it all?

An advert popped up. Did I want to order 250

business cards for the bargain price of $2? No, I did not. Click.

AshlynHale: Not quite. I think I'll need to go back again one day. Have you been?

WellRed: No, but there's a virtual gallery on their website. I like to look at the paintings.

AshlynHale: Maybe you could go in person one day?

And maybe I could go with him.

What? Where did that thought come from?

WellRed: I don't go out much, so I'll have to view from afar. Anyway, are you hungry? I could give you another cooking lesson?

Aw, he was such a sweet pervert. I almost wished I hadn't been out for dinner.

AshlynHale: Sorry, I already ate while I was out. But I'd like to cook another night if you're offering?

WellRed: Any time. At least you got a break from the kitchen tonight.

AshlynHale: Although eating out was almost as bad. Have you ever tried century eggs?

A pause.

WellRed: Okay, I just googled them. Tell me you didn't eat one of those?

AshlynHale: I did! I didn't realise what it was, and the guy I was with didn't tell me either.

Another pause, longer this time.

WellRed: You were on a date?

Hey, WellRed was a guy. Perhaps he could help me out here?

AshlynHale: Well, I'm not sure. It wasn't like he asked me out or anything, but then he wouldn't let me pay for the meal. Do you reckon that counts as a date?

Another advert popped up, this time offering discounted trainers. No, I didn't want those either. They were far too sensible for Ishmael's morning workouts in any case. Click.

WellRed: How did you meet the guy?

What did I say to that? I could hardly tell Red that my freakishly overprotective pseudo-sister didn't trust me to stay sober and therefore assigned me a bodyguard, could I?

AshlynHale: He's a friend of a friend. I'm new to the city and he got tasked with showing me around. But it was him who suggested dinner.

WellRed: He's interested. A guy wouldn't take a girl out for dinner like that if he wasn't.

AshlynHale: Are you sure?

WellRed: Well, I wouldn't.

Oh. Shit. Now what was I supposed to do? I mean, Cade was hot—really, really hot—albeit in a grumpy kind of way, but I couldn't go out with him again. Not when I had Ryan to think about. I didn't want to sully his memory. And especially not when Cade made heat pool in my belly the way he did.

"But Ryan's gone," the devil on my left shoulder piped up. "What are you going to do, date your battery-operated boyfriend for the rest of your life?"

Well, maybe not the rest of my life, but you know, things were still sinking in.

"You were with Ryan for two years," my angel said from her perch next to my right ear. "It's understandable that you don't feel ready."

"There are parts of you that do feel ready though, aren't there, Tia?" the devil said. "A quick roll between the sheets with Cade would ease that smouldering between your thighs."

But what about Ryan?

"Ryan was the one who knew how to stoke that fire," the angel said.

"Well, Ryan's not coming back, and those flames feel like they're leaping plenty high enough to me."

Shut up! Shut up, both of you!

The computer beeped.

WellRed: Are you still there?

Time to stop daydreaming. Except it wasn't day anymore. I needed to stop, well, dreaming.

AshlynHale: Yes, I'm still here. Just got distracted for a moment.

WellRed: Easily done. So, tell me more about the Met. What was your favourite piece?

It wasn't hard to get me to talk art, and I rambled on about Picasso until I realised with horror that I probably sounded like Bryce the Shakespearian twat.

Nice one, Tia.

AshlynHale: Sorry, I got a bit carried away...

WellRed: Lol. It's nice to hear someone so passionate about the subject.

AshlynHale: You're an art fan, then?

WellRed: I love to look at it, but I'm not so good at creating it. Do you paint?

Maybe I should try picking up a brush again? I really needed to get my paints shipped over from Emmy's house. Mental note: Speak to Bradley about that.

AshlynHale: Yes, but only for fun. Once, I dreamed of doing it for a living, but I'm not good enough for that.

WellRed: Have you tried?

Another ad. Grr. Go away!

AshlynHale: Not exactly, but when I look at other people's work in galleries, I know mine isn't up to scratch.

WellRed: Everyone has a different view of beauty. Someone out there will love it.

AshlynHale: How about you? What do you think is beautiful?

WellRed: I think beauty comes from the inside.

Just like Ishmael did. Once, I'd been obsessed with the outside, but two years with Emmy had taught me Red and Ishmael were absolutely right. Beauty was more than stylish hair or straight teeth. And a person could be gorgeous on the outside and still have a hideous soul. Sure, I still loved fashion, but not with the passion I once did.

AshlynHale: I wish more people shared that view. What about you? What do you do for a hobby? Reading?

WellRed: Reading?

AshylnHale: Because of your username—isn't it a play on words?

WellRed: Yes, I like to read, but I prefer messing around on my guitar. Sometimes the piano too.

AshlynHale: What kind of music do you like?

WellRed: A bit of everything. I was brought up on my grandmomma's country songs, but I branched out.

As a teenager, I'd been more of a pop fan, although I'd never been into the whole boy band, screaming-groupie thing. I wanted to hear people sing, not listen to them talk in interviews or watch them prance about on stage. Since I'd met Emmy, I'd expanded my tastes —she preferred rock while her husband often played classical piano. There was usually music playing somewhere in Riverley, and I kind of missed that.

AshlynHale: If we're not going to have dinner together, why don't we listen to music together instead?

Even though Red was only a virtual friend, talking to a stranger was what I needed right now. He didn't know my history, and therefore he didn't judge.

WellRed: Music? Great idea. How about we start with "Autumn Leaves"? Eva Cassidy?

I wasn't familiar with that song, but I didn't want to admit it to Red. Bradley had installed my stereo, so I bet it had every track ever recorded. Maybe it was time to step out of my musical comfort zone? I carried my MacBook over to the sofa, and now I was sober and I'd found the instruction manual, I managed to operate the stereo with only a few minor hiccups.

AshlynHale: Loading it now. Do I get to pick next?
WellRed: Sure thing.

Thank goodness Bradley had also provided tissues, because I was blubbing by the end of the song. Beautiful, but so, so sad.

I wiped away my tears and looked down my list of music. One song caught my eye. Perfect. Something kooky was exactly what I needed.

AshlynHale: Do you have "Red Alert" by Basement Jaxx?

WellRed: I have iTunes, therefore I have everything.

The music blasted out as I danced to the kitchen to make myself a coffee. The nausea from earlier had subsided, and now I wanted to stay awake. One cup of espresso, two sugars. I got back to the sofa just as the song ended.

AshlynHale: What's next?

WellRed: Etta James—At Last.

I know the words were supposed to be happy, but I still reached for the tissue box again. The song made me think of everything I'd lost. As the final bar sounded, I was damn glad Red couldn't see the state I'd got myself into.

Upbeat. I needed something upbeat. And loud. Please, say this apartment had good soundproofing because my neighbours were gonna be pissed otherwise.

AshlynHale: Bryan Adams. Summer of '69.

WellRed: Good choice. You're a rock fan?

AshlynHale: It's grown on me over the years.

And the guitar riffs made me get up and dance again. I was breathless by the time Bryan finished singing, and far happier than I'd been when I arrived home. Whoever Red truly was, he knew how to cheer me up and turn a bad evening into a better one.

AshlynHale: What's next?

WellRed: Let's stay old school with Def Leppard—Pour Some Sugar on Me.

AshlynHale: Def Leppard? How old are you?

WellRed: 22. But a good song is a good song.

Twenty-two. The same age as Ryan, and three years older than me since I'd just had a birthday, minus the party of course.

Ryan had been more into dance music, kind of fitting since we'd met in a nightclub. He said those tracks motivated him in the gym, and I'd taken to borrowing his iPod and listening to the same songs while I painted. But Red was right. Good music was good music. Perhaps I should expand my tastes?

AshlynHale: True. Although I really should cut down on the sugar—I always put too much in my coffee, and it's bad for my teeth.

WellRed: You don't need sugar—you're sweet enough as it is.

And he was saccharine. Yes, his words may have been kind of corny, but they still made a warm fuzz spread through me. The opening bars played. I took a sip of coffee, but before I could drink any more, Red typed another message.

WellRed: Do you keep getting all these annoying adverts?

AshlynHale: Yes. For trainers and business cards.

WellRed: That's tame. I've been offered a cock extension and Viagra. Do you think they're trying to tell me something?

I spat the mouthful of coffee I'd just taken all over the screen then frantically grabbed some tissues from the "Autumn Leaves" box to wipe it up. Please, don't let my computer be dead. I tapped a few keys and breathed a sigh of relief. Phew.

AshlynHale: Lol, I hope not!

I hope not? Why the hell did I type that? Oh shit, he'd think I hoped he had a big cock. *Way to go Tia.*

AshlynHale: Uh, I didn't mean that the way it sounded. I meant for your sake.

Now it sounded like I thought he was the one who wanted a big cock.

AshlynHale: That still came out wrong. I just meant it could be a bit awkward if you were in a situation where you needed to use Viagra.

Oh FFS. I leaned forward and smacked my head on

the table in an attempt to knock some sense into myself. Then, just for good measure, I did it again.

The computer pinged.

WellRed: Keep digging, sugar.

He thought I was funny? Well, it was better than thinking I was a slut.

AshlynHale: Can we start that part over?

WellRed: Sure, when I've finished wiping up the coffee I snorted over the keyboard.

At least it wasn't just me, then.

AshlynHale: So, any ideas on how to get rid of these adverts?

WellRed: I don't know if it's possible. I haven't used the site much, and I've never talked to anybody outside the chat rooms before.

I was his first? A little shiver ran through me.

AshlynHale: Same! I'll take a look at the Help page.

Five minutes later, we both came to the conclusion that the pop-ups were there to stay. An apologetic paragraph explained that the site owners needed the revenue they generated to fund the site.

WellRed: How about we switch to another site? Or iMessage?

iMessage? Did I dare to give him my number? If I'd met him at a party, I wouldn't have hesitated, in my pre-Ryan days at least. Ryan whose phone I'd "borrowed" and entered my details in an hour after our first conversation.

AshlynHale: I don't even know your name.

WellRed: Eli. My name's Eli.

Eli. I rolled it around on my tongue. Tasted it. Imagined a ranch hand sitting on the porch of a farmhouse somewhere a couple of states away. Cowboy hat, checked shirt, tight jeans clinging to an ass toned from working with horses. Maybe some chaps.

"Tia!" the angel said. "Put that dirty mind away."

"Mmmm, chaps," put in the devil.

Before the angel could interfere any further, I quickly typed my number out on the screen. Eli's came back immediately, and a few seconds later, the Messages program came to life.

Eli: This is better.

Me: Much!

Eli: But I just saw the time. I'm gonna have to get some sleep.

I glanced at the clock in the corner of the screen. How had we talked until one o'clock in the morning? I had work tomorrow, well, today, starting with an 8:00 a.m. yoga session. Ishmael had emailed me earlier reminding me to wear clothes I could bend in. Super. That wouldn't be embarrassing at all.

Me: Same. Talk tomorrow?

Eli: Wouldn't miss it for the world.

Me: Sleep well.

This time, I got his final message.

Eli: You too, sugar x

My legs wobbled as I walked up the stairs to bed. That *x*. And "sugar?" Eli had given me a nickname?

I gripped the bannister as I climbed, growing ever more tired as the caffeine wore off. Where was Cade when I needed him? He'd have carried me to bed in no time. Oh, hell. Cade. While I was talking to Eli, I'd forgotten all about Cade and our almost-maybe date.

I'd planned on being single forever, yet I'd managed to get hopelessly wrapped up in not one but two men today. What was I playing at? I'd come to New York to un-complicate my life, but all I'd succeeded in doing was tying it up in knots again. No, not just knots. More like macramé.

If only I could talk to Emmy right now. I needed help.

CHAPTER 13

A WEEKEND OFF was supposed to leave you feeling rested, right?

Right.

But it didn't. I'd lain awake half the night thinking about two very different men, and at five past eight in the morning, I found myself being folded in half by a third.

"Butt in the air, Tia. Higher. Higher!" Ishmael squawked at me. "And Myrna, what do you call that? This is downward facing dog, not the funky rhino."

Myrna grunted as she tried to straighten her legs. Nope. Her rhino was still funky. Ishmael shuffled onto his own hot pink yoga mat, straightened his headband, and proceeded to lead us through ten torturous rounds of sun salutations and a series of warrior poses. My thighs were quivering by the time the session ended, and not in a good way.

"Is it safe?" Jenna poked her head around the door just after Ishmael had bounded off for his power nap.

I raised my head off my desk to nod.

"What was it this morning? Kickboxing? Indoor ice skating?"

"Yoga."

"Glad I missed that. Are you ready to do the next lot of photos?"

"Could you give me a minute?"

"Oh, sure, sure. Meet you downstairs?"

"Yup."

If I asked nicely, would Ishmael let me have a nap too? Because I sure needed one. Although that was mostly because I was in terrible shape. Perhaps I should have taken Bradley up on his offer to install gym equipment in my apartment? Or I could go jogging—you know, see the city or explore Central Park.

But if I went jogging, would Cade come too? He'd been waiting outside my apartment again, looking far perkier than should have been legal on a Monday morning. Hmm... On balance, the drawbacks of huffing and puffing in front of him outweighed the benefits of seeing his ass in a pair of running shorts.

I dragged my mind out of the gutter. "Myrna, I'm going to do Ishmael's paperclips then sort out more photos. What else do you want me to do today?"

"Nothing. I'll do everything else. I'll even do the paperclips."

"It's no bother for me to do them."

"Really, it would be my pleasure. Is there anything else you need help with?"

Well, wonders would never cease. I resisted the temptation to whistle as I headed for the lift with a new spring in my step. Who said drunk me didn't make good decisions? Visiting that chat room on Friday night was the best idea I'd had in a long time.

And not just because of Myrna's stunning personality transplant. I snuck another look at the message I'd received while I drank my first cup of coffee this morning.

Eli: Morning, sugar. Hope you got more sleep than

I did last night.

So, he'd been lying awake too. If I'd known that, I could have messaged him. Except I wouldn't have, would I? Because that would have bordered on stalker.

Me: No, but it was worth it.

Jenna was waiting when I reached the workshop, as were half a dozen dresses.

Wow.

Just. Wow.

If this was what Ishmael got up to alone, then we should all just go home. Permanently.

Six gorgeous, ethereal creations graced the mannequins, and despite the skull print on the chiffon, they managed to be both feminine and elegant. I bet myself ten pounds Emmy would be wearing one soon after the show. They'd suit her down to the ground, quite literally—the swishy skirts meant there'd be plenty of room to hide her gun.

I helped Jenna to arrange the dresses under the lights then watched as she worked her magic. An hour later, she'd filled a memory card, and I had the difficult decision of deciding which pictures to use. Over the weekend, Professor Ito had emailed his photos as well, so I could add the corpses alongside the clothes. The catalogue would be two-thirds full by the time I left today, and I needed to get it proof read and book the print run. Maybe I could delegate the boring bits to Myrna?

Lunch was a Mars bar, and I drank so much black coffee I couldn't keep my hands steady by mid-afternoon. And every time I drank a cup, a certain guy from the internet popped into my head. I'd turned into Pavlov's dog—smell coffee, think of Eli. Which was crazy. For all I knew, he could be a fifty-year-old alcoholic with a good line in bullshit, farting and eating Cheetos while he typed at me from his trailer in Kansas.

But Cade was real. And Cade was waiting for me in the atrium when I stepped out of the lift at the end of the day. He stared pointedly out of the window at the street, not paying the slightest bit of attention to the row of girls squashed onto the bed of nails with their tongues hanging out.

"Good night, girls," I said.

Glazed eyes flickered in my direction, and I did my best not to roll mine. Cade heard my words and turned around, lips tilted up in a half smile.

A chorus of sighs came from behind me.

"Ready to go?" he asked.

"Lead the way."

"We're on the subway tonight. Traffic's murder. There's been a big accident a few streets away and everything's gridlocked."

Sure enough, nothing was moving on the street outside. Tempers were heating up along with the car engines, irate shouts mixing with car horns as we descended underground.

If the streets were packed, so was the train. I ended up plastered against Cade, gripping his leather jacket while he hung onto a rail overhead. At least he was tall. And my imagination was right—he did have muscles on muscles. I could feel every delicious bump of his six-pack as it pressed into me. And further down...

No, I didn't even want to think about that. I tried to move back a bit to open up a gap, but we were both wedged. *Deep breaths, Tia.* I forced myself to relax and melted right into Cade. Oops. My turn to sigh. Then I realised that if I could feel every bit of him, he could feel all of my *ahem* assets too. Bad news, right? So, why did I find myself saying a silent thank you to the businessman who shoved me further forward?

The awkwardness only increased when Cade walked me to my apartment, standing close behind as I took three attempts to get the key in the lock. It was definitely the caffeine making my hands shake. Nothing at all to do with the heat radiating from Cade's body and seeping into mine. No siree.

"Er, do you want to come in?" I asked.

"I'd better not."

Oh. "Well, bye."

"I need to get to work. I've got a couple of hours to do yet."

"At Blackwood?"

"No, a sideline. I'm the fourth member of an all-male dance troupe called The Hotshots. We've got a show."

What? He was joking, right? I studied his face, but he looked deadly serious.

"That's...surprising?"

"Pays well."

"Where are you performing?"

"Why, do you want a ticket?"

"Definitely not. No way. Is it sold out?"

His face creased into laughter, the first evidence I'd seen that he had a sense of humour.

"Seriously? You believed me?"

"I, uh... Well, you've certainly got the body for it."

His chuckles turned into guffaws, and he put out a hand to support himself on the wall as he doubled over at my expense. Dammit. *Think before you speak, Tia.*

"Wasn't sure whether you'd noticed."

I shoved him in the chest. "That's not funny."

"It's fuckin' hilarious. I can't believe you fell for that one."

He gyrated his hips and warbled an off-key rendition of Tom Jones's "Sexbomb" until I retreated into my apartment and slammed the door. I could still hear him singing as I headed for the bottle of wine in the fridge. Asshole. Although there was a small part of me that would have liked to see him strip.

Dammit. My mind had gone straight to the gutter again.

I kicked off my shoes and padded across the lounge, desperate to put on a more comfortable outfit. After the photos, I'd changed into a dress Ishmael had dropped into my lap, and while it looked stunning and sucked all my wobbly bits in, it wasn't made for sitting down. I'd just stripped off when my phone beeped. *Eli.* I covered myself up with my hands then rolled my eyes at my stupidity. Of course he couldn't see me.

Eli: Dinner tonight?

Well, I needed to eat, didn't I?

Me: What did you have in mind?

Eli: Let's take a look in your refrigerator.

As if by magic, the fridge had restocked itself while I was out at work. Bradley again. Living at Riverley, I'd got used to random people turning up and letting themselves in, and it seemed New York was no different.

Me: Bread, milk, cheese, some sort of fish, chicken, minced beef, green stuff, carrots, chocolate gateaux. Any good?

Eli: Do you have spaghetti? Canned tomatoes? An onion?

I rummaged through the cupboards.

Me: Yes!

Eli: Spaghetti bolognese it is, then. You'll need a frying pan to start off with.

He talked me through each step, from frying the onions, adding the mince and tomatoes, to boiling the pasta. At the end, I'd made a passable meal with just one slight problem.

Me: It looks good. It smells good. But I've made enough for six people.

My mind flicked to Cade. What time did he finish work? Did he like spaghetti bolognese? No, that would be kind of weird.

Oh, who was I kidding? This whole situation with Cade and Eli was weirder than a kitten riding a unicorn through the Lost City of Atlantis. What was I even thinking?

Eli: You can freeze it. Then if I'm not around, you'll still have something to eat.

If he wasn't around. *If?* Did he plan to be around a lot, then?

Me: Have you got dinner as well?

Eli: Same as you.

Aww, he'd been cooking too, almost as if he was there with me. I had a thought. A brainwave, if you like.

Me: Do you want to use FaceTime?

That way, I could satisfy my curiosity once and for all. Was Eli really the twenty-two-year-old cowboy he'd claimed? Or had I been whiling away my evenings with a fourteen-year-old school kid or a sixty-year-old reverse cougar? I quickly checked my hair in the mirror beside the fancy stainless steel fireplace that I had no idea how to turn on. Not too shabby. I grabbed my handbag and added an extra layer of mascara for luck.

Why hadn't he replied? Had he gone off to straighten his toupee or something?

Nothing.

What was wrong?

My spaghetti was almost cold when my MacBook finally pinged.

Eli: I can't.

Me: Can't? Or won't?

Shit. Eli really was an ancient pervert, wasn't he? And worse, he wasn't even open about it like Brad from San Fran-bloody-cisco. I sure knew how to pick them, didn't I?

Eli: Won't. It's not what you think, though. I can imagine what's going through your mind right now.

Me: Enlighten me.

Eli: I don't let anyone outside my family see me anymore. It's not just you.

Okay, this was getting weird.

Me: Why not?

I tapped my heel under the chair, waiting. Would he tell me or not? I'd been stupid enough to think we had a connection, even across the web.

Eli: I was in an accident. I don't look how I used to.

I froze, staring at the screen. Of all the things I'd been expecting... My heart cried for a man I'd never met and now, it seemed, I never would meet, even if I wanted to. What should I say? Words on a screen seemed so inadequate in a moment like this.

Me: I'm sorry. For what happened and for pushing you to tell me.

Eli: No reason for you to be sorry. It happened a few years ago, and I've learned to live with it. Well, kind of. And don't apologise for pushing me either. Sometimes I need it.

Me: My brother's always told me I'm good at being pushy.

Eli: Lol. Do you have any more siblings?

Me: No, one brother's quite enough. How about you? You said you had a sister?

Eli: Marley—she's fourteen. I should be out giving her potential boyfriends "the talk," but I'm stuck at home instead.

Me: My brother never did that. He delegated that to...

How did I describe Emmy? Did I even want to? Well, Eli had opened up to me, so I owed him something in return.

Me:...his ex-girlfriend. She's like a sister to me.

Eli: She threatens your boyfriends?

Me: Yes.

Eli: She must be tough.

In a way, the knowledge that I'd never meet Eli in person made me braver. And talking to him was cathartic—a stranger who listened but didn't seem to judge. Should I unload? Emmy always told me to trust my gut, so I start typing.

Me: She only ever had that talk once. There was only ever one boyfriend.

Plus one more mistake who she dealt with in a harsher manner by all accounts. Best not to mention that. She'd assured me she didn't do anything that left permanent damage in any case.

Eli: Only one? How old are you?

Me: I just turned nineteen.

Two weeks ago, in fact. Bradley had offered to throw me a big party, but what did I have to celebrate? My gifts were still wrapped, stacked in a corner of my bedroom at Riverley.

Eli: And this guy, is he still on the scene?
Me: He died.

Might as well get it out there as tiptoe around the truth. I waited for Eli to reply, but there was nothing.

Silence.

The cursor blinked back at me, a reminder that life went on no matter what I said or did. I poked at the remains of dinner with my fork. It was cold now, and my appetite had vanished anyway. Along, it seemed, with Eli.

Then my phone rang, making me jump.

I stared at the screen, which informed me in bland white letters that Eli was calling. Twenty minutes ago, I'd wanted to talk to him. I'd prepared myself for it. Hell, I'd even refreshed my make-up.

But now? Now, my heart raced as the phone chirped away.

To answer or not to answer, that was the question...

CHAPTER 14

THE PHONE CARRIED on ringing, oblivious to my turmoil. Sending Eli to voicemail would be the coward's option, but I could hardly pretend I didn't hear the phone, could I? He knew I was there. I only had a few seconds to make up my mind, much like on SpeedChat when I'd considered adding him as a friend.

This time, I'd make the right decision. I snatched up the phone and held it to my ear.

"Hello?"

"I'm so sorry."

Holy hell. I almost dropped the phone. If Cade had the body of a girl's dreams, Eli had the voice. Smooth yet husky, a hint of a Southern drawl; it could have belonged to Morgan Freeman's vocal coach. A tingle started between my ears and travelled all the way down to my... *Tia!*

What did he just say?

"Uh, sorry for what?" Not that I cared. I'd forgive him for anything as long as he kept talking.

"That you lost your boyfriend."

"It's okay." My voice came out as a high-pitched squeak.

"It's not okay. I shouldn't have pried."

"Like I did earlier, you mean? I'm doing my best to cope. Life goes on, or so people keep telling me."

"How long ago did it happen?"

"About two and a half months." At least I'd dropped thinking of it in terms of days, hours, and minutes now.

"Hell, sugar. You must be raw."

My eyes began to water. "It's not been the best time," I admitted. "I'm just trying to get on with things."

"Keeping busy is good. It's when you stop that everything catches up with you."

"Exactly."

I grabbed a tissue from the "Autumn Leaves" box on the coffee table and wiped away the mess of mascara dribbling down my cheeks.

"Time will heal, though. Little by little. Today, you'll feel like you've been through a meat grinder, but in a few months, the pain will start to fade. Each day that passes is another step."

He spoke from experience, that much I could tell.

"What happened to you?" I whispered.

"The accident I was in? It was a car crash. I survived, but my girlfriend didn't."

How many more tears could I cry? They flooded out of me as I paced the room with the phone clamped to my ear—for myself, for Ryan, and most of all, for Eli. He'd been through his own hell, and while my friends had rallied around to find me distractions, he was stuck at home.

"I-I-I don't know what to say."

"You don't need to say anything. It happened almost three years ago, and I've had more time than you to deal with it."

"But even so..."

He had to live with the reminder every day, every

time he looked in the mirror.

"Shhhh," he said, and the sound arrowed straight to my core. "Don't worry about me."

"But..."

"Another day. Tonight is about you. What can I do to help?"

I gave an overly loud sniffle-snort. Dammit. Why did he have to be so nice?

"Just talk to me. Please."

"What do you want to talk about?"

I only wanted to hear his voice. He could have read the dictionary for all I cared. Or a vacuum cleaner manual. Or flat pack furniture assembly instructions. As long as the auditory equivalent of chocolate fondue kept pouring out of his mouth, I'd be happy.

"It doesn't matter. Uh, tell me more about you. Start at the beginning."

He took a deep breath at the other end of the line.

"Well, I was born in the ranch house one snowy day in March. My parents named me Elijah after my granddaddy. On my momma's side..."

I left the dirty dishes where they were and struggled up the stairs. I was in no mood to clear up. In fact, I only just had enough energy to change into my pyjamas and crawl under the duvet, where I curled up into a ball while Eli's silk-and-honey voice told me stories of his life growing up in rural West Virginia.

"I first sat on a horse when I was three years old. My daddy lifted me up in front of my momma. I don't remember it, of course, but I've seen the photograph. Momma keeps it in a silver frame on the piano..."

As the hours passed, I heard about his first fall off a horse, a naughty cow pony called Bess, his antics at school, his sister Marley's refusal to wear anything but jeans, and...

I woke up in the dark. When I rolled over, the clock on my nightstand said 3:00 a.m. and the stars twinkled in a clear sky outside the window.

Shit. I'd fallen asleep on Eli.

I hunted through the covers until I found my phone then plugged it into the power cable because the battery was dead. When the screen came back to life, I found I had a message.

Eli: Sugar, from the lack of response, I guess you've fallen asleep. So I'm going to wish you sweet dreams and do the same myself x

Another *x*. At least he wasn't mad at me.

Me: Thank you for healing my wounded soul. Sleep tight x

Seven-freaking-thirty. I'd woken up late again, which meant I had to skip my coffee and run around like a headless chicken. Perhaps I should set all the clocks I owned forwards by half an hour? That way, I might actually make it somewhere on time.

Shower, underwear, make-up, clothes... Where was my damn handbag?

On the plus side, I shaved five minutes off my record time for getting ready. I might even be able to give Emmy, Mrs. I-can-go-from-sleeping-to-supermodel-in-ten-seconds-flat, a run for her money.

Today, Ishmael had decreed we'd be doing ballet. I'd taken lessons when I was a little girl at Mother's insistence, so at least I knew what I was letting myself in for. I didn't have any ballet shoes with me, so barefoot would have to do.

"What's with the leg warmers?" Cade asked when I got downstairs.

"We're doing ballet this morning."

"Ballet? I thought you were organising a fashion show."

"Ishmael believes in keeping fit. I'll warn you now, we're going roller skating tomorrow, so if you intend on sticking with me, you'd better bring your own wheels."

Cade scowled and muttered under his breath. "Fuck me."

And seeing the way his jeans hugged his ass as he bent over to open the car door for me, I was somewhat surprised to find I wasn't completely averse to the idea.

Mind. Gutter.

Cade spent most of the journey on the phone, and I heard Emmy's name mentioned more than once. When we reached the office, he didn't hang up, just covered the mouthpiece as he pushed open the door to the building for me.

"See you later, yeah?"

"Have a good day," I said, but he'd already gone.

Upstairs, Ishmael was bouncing up and down in his pink tutu. He'd pushed the couch over to the side and set up a portable barre in its place.

Before I could put my handbag down, he handed me a pair of pink satin ballet shoes. "I brought you a gift."

I peered inside one of them.

"They're the right size."

"Of course they are. I'm a fashion designer, darling. I could give you your measurements just by looking at you."

"Go on, then."

"You're five foot five inches tall; thirty-six, twenty-five, thirty-six—a classic hourglass shape. You'll look fabulous in pencil skirts and low-cut dresses, but you need to be careful with your arms. Capped sleeves are a big no-no."

Spot on, and right about my arms too, unfortunately. I opened my mouth to congratulate him, but he'd already turned back to the barre. He knew he was right.

I changed my shoes and took my place next to Myrna, who'd dressed as a cheerleader for some inexplicable reason.

As he got to the bottom of a plié, Ishmael said, "If you're borrowing clothes, Emmy's not the same shape as you. Try Dan's wardrobe."

"You know Dan?" Dan was a close friend of Emmy's.

"And Mack. I've been dressing all three of them for years."

"I'm not sure I'm brave enough for Dan's wardrobe."

She tended towards hooker-chic and somehow managed to get away with it.

Ishmael chuckled, no mean feat as he held a perfect arabesque at the same time. "If you rummage around at the back, she's got some nice pieces in there." He made a face. "It's just a shame she doesn't wear them much."

"She drives Bradley crazy. Every time she gets ready for a formal event, I see him gearing up for battle."

"More than once, he's called me in despair as she walks out the door. Now, you need to straighten your arms more. Think of your lines."

Myrna had been listening to our little exchange, but when I turned to look at her properly, she resumed her attempts at battement tendu. She may have been a fan of ballet pumps, but it was safe to say her penchant didn't extend to the dance itself. When the cuckoo popped out, she breathed a sigh of relief.

Ishmael tippy-toed across the room en pointe. "Next time, Tia, I'll bring you a tutu. So elegant."

Fantastic. I could hardly wait.

Myrna slumped onto the sofa.

"I hate ballet. Of all the things he makes me do, that's the worst. I'm going to get coffee. Would you mind doing the paperclips, please?"

Please? Was she feeling okay? Obviously not, because she returned from Starbucks with three cups instead of her usual two.

"I don't know what you drink, so I got you a cappuccino."

"Thanks. For next time, I always drink my coffee black."

As if on cue, my phone vibrated.

Eli: Good morning, beautiful.

What?

Me: You don't even know what I look like.

Eli: I told you, beauty comes from the inside.

Me: In that case, good morning...

No, I couldn't type "smooth-talking stud" even though he surely was, inside and outside.

Me:...handsome.

Eli: Sweet as well as beautiful. Do you have a busy day ahead?

I had to make the last arrangements with Professor

Ito and finish off the photos with Jenna. The seating arrangements needed to be finalised, and I had several irate messages on my voicemail from people who hadn't been allocated tickets.

But suddenly, texting a guy who was gorgeous to his core shot to the top of my to-do list.

Me: Yes, I have. I have to arrange corpses for a fashion show and put some photos into the brochure.

Eli: Am I distracting you, sugar? You made a typo there.

I read back over the message. No, everything was spelled right.

Me: There's no typo?

Eli: What about corpses/clothes?

Me: No, that's right.

Eli: CORPSES?

Me: It's a long story. I'll tell you all about it later.

Eli: This I can't wait to hear. I have to go work, but I'll call you later.

Me: Okay.

Dammit. Why had I just said "okay?" That was so lame. He'd think I didn't care.

Me: xx

Eli: :)) x

My stomach flipped. How could an *x* on a screen have such an effect on me?

It was at the forefront of my mind all day, as I tried to organise a seating plan that would keep everybody happy.

Emmy was coming along with the rest of the girls— Dan, Mack, and Ana, plus Carmen, Lara, Georgia, and Chess who were all either dating or married to guys from Blackwood. I put Emmy in a prime position at the front so she'd get the best view, but the flutters in my belly turned to full on butterflies when I realised how nervous I was about seeing her again.

What with that and having to deal with the pissed off manager of a Z-list starlet who wasn't invited but was convinced she should have been, I barely had the energy to sit upright by the end of the day.

I was looking forward to a nice soak in my ridiculously oversized tub complete with the bath bombs and bubbles that Bradley had bought for me when Ishmael came in.

"Tia, will you come with me to meet the jewellery designer this evening? I need a second opinion. We can get dinner afterwards."

Myrna gave me an angry glare, and I figured Ishmael didn't make a habit of asking for her opinion.

Which made me say, "I'd love to. What time?"

"I'm due at Kamal's by seven to view the pieces. So we need to leave here by six thirty."

That gave me twenty minutes to freshen up, and even though I'd yawned six times in the last half hour, I couldn't help being intrigued to see what kind of jewellery Ishmael planned to use in the show.

And where would we go for dinner? Somewhere fancy and experimental or more conventional fare? Italian, Indian, Chinese?

Chinese... Dammit, I'd forgotten about Cade. He'd be on his way to meet me, and I didn't have his number to stop him. All I could do was apologise on my way out.

I topped up my lip gloss and hurried downstairs with Ishmael, finding Cade in the same place as yesterday. And his fan club, which swiftly gained a new member. Ishmael stopped short, and I walked right into him.

"Who. Is. That?"

"You mean Cade?"

"If Cade's the hottie over by the window, then yes, Cade."

"Emmy sends him to see me home. I'll just tell him I'm going to dinner instead."

"Why don't you invite him along?"

"He's straight. You can put your tongue away."

Ishmael pursed his lips. "Are you sure?"

I thought back to the stirrings I'd felt against my hip when I was squashed against Cade on the subway.

"Ninety-nine percent."

"What a waste. I'll make sure you get home safely. Your man can go to bed and get his beauty sleep, not that he needs it."

I left Ishmael nursing his disappointment and walked over to Cade.

"Hey."

He gave me a heart-stopping smile. "Ready to go?"

"I've got to head out with Ishmael instead. Jewellery shopping then dinner. I'd have called if I had your number."

An expression of...something crossed his face. What was it? Disappointment? Peevishness that he'd been dragged all the way here for nothing?

"Look on the bright side," I said. "You can have an early night."

"No, I can't. I'm going straight back to Blackwood. We're busy as hell."

So that was it. He'd wanted a break from the office.

"Sorry."

He got out his phone, and seconds later, mine buzzed in my pocket.

"Now you've got my number. Do me a favour and message me when you get home? I need to know you're safe."

"Of course. I promise."

Anything to keep him from being grumpy. Which it seemed was easier said than done as he strode off without looking back.

Chapter 15

WELL, THAT WAS an interesting evening. And thank goodness I hadn't brought Cade.

I'd expected the jewellery to be quirky, and Ishmael hadn't disappointed me. Platinum hearts, silver lungs, and rose gold brains studded with rubies and diamonds, emeralds and sapphires. Some might have found it shocking, but I was beyond that as I picked up a matching pair of kidney earrings.

At least that was what I thought until we got to the restaurant.

"We're going for Japanese," Ishmael had said. "Atomic Sushi serves it like no other."

He wasn't kidding. I'd never eaten maki rolls off a naked man before. But there he was, laid out along the table like a giant platter. I didn't know where to look, much to Ishmael's amusement.

"Just eat from the good bits, darling," he told me, using his chopsticks to pluck a sliver of salmon from somewhere unmentionable. Ishmael had no shame. I risked a quick glance, relieved to see that nude-dude had shaved down there at least. Choking on a pube would have been beyond mortifying.

Turned out I had no shame either once I got a few glasses of sake inside me. And a scoop of green tea ice cream, which I may have eaten off a well-toned stomach. Licked. Okay, I licked it.

It was almost midnight when I tripped back up the stairs to my apartment building, clutching a bag of mochi and my souvenir chopsticks. Both went flying from my grasp as I tripped over Cade, sitting with his legs outstretched beside my front door.

Ooh, Cade... He could be my sushi platter any day.

Tia! Stop it! No, I absolutely did not just have that thought.

Cade sucked in a breath as I landed in his lap, and I hurried to remove my hand from between his legs while having a surreptitious feel at the same time. Flipping heck, did he keep a salami in there?

"Sorry, sorry. Oops. What are you doing here?"

"You said you'd tell me when you got home safe."

"And I planned to message you as soon as I got inside." Except I may have forgotten completely.

"I didn't know that. I was worried."

"Why didn't you call me?"

"I did."

I tried and failed to squelch down a hiccup as I pulled out my phone. Eight missed calls from Cade and two messages from Eli. Whoops.

I really, really wanted to know what Eli had to say, but I also didn't want to read his words in front of Cade. Two men, one phone—super weird. I tried to get my key into the lock, but the keyhole had shrunk. After I'd made a couple of attempts, Cade took the key off me and opened the door himself.

My fingers burned where his hand brushed against them, and where he put his hand on the small of my back to guide me inside, I got the same feeling I'd had when the sake seared my throat earlier in the evening.

"Can you walk up the stairs?" he asked.

Probably, but the question was, did I want to when I could be tucked against him and carried instead?

Drunk me was thinking all sorts of dirty things. Sake was my new best friend. Really, I should buy my own bottle. Tomorrow. I'd do that tomorrow.

While I dithered, Cade's patience ran out. He picked me up anyway, and I clung on to his neck as he transported me to my bedroom. He smelled so...so...so *male*. All woodsy cologne and man musk. When he leaned over and deposited me on the bed, I forgot to let go, and our lips ended up mere inches apart. Heat rolled off him in waves.

He leaned closer.

"Tia," he whispered. "You have to let go."

It took a few seconds for his words to filter in, and I slowly untwined my fingers.

Just as slowly, he drew away from me.

His footsteps retreated into the distance, down the stairs and across my apartment. I heard the bleep of the burglar alarm followed by a quiet click as he locked the door behind him. Goodnight, Cade.

My thoughts churned in the still air. What just happened?

I'd wanted Cade to kiss me. And I'd wanted to kiss him back.

The sake. It must be the sake. That was the only explanation. Why else would I have been tempted to drag a grumpy former Navy SEAL into bed with me?

"Because he's undeniably hot," the devil on my shoulder told me.

"Ryan was hot," said my angel.

"But Ryan's not here."

Their argument was interrupted by my phone buzzing again. Eli. How could I have forgotten about Eli?

I quickly checked his messages. The first had arrived at seven o'clock.

Eli: Sugar, do you want pasta this evening?

At nine...

Eli: Okay, I'm going to take that as a no. Busy night?

And just now...

Eli: Sugar, are you all right?

No, I was anything but all right. I was drunk and inexplicably horny. Perhaps his deliciously smooth tones could help with that?

I hit dial.

"Thank goodness. I was getting worried," he said, and I melted into the mattress.

"I'm so sorry. I had to work late. My boss wanted me to visit a jewellery designer with him then we grabbed a bite to eat."

Best to leave out the part about my plate being a ripped, tanned—and most likely very gay, since he'd given Ishmael his number before we left—hunk of deliciousness.

"At least you've eaten. I thought you might be hungry."

I *was* hungry, just not in the way he thought. The vibrations from his voice were doing strange things to my insides.

"No, I'm good. I had sushi."

"Did you eat enough? I always found those little tiny portions never filled me up."

"I got enough to eat, yes."

I still needed to be filled up, but that wasn't exactly something I could talk about with Eli, even if he did have the perfect voice for a sex chat line. If he ever decided to change profession, he'd be able to retire at thirty.

"So, are you home now?"

"Mmm hmm."

"You sound sleepy."

"I am, a little. It's been a long day."

"Do you want me to go?"

Hell, no. I wanted him to talk to me forever and a day.

"No. I... I... I'm addicted to the sound of your voice."

Silence reigned briefly then Eli cleared his throat.

"I grin like a possum eatin' a sweet tater every time I hear you too. You sound like the sun rising on a summer morning."

"You sound like sex."

I clapped a hand over my mouth. What the hell just came out of me? I needed to engage my brain-to-mouth filter from now on, and I was never, ever drinking sake again. Mortified, I turned over and buried my face in the pillow, hoping for suffocation.

But I still had the phone to my ear. Eli's voice dropped an octave, and I felt it to my core.

"Sugar, you're doing bad things to me. Best we say goodnight now, and I'll speak to you tomorrow."

Hang up? I could no sooner hang up than stop breathing.

"I can't," I whispered.

He let out a low groan. "Hell, you don't want to know where my hand's heading right now."

"Tell me," I said, so quietly I could barely hear myself. My own hand inched downwards.

So he did.

I woke the next morning with a killer headache, although the rest of me felt oddly relaxed. Why was that?

I caught sight of the phone, still on the pillow next to me, and the horrors of my phone conversation with Eli came flooding back to me. Literally, came.

Shitting. Hell. I'd had drunk phone sex with an almost-complete stranger. One day I was crying my eyes out to him, the next, I was encouraging him to... I didn't even want to think about it. Thank goodness he lived a couple of states away. Maybe I could leave my phone turned off for a bit. Or throw it in the Hudson.

Except, it seemed, Eli didn't share my panic. My phone buzzed while I was snarfing down a bowl of Coco Pops.

Eli: Good morning, sugar.

Then, a second later...

Eli: No, changing that. Good morning, sexy xx

Oh, hell. The vague notion he might have written our little chat off as a particularly graphic dream died in its tracks. Now I had a choice—I could either toss the phone out of the window or reply. Ignoring him wasn't an option. Some parts of my upbringing had stuck with me, even if the DeBrett's etiquette guide mentioned nothing about what to do the morning after phone sex.

Me: Good morning...

What should I write? If I simply put "Eli," it would

trivialise what happened. Writing nothing would come across as grumpy. My loins suggested "sex machine," but that would sound like I wanted a repeat every night.

"You do," said the devil on my shoulder.

I shut her up by writing "gorgeous," then hit send before I got tempted to change it. The phone rang a few seconds later, and I put it on speaker, filling the kitchen with the voice of my dreams.

"I wanted to call and check you were okay. You know...after... Well, things escalated."

That was putting it mildly.

"I'm okay." Perhaps even a little better than okay.

Eli let out a whoosh of breath on the other end of the line. "Thank goodness. I just thought... I don't know, really..."

"You were amazing," I whispered. My filter was well and truly broken. What was it about this man that made me blurt out my true feelings?

Silence.

Then, "I've never done that before. I mean over the phone...with another girl. I just wanted you to know that."

Whew. Not that I'd have any right to complain if he'd made a habit of it, but still... I was glad.

"I haven't either. Not with any other guy. Or girl."

He chuckled. "I reckon there's still room for improvement."

"You do?"

"You know what they say about practice?"

"Makes perfect," I said softly.

He wanted to do it again.

My brain was a hot mess as I rode to work. The fact that Cade was sitting next to me didn't help, his muscled thighs encased in a pair of tracksuit bottoms and his six-pack and pecs outlined by a tight top which left nothing to the imagination. And me? I'd cocooned myself in a white tiger-print onesie. Every time I went out, more clothes appeared in my wardrobe, and Ishmael's influence over Bradley was showing through.

I replayed the conversation with Eli in my mind. He'd said he wanted to...what? Have phone sex every night? Well, perhaps not every night, but I got the impression he was hoping for more than once a month.

Where would it lead? Sure, I got an instant rush followed by the relaxed glow of a mind-blowing orgasm, but how about long-term? Nothing about our relationship was normal.

Whoa, whoa, *whoa!* Relationship? Since when were we having a relationship? My subconscious had taken one crazy night and run wild.

Then there was Cade. Cade who made me check the corners of my mouth for drool every time I laid eyes on him. Eli sure was easy to talk to, but with Cade oozing pheromones from every pore next to me, I forgot how to form words. All except one: hussy.

And how did Ryan fit in? He'd said in his letter he wanted me to move on, but I doubted this was quite what he'd had in mind.

"Tia?" Cade snapped his fingers in front of my eyes. "What?"

"Earth to Tia. We're here. Are you getting out?"

How did we reach the office so quickly? I climbed out in a daze, and it barely registered when Cade lifted a pair of rollerblades out of the boot, nor when he followed me into the atrium. Only when Ishmael's eyes saucered did I take a good look behind me.

What the...?

"Aren't you going back to Blackwood?" I asked Cade.

"You said we were going roller skating."

"Hell, yes, we're going roller skating," Ishmael interrupted. "Tia, I brought you a pair of skates."

He held them out, hot pink with sparkly silver laces. Any hope of blending in with the early morning jogging crowd quickly evaporated. Not that Ishmael did the whole "blending in" thing. He'd worn a tracksuit the colour of a satsuma, and his skates had bells on. At least my onesie came with a hood.

"Reckon he'd notice if we went in a different direction?" Cade muttered.

"I guess we could hang back a bit."

Like, maybe a mile or two.

"How about the next state?"

Why stop there? We could skip one and end up in... West Virginia. Oh, I was so not going there.

"Why don't you two go in front?" Ishmael suggested. "Myrna and I can follow on behind."

I shot him an evil glare because I knew exactly why he'd suggested that. Yes, I'd seen him eyeing up Cade's rear, which admittedly looked rather pert.

Dammit. My mind had gone past the gutter and was well and truly down the drain.

"Sorry, we need to go at the back," Cade said. "I learned that in my bodyguard training course."

He was talking absolute rubbish, I could tell. But Ishmael swallowed it up with a look of disappointment.

"Why don't you join us for coffee when we get back?"

"Afraid I need to go straight to the office afterwards. I have a meeting."

"Perhaps another day, eh?" I put in, trying to keep the peace.

"Yeah. Sure."

Cade's glare said that day would never come.

After a few hiccups with the revolving door, we finally made it onto the street. Myrna didn't look happy on roller skates. I mean, Myrna didn't look happy ever, but right now she looked like a thundercloud. Ishmael took off, gliding like an orange swan while she tripped along behind him.

I wasn't particularly comfortable on wheels either, but Cade grabbed my hand to hold me up when I nearly fell over a kerb. He, of course, looked like a pro.

"Where did you learn to skate?" I asked him.

"I played hockey in school. It's kind of the same."

We didn't go particularly fast at first because the paparazzi needed time to get their photos, but once we got to the park, Ishmael scooted off, yelling at Myrna to keep up.

Cade spun around and skated backwards. Show off.

"You look as if you're doing better now," he said. "Shall I let go?"

I'd barely noticed his hand still in mine, but now sparks shot up my arm again.

"Okay."

I didn't feel like I was about to face-plant anymore, and better still, my concentrated efforts to stay upright had pushed thoughts of Eli to the back of my mind. At least, until we skated past a coffee vendor and I smelled the delicious aroma. I tripped over a bench and was heading straight for a flower border when Cade caught me, bringing me hard up against him. Warm breath puffed against my ear as his heat seeped into me.

"Careful, tiger," he whispered.

I shivered.

"Cold?" he asked, holding me tighter.

Nope, definitely not. One could even go so far as to say I was hot. The temperature wasn't why I'd shivered. No, I'd shivered because I could feel every glorious inch of Cade in painstaking detail. The outline of each taut muscle, the vibrations in his chest as he spoke, and the not entirely soft length of his cock. Holy hell. I needed to go for a long lie down on an ice rink.

But I could hardly tell him that, could I?

"I'm just a little chilly."

He took off his jacket and wrapped it around me, which left him standing in the tight top he'd been wearing in the car. Except the chilled air made things even more graphic. Bordering on pornographic.

"Really, I'm fine. You should put your jacket back on."

"Not if you're cold."

"I'll be okay."

If "hot and sweaty" counted as okay.

"I'm not letting you get a chill." He slung his arm around my shoulder and pulled me tight against him, putting in enough effort for both of us as he guided me along.

Oh, yes, this was totally helping.

I'd be a jellied mess by the time we got back to the

office.

CHAPTER 16

"WHERE DID YOU two get to?" Ishmael asked when I crept barefoot into his office, roller skates in hand.

He'd already got back from his nap—that's how late I was.

"I nearly fell over in the park, so we went more slowly on the way back."

He peered at me over the top of his sunglasses. "You look very pink."

"It's the cold air. Honestly. I always turn this colour when I go outside in winter."

"Hmmm. You didn't take a detour?"

"Cross my heart." My furiously pounding heart.

Obviously, Ishmael didn't believe me, and I could understand why. Cade was the type of man who would make any woman with eyes and a pulse want to run off into the bushes with him.

"Myrna's gone for coffee," Ishmael said. "When she gets back, I want to head over to the Lincoln Center to run through the layout. Monday's fast approaching."

Tell me about it. Yesterday afternoon, the three of us had drawn up a list of all the things left to do, and it ran to four pages. I needed Valium.

"Aren't we still a few models short?" I asked Ishmael.

"Yes, but we have another casting this afternoon.

I'll pick the final two from that. Are the male models sorted? The ones for the goody bags? I've already picked the four for the runway."

"They are indeed," Myrna announced as she walked in the door with three cups in a cardboard tray. "They're booked and briefed, and the goody bags for them to give out are totally organised."

"At least that's one thing we don't have to worry about," Ishmael said. "Tia, can you do the final photographs with Jenna today? All the pieces are finished now, and you should have pictures of the jewellery dropping into your inbox any minute."

"No problem."

The day sped by. Keeping busy helped, but even so, I had two hot guys fighting for space in my head. One had the looks, the other had the voice, and both gave me goosebumps.

Eli messaged me a shopping list, which meant I needed to find a supermarket on my way home. Such a simple task, but as all the food I'd eaten in New York either came from a restaurant or magically appeared in my fridge, I didn't know where to begin.

Of course, Cade did. He pushed the trolley, looking utterly out of place as I hunted for ingredients. No, this wasn't awkward at all, shopping with one man before cooking dinner with another.

Just concentrate on the food, Tia.

Asparagus, an orange, pancetta, a jar of truffles. "Where do I find robiola cheese?"

"No idea. What the hell are you making, anyway?"

Good question. "Uh, I forget the name. Something Italian."

"Been ages since I ate a home-cooked meal."

Was Cade angling for an invitation or merely feeling nostalgic? I kind of liked the idea of eating dinner with him again, but I couldn't invite him over with Eli on the phone. Especially as I had a good idea where dinner would lead. Weren't truffles an aphrodisiac?

Cade spotted the cheese, and I began to feel guilty. I bet he wasn't on the clock at Blackwood this evening, which meant he was giving up his time to help me.

"Why don't you come over tomorrow night?" I suggested. "I'll cook you dinner. Or at least, I'll try to. I'm not promising it'll be edible."

He gave me one of those special smiles, and my knees weakened.

"Reckon I'd like that."

Dammit, I was turning into such a slut. I'd be ringing Dan for advice soon.

Dating over the phone had one advantage—I didn't have to cake on make-up, and I could wear slippers instead of stilettos. What was Eli wearing? I imagined him coming in from the fields in a pair of worn jeans, soft from being washed too many times. His checked shirt hung open at the neck, revealing a taut, golden chest covered in a smattering of...shit—I didn't even know what colour his hair was.

Yes, I'd gone insane. What the hell was I playing at?

The answer? I had absolutely no idea. Everything was happening so fast my thoughts had ended up in a jumbled mess.

But I didn't have time to begin unravelling them

because the phone rang. I snatched it up.

"Sugar, I've been waiting to hear the sound of your voice all day."

He'd been waiting to hear *my* voice? It was his that melted underwear. One sentence, and already an ache was spreading through me.

But I had to focus. First, we needed to talk about more serious things.

"I couldn't wait to speak to you either."

"But..."

"But what?"

"There's a but coming. I can hear it in your voice."

Eli was so perceptive. Maybe because he couldn't see people's faces, he'd learned to pick up on the nuances in their voice.

"Okay, there is. What we did last night, it was, well, I don't really have words. But I've been thinking, I barely know you. I'm opening myself up to a virtual stranger and it scares me."

"So what are you saying?" His voice cracked along with my heart. "That you don't want to do this anymore?"

"No! Not at all. I just want to get to know you a bit better. I mean, I understand why I can't see you, but if we're going to carry on like this, I need to know who I'm carrying on with."

His sigh sounded clear down the line. Relief, I hoped.

"Sugar, I want to get to know you better too. There's something between us... I don't know what it is, but I feel it. Tell me you do too?"

"Yes," I whispered. "I do."

"Ask me anything."

"What do you look like?"

He chuckled. "I want to hear that from you too."

"Okay."

As I was never going to meet him, I could describe myself as a supermodel. All legs and ribs rather than tits and ass. Mind you, he could embellish the truth too. Maybe he'd turn out to be the cowboy equivalent of Zac Efron?

"Right, so I'm six foot one. A little tall for riding the cow ponies, really. Ideally, I could do with being a couple of inches shorter. But the height's good when it comes to maintenance work."

I lay back on the sofa, imagining him reaching up to hammer nails into the side of a barn. Shirtless of course. In my fantasy, it was a hot day, okay?

"My hair's dark brown. About the colour of a buckeye."

When I first came to the US, it took me ages to work out what a buckeye was. As a Brit, I'd always called them conkers. But as a hair colour? Nice. I adjusted fantasy-Eli accordingly.

"Is it short?"

"No, longer. To my shoulders. So it covers up...you know."

"Do you have a beard?" Maybe it would hide some of the scarring?

"I tried it, but it looked worse. The hair didn't grow on the scarred patches."

"What colour are your eyes?"

"Same as my hair. Nothing exotic."

"And your build?"

His voice said he shrugged before answering. "Average, I guess. I don't go to the gym or anything.

Working on the ranch keeps me fit enough. Now, it's your turn. I want to know about you."

"Ishmael says I should wear pencil skirts," I blurted.

"Ishmael?"

"My boss. The fashion designer."

Eli laughed. "That's the best you can come up with?"

Suddenly, I didn't know where to start. "Ishmael says my figure is an hourglass, but I've always thought my bum was too big."

"Men like something to grab hold of, sugar."

"Why do you call me sugar?"

"Because you're so damn sweet."

He said that, and I was supposed to be the sweet one?

"Okay, I'm blushing."

"Like an English rose. What colour hair do you have?"

"Brown, maybe a touch lighter than yours. It's kind of long at the moment. I need to get it cut."

"More than anything, I wish I could tangle my fingers in it right now."

I swallowed hard as his words heated my core. "Do you want to skip dinner?"

"What, and go straight for dessert?"

"Mmm hmm."

"Don't tempt me." A pause, and I imagined his pulse racing along with mine. "If we plan on eating tonight, we really need to get started with the preparation. Three courses won't be quick."

My raging hormones waged a battle with my appetite, lust against hunger. A glass of wine would help to calm me down, right? I poured myself a generous measure.

"Are you cooking as well?" I asked Eli.

"Same as you. If we mess up, we do it together."

"Doesn't your family think it's weird?"

"Think what's weird?"

"The amount of time you're spending on the phone in the kitchen."

Tell me his mother wasn't helping.

He laughed. "My family doesn't have a clue what I'm doing. I live on my own."

"But I thought you said you lived at the ranch you grew up on?"

"I do. But I converted one of the old barns into a home for myself. It's mine and mine alone. So, when we're in bed later and I've got you on speaker because my hands are otherwise engaged, you can scream as loud as you want."

My knees went weak. "I don't think I want dinner anymore."

"Sugar, you're eating. You'll need energy for what I have planned."

I plopped onto a stool. Maybe I could just order takeout?

But Eli insisted we were cooking, and I managed to stand while he talked me through three ambitious courses. Pancetta-wrapped asparagus with citronette to start—I'd never made my own dressing before, and it was easier than I thought.

Perhaps I could make it for Cade tomorrow?

The instant that thought popped into my head, I felt sick. Making this meal with anyone other than Eli would feel like cheating.

Could I be unfaithful in a relationship that consisted of phone sex and cooking?

"The talking, Tia, don't forget the talking," my angel said. "You bare your soul to this man."

And it was true. Through a main course of pasta with robiola cheese and shaved truffles, I told Eli about my childhood—how I'd grown up with a mother more interested in her social standing than her daughter, and a housekeeper who hated me.

Over chocolate soufflé, Eli told me more about his early years on the ranch. His first pony had tossed him into a pond, and when he'd walked home covered in duckweed, his grandma had fainted at the sight of him.

The whole time he was talking, an undercurrent of electricity ran through me, fed by *that* voice and my overactive imagination. As I took my last bite of a dessert I never could have dreamed of making alone, the sizzle exploded into full on desire.

"I'm going upstairs," I told Eli, shoving my chair back.

"And I'm joining you."

I lay back on my bed, naked, as Eli took talking dirty to a whole new level.

He said he hadn't done this before, which meant he must have natural talent. Holy hell, if his voice alone reduced me to this quivering mess, I could only imagine what he'd be able to do in person.

And that was the shame of it. I could only imagine. So could he, but as I came for the third time, I decided to help him along with that.

When his final message of the night came through, wishing me sweet dreams, I held my phone out in front of me and snapped a selfie. My hair splayed out over the pillow, and my make-up was far from perfect. I looked like I'd just been fucked, which effectively, I had been. Even I could see that my face was glowing.

Before I chickened out, I pressed *send* then quickly followed the photo up with a message.

Me: This is what you do to me. Xx

Oh hell, oh hell, oh hell. Before I could overanalyse what I'd done, I flicked the phone onto silent, turned over, and went to sleep.

And I did indeed have sweet dreams.

Chapter 17

THE NEXT MORNING, I snatched my phone off the nightstand and checked the screen. No message. My heart sank, but then the phone began vibrating to the tune of Justin Timberlake's "Sexyback." Okay, it was cheesy, but appropriate because Eli *was* bringing my sexy back.

His voice was thick with emotion as he spoke.

"Sugar, you can't send me pictures like that."

"Why not?"

It was my picture. I could do whatever I wanted with it.

"Because I've got nothing to send you in return. Unless I start sending photos of body parts, but that's just crude."

"I don't expect you to send me anything back. You already paid up-front with orgasms." Although the filthy girl who hid inside me was tempted to ask for a dick pic, crude or not.

"That was a fair exchange."

"I'll give you everything you'll let me give you."

"Hey, this is getting heavy for so early in the morning."

I forced a laugh. "We'd better lighten up, then. Did you know that each morning Ishmael plans a fun keep-fit activity for us? Yesterday we went rollerblading, and

Tuesday was ballet. Guess what we're doing today?"

"I give up already. What?"

"Hula hoops! They got delivered yesterday. Mine's green with glitter."

"You're kidding?"

"Nope. It's kinda fun. I've tried all these things I've never done before. We've got mini trampolines for tomorrow."

"You shouldn't have told me that. I'll be thinking of you wiggling around and bouncing up and down all day."

"You have a dirty mind, Eli."

"It's in the sewer, sugar."

A man after my own heart.

Not only had Ishmael bought us hula hoops, he'd got us fancy new onesies to wear while we hula-hulaed. His was pink camouflage. Mine had My Little Ponies on it. Myrna's was black.

"It's slimming," Ishmael told her, a little bitchily.

I kept dropping my hoop, and Ishmael's carefully arranged paperclips went flying along with a pot of glitter and a boxful of *Happy Birthday* confetti. The office looked as if a rainbow just escaped from the asylum.

On the plus side, Myrna looked more colourful by the end.

The catalogue had gone to the printers, so that was crossed off my list, and I spent the morning organising the logistics of getting the clothes and equipment to the Lincoln Center for the weekend. I had Saturday off work, but Ishmael's schedule saw us starting at 7:00 a.m. on Sunday. It promised to be a busy day for everyone.

The afternoon brought a new challenge. Ishmael had called in a million favours to get the Ghost to DJ the show. I'd never heard of him, but Myrna reckoned he was some legendary music producer, famous for hiding his face behind a freaky white mask in public. His team would be setting his equipment up on Sunday, but his rider had been delegated to me.

Everything had to be white. A white dressing room with white furniture, white accessories, and even white flipping food. White chocolate buttons and white caviar. Was he planning to eat them together? He sounded like a right diva.

All that rushing around barely left me enough time to Google a recipe to cook for Cade this evening. Seeing as I'd followed Eli's instructions last night and hadn't burned the apartment down or died of food poisoning, I felt pretty confident.

Since Cade undoubtedly went to the gym, I figured chicken was a safe bet. After all, that was what most of the men at Riverley lived on, along with egg white omelettes. Pinterest yielded the perfect recipe for spicy mango chicken served up with ginger carrots and brown rice.

At seven o'clock, I finally turned off my MacBook and hugged Ishmael goodbye.

"See you on Sunday."

"Don't forget we're starting early."

"I've already set my alarm."

Today, Cade was sitting on the floor, legs crossed at the ankles as he watched the door.

"Your apartment?" he asked.

"We need to make a quick trip to the supermarket first. I've got a new recipe to try."

I patted my handbag, a new Mulberry sample from Ishmael where I'd carefully stashed the printouts.

"Can't complain if I get to eat the spoils."

Cade pushed the trolley again, although today he kept getting distracted by his phone.

"Work?" I asked.

"Sorry. A big case is on the verge of breaking."

"Do you need to go back?"

He flashed a smile. "No. A couple more emails and I'm all yours."

I rounded up the groceries, and when we reached the checkout, Cade got his wallet out at the same moment I opened my handbag.

"This is on me," I told him. And for the first time in my life, I'd be paying with money I'd actually earned myself.

He shook his head and handed over his credit card anyway. "You don't pay. Simple as that."

"But you even put up with roller skating for me. I owe you."

"Call me old-fashioned."

His mouth set in a hard line, and I realised I'd have had more chance of moving the Statue of Liberty single-handed than winning that argument. Part of me appreciated his kindness, but his stubborn streak made me gnash my teeth. Another common feature among Blackwood men. Cade carried the shopping too, and once we got into my kitchen, he pushed up his sleeves.

"What do you want me to do?"

"Nothing. Sit down and relax. You're too uptight."

"I'm not uptight," he snapped.

"Listen to yourself."

He sighed. "I'm sorry. It's been a long week at work."

"Just sit, okay?" I pointed at one of the stools beside the counter.

He sat.

I propped my cheat-sheet against the kettle and set about making the sauce. Peel this, chop that, stir the other. I kind of wished Eli was there to help with instructions. Cade didn't offer any tips at all, just watched me like a hawk as I moved around the kitchen, and his gaze made me nervous. Wine was called for.

"Do you want a glass?" I asked him, fetching a bottle of rosé from the fridge.

"I don't drink while I'm working."

"Is that what tonight is? Work?"

"I guess not," he conceded. "Do you have any red?"

Of course I did. Bradley stocked the kitchen. I had everything from cooking wine to Dom Pérignon.

I fetched Cade a generous glassful, and he swirled and sniffed before drinking. So, he did have some culture even if he tried to hide it. His posture relaxed after he'd drunk it all, and I poured him another.

"Have you always lived in New York?" I asked. "Apart from when you were in the Navy, I mean."

"I grew up in Minnesota. I only moved to New York when I joined Blackwood."

"Why didn't you just work at their Minneapolis office?"

"Because for what I want, it's well known that the best place to get spotted is in Richmond or London. New York was the closest vacancy."

"What do you want?" I thought about it. Who spent a lot of time in Richmond and London? "Oh. You want Emmy."

"I don't want Emmy as such. But I do want to be on her Special Projects Team."

Memories flooded back, of another time, another place, and a conversation with Ryan. He'd shared that same dream, and the day he got selected, we'd celebrated with champagne.

I didn't feel so joyous now. In fact, I felt quite sick.

"But it's so dangerous."

"I know, but I want that challenge."

"Wouldn't you rather live a regular life? A safe one?"

"No."

"But what if you die?"

I didn't want to be having this conversation, but now I'd started, I couldn't stop. I'd asked Ryan the same questions many times, but he'd never given me a straight answer.

"Nobody lives forever. I'd rather shuffle off this mortal coil doing something that makes me come alive than be slowly suffocated by normality." He fixed his eyes on mine. "I guarantee every person on that team feels the same way."

"Even Emmy?"

"Especially Emmy. She's a warrior in the truest sense of the word."

"And Ryan?" I whispered.

"Ryan had the end we all hope for. He died quickly doing something he loved, and he didn't see it coming."

"You know what happened?"

He nodded. "The person who did see it coming was

Emmy. They say something broke inside her that day."

It did, and for too long I'd blamed her for what happened, pretending not to see the haunted look in her eyes. And what had I done after that? Run to New York and abandoned her. I yearned to get back to how we were before, but I didn't know how to start making things right.

The oven timer saved me from more awkwardness, and I used the oven mitt to wipe a tear from my eye as I crossed the kitchen. I refused to break down in front of Cade.

The chicken looked surprisingly edible, and I arranged it on a bed of rice with carrots at the side. I even added a sprig of parsley from the pretty pink pot that had materialised on the windowsill. Anything to avoid going back to our previous conversation.

"Enjoy," I said, sliding Cade's plate in front of him.

"Looks good."

He smiled and took a mouthful, chewed for a second, then started choking.

Huh? Did I leave a bone in it or something?

He clutched at his throat as he ran over to the sink and stuck his face under the tap. What the hell was wrong with him? I took a quick bite of my own chicken to find out.

Oh, cheese and rice! My mouth was on fire! I knocked back Cade's half-full glass of wine then ran to the fridge and drank the nearest cold thing I could get my hands on. Yeuch! I staggered to the sink and spat out the mouthful of lime juice I'd just taken.

Cade was still there, his wet hair dripping everywhere.

"Fuck, woman," he gasped. "How much chilli did

you put in that?"

"Uh, maybe four or five."

His eyes widened.

"They were really small."

He marched over to the counter and picked up the empty packet. "These are habaneros!"

I shrugged. That meant nothing to me.

"They're the hottest chillis you can get. Were you trying to kill us both?"

The emotions of the evening caught up with me, and I burst into tears.

"Don't rub your eyes!" Cade yelled.

I sank to the floor, and after a second, Cade joined me, bundling me up against him.

"I'm sorry I shouted," he mumbled into my hair. "I just didn't want you to get hurt."

"I'm sorry I tried to poison you."

"It's okay, tiger. You didn't mean it. I appreciate you trying to cook. Come on, we need to go scrub your hands."

Once again, he carried me up the stairs like I weighed nothing. Into the bathroom we went, where he stood behind me at the sink and lathered my hands with soap five times over.

"That should help. Just don't touch your eyes, or nose, or...any other sensitive parts for a day or so."

"Other sensitive parts?"

"Just be real careful when you use the toilet."

Thank goodness he mentioned that. Otherwise when Eli phoned, things could have got a little more explosive that usual.

When Eli phoned... At the moment, I had Cade pressed against me, his front to my back, and now I was one hundred percent sure he was straight. Shit.

I couldn't go there. I mean, I had Ryan to think of as well as Eli. But Cade held all the cards right now—he was alive, he was hot, and he was in my apartment.

Luckily, he stepped back, saving me from doing something utterly stupid.

Okay, stupider. Because in anyone's book, cavorting with a hot guy who reminded me of my late boyfriend—okay, fine, I admitted it, Cade and Ryan did share a lot of similarities—while having a weird online textual relationship with a virtual stranger counted as monumentally insane.

"We still need to eat," Cade said.

"I'm not sure I can be trusted in the kitchen."

"Let's make pancakes." He took my hand and led me downstairs.

"Do you know how to make pancakes?"

"Yeah, I know how to make pancakes."

It was my turn to take a seat while Cade found his way around the kitchen, fishing out eggs and milk and flour, and I poured myself a glass of wine while I watched. Yes, this was much better.

"Do you have any lemons?" he asked, head buried in a cupboard.

In the fridge—I'd seen them earlier. I hopped down from the stool and fetched one, tossing it in his direction, only the alcohol skewed my aim and it bounced off his shoulder instead.

"You little minx. You're gonna pay for that."

Cade reached behind him for the lemon and threw it back. His aim was better than mine, and it hit me square in the chest. Except it turned out not to be the lemon. It was one of the eggs.

His eyes widened. "Oh, fuck. I'm sorry."

Sorry? Yolk ran down my dress and dripped onto my pair of Jimmy Choos.

"Sorry doesn't cut it, hotshot."

I was standing next to the fridge, and before the words left my mouth, I'd reached inside. I had a whole arsenal at my disposal.

Bull's-eye!

Cade wiped away the cream running down his face as the pot rolled across the floor. Three more eggs came back at me, one after the other, and I retaliated with a bottle of chocolate sauce and a cream cake. He threw himself behind the breakfast bar, popping up only to lob a bag of flour that exploded on impact. White puffs mushroomed around me as I ducked behind the fridge door and threw two oranges and a stick of butter. Judging by the grunt, I scored at least one direct hit.

Cade's hands appeared above the counter in surrender.

"Truce?" he called. "I'd rather face the Taliban."

I left a trail of flour as I walked out to survey the damage. Aw, hell, it looked worse than Emmy's house after a fourteen-man assault team rampaged through it. Cade crossed the tiles to meet me, and I thought he'd stop when he got close. But he kept coming, pushing me back against the counter and pinning me there with his hips.

"Tiger, you need to be locked up."

I grinned at him. "Are you offering?"

He closed his eyes and a breath shuddered through him. "You make me lose my self-control."

"Is that a good thing or a bad thing?" I leaned into him and his eyes popped open. "You have cream on your face."

Unable to resist, I stuck my tongue out and licked a little bit off.

He closed his eyes again. "Tia, this is not a good idea."

Why not? He was here, and he was definitely ready. I was practically panting. What wasn't good about it?

"Really?"

He leaned his forehead against mine, our breath mingling. "I can't cross that boundary. You're still a client."

"I could get Emmy to fire you."

"Tempting." He groaned, long and low. "But I can't."

He pushed back, and the moment was lost. My runaway heart hammered in my chest, all too aware of what a close call that had been.

"You get in the shower," Cade said. "I'll clear up this mess and order a pizza."

"I'll help."

"You're dropping flour everywhere." He spun me around and gave me a gentle push towards the stairs. "Go."

By the time I'd shampooed my hair and dressed in smart-ish jeans and a sweater, the kitchen looked more like its former self.

"If you ever need a new career, I'm sure any maid service would be glad to have you."

"I'll have to pass on that. I can't get the egg off the tile."

"Don't worry. It's your turn for a shower. I'll put your clothes through the washer-dryer while we eat."

"Pizza's gonna be here in twenty minutes. Don't

open the door. I'll do it."

"Do you ever stop being bossy?"

His smile came back. "Nope."

I couldn't help smiling too, because I kind of liked him that way.

Eating pizza wasn't easy with Cade sitting opposite in only a pair of boxer shorts, especially when I saw what he was hiding under his shirt. Tattoos. A full sleeve on his right arm that spilled across his shoulder and onto his chest. A mermaid reclined on his forearm, and every time he took a bite of his spicy pepperoni, folding the slices in half so they didn't bend, she flashed her bare breasts at me. At one point, my pizza missed my mouth completely, but thankfully Cade was focused on the movie I'd put on in an attempt to avoid talking about what just happened. Once the credits rolled, I cued up a box set from Netflix and prayed for the tumble dryer to finish its cycle. If it didn't hurry, I might be tempted to crawl into Cade's lap, and that could only be a bad thing.

On screen, aliens invaded, but I didn't last the distance. The next morning, the only evidence Cade had been in my apartment was a note propped up against the parsley pot.

See you in the morning. C

And my phone, once I located it in my coat pocket, had two messages and two missed calls from Eli.

Chapter 18

MY FINGERS TREMBLED as I dialled Eli. What if he was upset I hadn't answered his calls? The cold dread crawling up my throat said just how much that worried me, and guilt prickled at my insides. I'd barely thought of Eli at all yesterday evening, and now that felt like a betrayal.

He picked up on the second ring.

"Ashlyn?"

Dammit, I still hadn't told him my real name, probably because he kept calling me sugar, which I'll admit I liked more than I should.

"Yes, it's me, but..."

"Sugar, I was so worried when you didn't answer. I know it's irrational, and I don't want to come across all stalker-like..."

"You don't, not at all. It's my fault. I fell asleep and left my phone in my coat pocket."

"Everything's okay, then?"

"I had a small recipe-related disaster, but apart from that, yes."

"What happened? You didn't set anything on fire, did you?"

"Only my mouth."

I recounted the story, leaving out the food fight and the part where I'd almost thrown myself at Cade.

"You really didn't know there were different kinds of chilli?"

"Cooking isn't something I've ever had to do before. Even you had to start somewhere."

"I did. I was lucky to have a grandmomma who loved the kitchen."

"I never knew either of my grandmothers. Maybe I should enrol in classes?"

"Or I'll teach you," Eli said quietly. "I've felt more alive this last week than I have in years, and it's because of you. I don't want this to stop."

The ache in my chest told me I didn't either.

"Tonight, then? We can cook something else tonight?"

"I'll be counting down the seconds."

Breaking the connection was hard, but Eli said he had to go herd cattle, and I needed to work. His voice echoed in my head as I hung up, the soundtrack to my heart.

While I got dressed, I pictured him on the ranch, walking out to the pasture to saddle up his horse. A sigh escaped my lips. Such a cowboy.

Then my mind turned darker and imagined Eli naked, spread out on his bed with his face in shadow. The moonlight reflected off his pecs, his abs, his...

Enough!

I was being ridiculous, but I couldn't stop myself. I wanted to know everything about Eli. Even if I couldn't see his face, I wanted to see his room. And his house. Was he neat and tidy or a secret slob?

I wanted to understand him as a person.

Would he give me that?

All that daydreaming made me late. Ten minutes,

according to my watch. Where was Cade? I'd expected to hear him knock by now.

I tried calling him, but his phone went straight to voicemail. Well, I couldn't wait any longer. I'd have to take the subway, which meant I'd arrive at work sweaty and a bit squashed.

I'd got halfway across the lobby when a tough-looking guy waved me down mid-run.

"Tia Halston-Cain?"

More or less. I rarely used the Halston part because it sounded poncey. "Yes?"

"Cade sent me. He had to go into the office this morning."

Was that true? Emmy had always drilled into me that I mustn't take things at face value. I'd already been kidnapped once, and I didn't relish the idea of it happening again.

"Do you have ID?"

He pulled out his Blackwood company pass and showed it to me under the watchful eye of the security guard in the lobby. The pass identified my new shadow as Bernard Howe from the executive protection division. I looked out to the kerb. The same black car as yesterday idled in front of the building, and the driver waved at me through the window.

I let out a breath I didn't realise I'd been holding. Things were okay.

Well, sort of okay. I'd much rather have had Cade beside me even if that meant arriving at the office with damp knickers. And why had he been called away?

"What's Cade doing at the office?"

"Sorry, that's all confidential."

"Is it dangerous? Can you at least tell me that?"

"Sometimes, working as a bodyguard can have an element of danger."

Bernard sounded like a bloody robot.

"Look, I didn't ask for Cade's job description. I just want to know whether he'll be back to look after me tomorrow or if he's likely to end up at the hospital instead?"

One day at a time, right? I had to take one day at a time.

Bernard's exasperated expression said he didn't get paid enough to deal with girls like me, but he angled his body away slightly and tapped away on his phone. What, did he think I'd look over his shoulder and learn state secrets or something?

"Cade's schedule says he's in the office, briefing a colleague on an upcoming job. For an *important* client."

Bernard's inflection was clear: more important than me. How much of my history had he been told? Did he know what a brat I'd been towards everyone lately? If so, I could understand his low opinion, but it still hurt more than I dared to let on.

Instead, I stared at the passing traffic as I let out a shaky breath. If Cade was in the office, he'd be safe.

He'd be safe.

Bernard didn't say another word the whole way, and I was kind of grateful for that. Small talk wasn't my thing either.

Thankfully, I could always rely on Ishmael to cheer me up, and when I arrived at the office, he didn't disappoint. Who knew mini trampolines could be so much fun? I was laughing and sweaty in a whole different way by the time we'd finished.

"What are we doing next week?" I asked him as we folded them away.

"I thought we'd try pole dancing."

Pole dancing? I nearly choked. Not at the idea of the poles, but at the outfits that Ishmael would undoubtedly come up with for us to wear. I could just imagine him in pink lycra hot pants and quite frankly that scared me a little.

"The poles aren't being delivered until next Tuesday afternoon, though, so we get a day off exercise. I've got a lady coming in at eight to do facials instead. We could do with a recharge after Monday's show."

Oh great, four whole days to work up a sense of dread. I couldn't hang from a pole. I couldn't even climb a rope in Emmy's gym. Perhaps I could go back to Virginia after the show ended? After all, I'd never planned to stay in New York for long. Except when I considered hitching a lift back with the Blackwood girls, I found I didn't actually want to leave. New York had grown on me. And despite overhearing Ishmael on the phone as he ordered three leotards, platform wedges, and extra glitter, I finished Friday in a good place. I'd crossed a lot of items off my list, and I was ready to face Sunday.

But first, I had to get through Saturday.

Downstairs, Bernard herded me out to the car, looking every inch the bodyguard in his black suit and earpiece. At least Cade made the effort to blend in.

And speaking of Cade, my phone buzzed with a message as Bernard shut my car door.

Cade: *Sorry I couldn't pick you up. Had to work, but I'm yours tomorrow. Call me when you decide what you want to do.*

I mulled over the wording of that all the way home. Cade was mine? Did he mean that in a purely work-related sense? Or something more?

Why couldn't he speak in black and white?

Why couldn't my life be straightforward?

The added complication of Eli didn't help either. We cooked again, and he talked me through how to make risotto. I was getting better at not sticking things to the pan, but worse at not melting every time he spoke.

By the time I fell asleep, or rather, passed out in a boneless mess on my mattress, I'd screamed Eli's name three times, and he had another photo to add to his collection.

On Saturday, I groaned at the sunlight glaring in through the window, tempted beyond measure to roll over and sleep for the rest of the day. But as I tucked my head under the duvet, Cade's message came back to me. I couldn't just ignore him.

Besides, here I was in the Big Apple, and I shouldn't waste an entire day in bed. Not alone, at any rate.

Mind. Gutter. Again.

No, I should go out and explore everything this amazing city had to offer. Another gallery, perhaps? The Guggenheim? I fancied that idea, but I didn't have the heart to make Cade suffer through more art. Shopping? A show? The Empire State Building? A carriage ride in Central Park?

I rolled over and dialled Cade.

"Have you decided?" he mumbled, sounding half

asleep.

"Yes."

"And? Which gallery is it today?" He didn't sound thrilled at the prospect.

"None of them. I've decided you can decide."

"Sorry?"

"Where we go. You can pick where we go."

"You're my client. It's up to you."

"Oh, would you quit with the client thing? It went beyond that the other night and you know it. Unless you have food fights with everyone you work for?"

He fell silent for a few seconds. What? Mr. Know-it-all had no clever comeback? Or was he still stressing over being my bodyguard? Because Emmy and co. were remarkably relaxed about that kind of thing as long as it didn't impact work.

Finally, he replied, "Right, I've decided where we're going. You're not claustrophobic, are you?"

"No, why?"

"Wear comfortable shoes."

"That's it? Wear comfortable shoes? Aren't you going to tell me what we're doing?"

"Nope. It's a surprise."

Great. I just loved surprises.

Half an hour later, Cade knocked on my door wearing jeans, a warm jumper, and chunky boots. Uh oh. Those looked suspiciously like outdoor clothes. He perused me slowly from head to toe. What would he think of my artfully distressed skinny jeans and velvet blazer?

"Lose the fancy jacket, tiger. You need something warmer."

"You haven't told me what we're doing yet."

He ignored that and climbed the stairs to my bedroom two at a time.

"Hey! Where are you going?"

I raced after him and found him rummaging in my wardrobe.

"What are you—?"

"This works." He tossed me one of the waterproof, breathable, padded jackets Emmy habitually wore when she headed out on a survival exercise. Why did I get a bad feeling about this?

"How about we visit the Statue of Liberty?" I suggested. "My treat."

"Nope."

Oh dear.

"Are we taking the town car or the subway?"

"Neither."

He shepherded me down in the lift, and when we got outside, I spotted an illegally parked Mercedes SLK at the kerb. Black paintwork, black windows.

"Is that yours?"

"Good to have an excuse to drive it. I rarely do in the city."

He opened my door then hopped in the driver's side. The engine roared as he rocketed forwards then braked sharply for traffic, and I gripped the sides of my seat until my knuckles turned white.

"You drive like Emmy."

"How so?"

"Obscenely fast, like you're on the verge of crashing all the time."

"I don't crash. Isn't it Dan who keeps having accidents?"

"She goes through a car a month."

City turned to country, and one hour turned into two. Out of the sprawl of Manhattan, Cade's driving didn't scare me quite so much, probably because there was less for him to hit.

"Won't you give me a clue yet?" I asked.

"Don't want to ruin the surprise."

Twenty minutes later, we pulled into the car park of a nondescript-looking hotel. Tell me he hadn't brought me all this way to have a dirty weekend?

Well, it turned out he had. Just not in the way I imagined.

"What are we doing at this place?" I hissed as we walked in the front door. Dinner? Room? Both?

Neither.

"We're going spelunking," Cade told me, his eyes lighting up like a five-year-old on Christmas morning.

"Spelu-what?" Tell me that wasn't some weird thing out of the *Kama Sutra*.

"Caving."

"Sorry? For a moment there, I thought you said we were going caving."

"We are. An old friend of mine runs this place. There's an awesome cave system right out back."

"Like actual caves? The dark, scary kind?"

"We'll have flashlights."

A blond-haired man ambled up to us. He was dressed like Cade, except his outfit looked more worn around the edges, and he needed a haircut too. Was this the caveman?

Seemed so, because he thumped Cade on the back. "How have you been, buddy?"

"Not bad. Busy."

The blond guy looked me up and down. "I can see

why."

"It's not like that. Tia's..."

Tia was what? I was curious to know, but Cade's friend had other thoughts.

"Tia? Pretty name for a pretty lady. I'm Andy." He stuck out a hand. "I'll be guiding you this afternoon. Follow me, and I'll get you both set up with equipment."

My feet dragged as I did as I was told. Caving? Cade had seriously brought me caving? I should have pulled rank and gone to the flipping Guggenheim. Now, I'd get to spend my afternoon in the pitch black with only Cade and his admittedly attractive-in-a-rugged-way friend for company. What if I had to feel my way around?

Hmmm... Actually, on second thoughts, this caving lark could have its advantages.

Andy fastened pads around my knees and elbows then fitted me with a helmet.

"Your light goes on the helmet. That way you can keep your hands free," he explained.

"Why do I need the elbow and knee pads?"

"There are some parts where we have to crawl."

Crawl? He was kidding, right? "Is it too late to go home?" I whispered to Cade.

"You're not backing out now, tiger. I'll be with you every step of the way."

And he was.

He held my hand as we descended into the darkness, and even though we all had torches, he kept some part of himself in constant contact with me.

A squeeze of his hand, a brush of his fingers, and when we stopped in a huge cavern, he stood behind my back and wrapped his arms around me, resting his chin on top of my head.

"Wow. Just wow."

Crystals glittered from the walls as we shone our torches from left to right, and a small stream running through a rocky channel it had started carving centuries ago provided a burbling soundtrack.

"Every time I come down here, it's like visiting another world."

"It's amazing."

"Yes, it is."

His lips brushed my ear, and I got the feeling he wasn't only talking about the cave. Holy hotness.

Good job I wasn't claustrophobic, because the parts we had to crawl through were barely roomy enough for a mouse. I tried to make Cade go in front so I could at least enjoy the view, but he insisted on bringing up the rear. For safety, apparently.

I thought I'd hate the two hours we spent underground, but despite the dampness, the sharp rocks, and the slimy walls, I didn't. Probably something to do with the company.

Over hot chocolate in the hotel restaurant, I watched Cade as he talked to Andy. Out of the city and away from his duties, he was more relaxed, smiling and joking. His frown lines disappeared, and the tension normally evident in his posture eased.

I liked this new side of him.

I just liked, well, him.

Ryan had told me to meet a man who put me first every time. Did Cade do that? He'd made a few work-related slip-ups, but he'd been around to save me from myself in the evenings, and now he was spending his

Saturday with me too. If I was honest with myself, Ryan had put Blackwood first more often than not, although I'd never minded because I loved him.

Without Eli on the scene, my decision would have been straightforward. I'd have checked my hair, touched up my make-up, and suggested booking a room.

But Eli did exist, and like it or not, I was hung up on a faceless guy who lived in West Virginia.

Which meant when Cade headed back over, I smiled politely and kept the distance between us.

"Andy's gonna make us a late lunch."

Right on cue, my stomach let out a grumble, and Cade laughed.

"Sounds like that's a good thing."

"I didn't eat much breakfast." Just coffee and a bar of chocolate.

Torn as I was between two men, I stuck to safe topics of conversation as we ate omelettes with french fries and salad. Attractions in New York, Cade's motorbike, the upcoming fashion show. I tried to ask Cade about his childhood, but he shut me down and asked about my horses instead. It seemed his past was a touchy subject.

All the while, I pushed Eli out of my head. Not because I didn't care, but because I didn't want to spoil the most perfect day I'd had in ages by torturing myself.

"Will I see you back again?" Andy asked me after we'd finished eating.

Despite all the crawling, I wouldn't mind another visit, but not on my own.

"If Cade wants to bring me."

Cade smiled, and he smiled big. "We'll both see you soon."

He put his arm around me as we walked back to the car, and I returned the favour. I couldn't resist slipping my hand into the back pocket of his jeans. Purely for warmth, you understand, nothing to do with the firmness of his sexy ass underneath it.

Once we'd got onto the highway, Cade flipped on the radio and twined his fingers through mine, resting his hand on my thigh.

"Classical?" I asked. "I'd have had you pegged as a rock fan."

"Classical's relaxing. I always listen to it when I need to think."

He needed to think, and so did I. About him. Was he thinking about me? We barely talked on the way back, but it was a comfortable silence, both of us happy to be in the other's company.

When we reached the city, my mind wasn't any clearer. Then Cade drove past the entrance to my apartment building, around the block, and aimed a key fob at a roll-up shutter.

"Where are we going?"

"Your parking garage. You've got two allocated spaces."

"I do?"

Nobody had mentioned them, probably because I'd left my car at Emmy's. Chances of me driving in New York without getting lost or crashing? Zero.

But now Cade was parking at my apartment. Why? Did he plan on staying long?

And if he did, how did I feel about that?

Tension hummed between us in the lift, and I didn't

bother trying to unlock the door myself, just handed the key to Cade. Neither of us said a word, and once inside, he didn't hesitate. He came at me, pushing me back against the wall and pinning my hands over my head with one of his.

Helpless. I felt helpless and hopelessly turned on.

So was Cade. It wasn't hard to tell. Or rather, it *was*.

The only light came from a giant fish-shaped lamp that had appeared by the TV courtesy of Bradley, and even in the dim light, I could see the wide chasms of Cade's pupils staring into mine. He ran the fingers of his free hand lightly up my side, making me squirm.

"Tia," he breathed, and his lips came closer, closer.

Something twitched on my hip as he pressed against me, and I thought he was just happy until the vibrations started.

"Fuck," he muttered.

Weren't we about to?

He stepped back and yanked the phone out of his pocket, cursing again as he held it to his ear. A series of yeses and mmm hmms followed before he hung up and thumped the wall.

"I have to go to the office."

Now? Seriously? He had to go to work now? But my nether regions were on fire, and thankfully it wasn't from habanero sauce.

"Can't you tell Blackwood you're busy?"

He leaned his forehead against mine the same way he had the other day, his jaw tense.

"I'd love nothing more than to stay right here and screw you senseless against this wall, but I can't. The boss is in town."

"The boss?"

"Emmy."

Emmy was in town and nobody had told me? I knew she was due in for the show, but that wasn't for another two days. Tears pricked at the corner of my eyes as I realised just how strained our relationship had become. Pre-tragedy, she'd have called me for sure if she planned to be nearby.

A single tear rolled down my cheek, and Cade wiped it away. "I'm sorry, tiger. I'll be thinking of you all night."

He gave me a quick, chaste kiss on the lips, and then he was gone.

So much for putting me first.

CHAPTER 19

I GLANCED AT the thermostat on the wall by the coatrack. Had I accidentally turned up the heating before I left? I kicked off my boots and tore my jumper over my head as I stomped up the stairs, hot, bothered, and desperate to find the release I craved.

I felt like an absolute bitch as I dialled Eli's number. What kind of girl got turned on by one guy and got off with another?

Not this one, it turned out. Eli didn't answer.

I threw the phone down and cursed myself as I tossed my remaining clothes onto the floor. Now what? Everything about this situation was insane. Thinking quickly, I climbed into the shower and turned the knob all the way to freezing. Even that didn't cool my overheated libido. I pressed my thighs together as I shrugged into my bathrobe, shivering and not in a pleasant way. Wine. If I couldn't have an orgasm, I needed wine. I grabbed a bottle from the cupboard, flopped back on the sofa, and drank the entire thing while watching *Gossip Girl* reruns.

This was the life, eh?

I woke in the early hours, face down on the sofa, the

pattern of intricate stitching from the cushion imprinted on my forehead. The wine bottle lay on its side on the coffee table, the last dregs of red trickling out across the pristine white surface.

I tilted my head to admire my handiwork. Probably it wouldn't look out of place at MoMA. I could call it "Portrait of my fucked-up life."

Sleep eluded me for the rest of the night, and on Sunday morning, Bernard only added to my headache. To be fair, he looked about as thrilled to be on my security detail as I was to have him there.

Would it have been any better if Cade had turned up? I didn't know what to say to him after his hasty exit last night. At least I'd get a day to think about it.

At the Lincoln Center, Ishmael was on top form, whizzing around on a pair of roller skates teamed with a tutu. He'd plaited the left-hand side of his afro into cornrows and accessorised with a pair of pink skulls sticking up from a headband on springs. At least the pole dancing outfits hadn't arrived yet. Thank goodness for small mercies.

"What should I do, Ishmael?"

"Could you check on the Ghost's rider? His manager's on the way over, and I hear that man gets more anal than the crowd at NYC pride."

"Sure, I'll get right on it."

Okay, the entire room was white. If someone dropped one of the mint Tic Tacs the Ghost insisted on having laid out in white Venetian glass bowls, they'd never find it again. Perfect. It was perfect.

At least, that's what I thought until Harold Styles turned up. A miserable-looking man in his fifties, he wore a suit that might have been made to measure but did nothing for his paunch, and he proceeded to find fault with everything I said and did.

"This couch is cream."

"The brochure said it was white."

"Yes, but if you stand back and look at it from this angle, it's definitely cream."

"Well, what do you want me to do?"

"You'll have to find a white throw. *Pure* white. Not off-white, not calico, not magnolia."

I found a white throw, got it couriered over by the furnishing shop, and his next problem was the floor.

"There's dirt on it. See?" He pointed at a barely perceptible brown streak.

"I'll organise a cleaning crew."

Three men turned up with buckets and mops, and ten minutes later, the floor was streak-free and sparkling. Were we done now?

Of course not.

"The room smells of bleach." Harold wrinkled his nose. "You'll have to light a scented candle." He wandered over to the white sideboard, picked one up, and sucked in a breath. "What's this?"

"A candle?"

"But it's vanilla and blackberry. The rider specifically says vanilla and raspberry."

I balled my fists up. "Does it honestly matter?"

Harold's mouth set in a hard line. "Yes, it does."

I left the room before Harold got the soothing scent of vanilla and blackberry shoved up his rectum, and I marched over to Ishmael.

"I'm going candle hunting."

"I thought we had the candles?"

"We have vanilla and blackberry. We need

raspberry."

"Are they really that different?"

Probably not, if Ishmael didn't think they were.

"Apparently so."

Frustration seeped out of my pores as I stormed out of the building and into the nearest cab. At least my annoyance had one benefit—I stuck my arm out, and the driver stopped instantly.

"Bloomingdale's. Please."

I was on the first floor, hunting fruitlessly, when Bernard materialised behind me with a scowl on his face.

"You're not supposed to be out alone."

He sounded so prissy, my irritation simmered over into anger.

"I'm nineteen years old," I yelled. "I'm capable of holding my own in a department store."

All around us, shoppers stopped mid-stride and stared. I abandoned the Coach handbag I may have accidentally picked up and lowered my voice a few decibels.

"Look, you can go back to Blackwood and tell Emmy, or Cade, or whoever just tracked my mobile phone that if I want to go shopping by myself, I will."

I turned on my heel and strode to the nearest escalator, leaving Bernard fidgeting behind me. Before he disappeared from view, I saw him take out his own phone, calling the control room for advice, no doubt. Heaven forbid he should have to think for himself.

In the fifth-floor furniture department, I plopped down into a brick-like Beekman chair and weighed up my options. Should I admit defeat on the candle? Keep searching? And what about Bernard? He needed a return-to-sender option, and I needed divine inspiration.

It came in the form of Eli. I hadn't heard his velvet tones since Saturday morning, and even his voicemail had a generic message that left me feeling cheated. But now my phone vibrated in my hands.

"Sugar, I wouldn't normally disturb you during the day, but I've been up all night with a pregnant mare, and I just wanted to hear your voice before I went to sleep."

My heart flipped. "Call me any time. And it's me who likes listening to your voice."

"Sounds like sex, right?" he said, totally straight-laced. Then he lowered the volume, and a ripple of pleasure shuddered through me. "That comes later."

"Please stop. I'm in a department store."

He chuckled, and even that gave me shivers. "Rain check, huh? Why are you shopping? I thought you had to work today?"

"I'm looking for a bloody candle." Teeth gritted, I told Eli the story of the Ghost and his asshole of a manager.

"Don't worry about it. I bet the Ghost won't notice."

"But what if he does? What if he yells at me on Monday in front of everyone? It's bad enough having to deal with models and their egos without having to cater to an overinflated pop pixie."

"He won't care. Trust me."

"How do you know? He could be a total nutcase."

"He's not. Look, I had a friend who worked with him once, and he said the guy was okay. Down to earth. It's that manager of his who whips everything up into a frenzy. The Ghost's all about the music."

Curiosity: piqued. That was the first time Eli had mentioned anyone outside of his family and his dead girlfriend.

"Who's this friend?"

"Doesn't matter. He's not around anymore. Promise me you'll stop worrying, sugar? Go home and relax."

How could I say no to him? I'd probe more later, but for now, I'd just peel the labels off the sodding candles.

"I've got three or four more hours to do at work, then I'll relax. Will you call when you wake up?"

"Wild horses couldn't stop me."

Downstairs, Bernard was waiting by the exit, looking even grumpier than earlier. I hadn't believed that was possible.

Well, two could play at that game.

"I thought I told you to go back to the office."

"You were overridden."

"By who? Emmy? Cade?"

"You'll have to speak to the control room about that."

Gah! I'd had enough of this. "Fine. Follow if you must, but I'm not hanging around to wait for you."

Back in the Lincoln Center, I spent the rest of the afternoon taking notes for Ishmael, who from his demeanour, appeared to be on the edge of a breakdown. But at one point, he turned to wink at me and I knew it was all an act. Yes, I know he was gay, but I loved that man.

And when I got home, I kept my word to Eli and ran myself a bath. A bath bomb, plenty of bubbles, a few whatever-scented candles, and maybe, just maybe, a glass of rosé.

As if on cue, my phone buzzed.

Eli: Hope you're getting some rest, sugar. Call me whenever you're ready?

Oh, I was ready all right. I was ready two long days ago. I checked the bubbles covered the good bits then snapped a photo of myself and sent it over.

Eli: You're killing me.

Me: A pleasurable death, I hope?

Eli: With you, there's no other kind. Apart from dirty, maybe.

Me: I'm feeling very...

Me: ...wet.

I drummed my fingers on the rim of the bath as I waited for his response. That had to get one, surely?

Oh, it did.

Eli: I need to watch you. Just your face. Please?

He wanted to watch me? What, in the bath? I'd never had anyone see me do...what I was undoubtedly about to do, not even Ryan. Eli had listened on the phone, yes, but on camera? Did I want to cross that line?

My pussy answered for me, clenching at the mere thought. Yes, I did want Eli to watch. I wanted to put on a show and let him see the pleasure he gave me.

Me: Okay. FaceTime?

I propped my iPad on a stool next to my lotions and potions, angled it at my face, and settled back into the water. Eli was going to see me, but would I see him?

FaceTime buzzed.

I answered

A fuzzy image of Eli's room appeared, lit only by the glow from his screen. The contrast made me feel exposed by the bright spotlights above my bath. On display.

But my nerves vanished when he spoke.

"I knew you were beautiful, but lying there... I don't have words."

"Please, keep talking. It feels odd with you watching me."

"If this is awkward, I can always call instead. I never want you to feel uncomfortable."

"No, it's okay. Let's try this. Tell me what you want me to do."

A month ago, if someone told me I'd enjoy this— being told by a shadow how to move, where to touch, how to feel—I'd have drawn them a map to the nearest asylum. But as we got down to it, I'd never felt anything so...so...so right in my life.

At some point, when Eli told me to hook one leg over the side of the bath, I knocked the stool. The bubbles had mostly gone by then, and he could see everything. Ev-e-ry-thing. And I didn't care.

Let him see.

I wanted him to see.

Eli adjusted his screen too, and as the moon rose through his window, I saw he was as naked as me. His actions mirrored mine, and when that almost unbearable ball of energy built inside, he reached the same place. My final scream was answered by a long, drawn-out groan from him. Then silence.

Finally, he stole my words. "Damn. That was the hottest thing I've ever done in my life."

As the world came back into focus, Eli's silhouette resolved on the bed, propped up against his pillows. Starlight played over the planes of his chest, his abs, his... Yes, he was everything I'd imagined. A little more, if we were measuring.

I shivered again, but this time it *was* because of the cold. The water temperature had dropped, and not only that, I'd gone all pruney.

"I need to find my bathrobe."

"I've never wanted to be an item of clothing more than I do right now."

All of a sudden, the cooling water seemed rather hot. Steamy, in fact. Eli may have been two states away, but he set me on fire with words.

I stood up, rivulets of water and a clump of stray bubbles pouring off me, and stepped out of the bath. So much for the grand finale. I went base over apex in a puddle of water and landed on my ass.

Eli gasped on screen. "Are you okay?"

I scrambled to my knees, gripping the side of the tub.

"Yes. Yes, I'm fine." Just mortally embarrassed, that was all.

"I wish I could hold you in my arms right now. Just to sleep."

"You like that kind of thing?"

Ryan had been many things, but cuddly wasn't one of them. Secretly, I'd always craved that closeness.

"Second best bit."

My heart had already melted, but now it slid down my leg and pooled in my foot.

"This is real, isn't it?" I asked Eli.

For me, it was. We may not have been physically next to each other, but what I felt for him... Distance didn't matter.

"It is for me, sugar. It is for me."

"What do we do now?"

"You hungry?"

He wanted to eat rather than talk? Well, that was a rather abrupt subject change.

"Uh, I guess."

In the kitchen, I propped my iPad up on the fridge so Eli could see what I was doing. In return, I got a view of his hands, which was better than nothing.

"What are we eating?" I asked.

"Pasta bake. It's quick and filling."

"I like the filling part, but I prefer it slow." Yes, I'd turned into a complete hussy.

Eli's fingers clenched at the edge of the counter. Oh, I did love winding him up.

And as I watched those long, elegant fingers slicing and dicing vegetables, I imagined them running along my arms, up my sides, across my...

"Ouch!" I yelped.

"Are you okay? Is that blood?"

"Just a tiny cut." I'd nicked the end of my finger with the knife. "I got distracted."

He didn't need to ask what by. "I'll turn the camera off if you don't concentrate on what you're doing."

"Fine."

"And stop pouting. Although it is kinda cute."

I turned to the camera and grinned at him. Then pouted. Then grinned again.

"Do you want dinner or not?" he asked.

I focused on what I was doing and managed the rest of the prep without adding fingers as a garnish. Eli put his dinner in the oven too, in a blue earthenware casserole dish—rugged and manly just like him.

"What shall we do while it cooks?" I asked. "Round two?"

"I thought you said you liked it slow?"

"I suppose burnt and crispy pasta wouldn't be that palatable."

"I've got a better idea. Wait there."

Five minutes later, he came back and moved the camera. This time, I saw him from the neck down, sitting on a wooden chair in a checked shirt and worn blue jeans. Dark brown hair brushed his shoulders as he got comfortable. Then he leaned over and picked up a guitar.

"You're going to play me a song?"

"I'm gonna sing you a song. I've wanted to do this for days, and I've been waiting for the right moment."

Aww, sweet. Nobody had ever sung for me before, unless you counted Dan when she was drunk, which I didn't. I expected a nervous cough, fumbled chords, and a mangled attempt at lyrics, but that wasn't what Eli gave me.

Holy hell, the man could sing! When he started the first verse of "At Last," goosebumps popped up all over my body. I froze to the spot as I listened, and even after he finished, I couldn't move.

If his speaking voice was sex, his singing voice was multiple orgasms. And a little niggle in the back of my brain told me I'd heard it somewhere before. Perhaps not exactly the same—I'd never forget the huskiness that left my knickers damp—okay, damper—but I'd definitely heard similar. I just couldn't put my finger on it.

"Well?" he asked.

"Words...gone."

"In a good way?"

Oh, he had to know he was beyond good. He sang

without any of the hesitation that had dominated his speech when we first began talking.

I nodded, and although I couldn't see his smile, I felt it. Finally, I found my tongue.

"Where did you learn to do that?"

"Play the guitar? I taught myself when I was a kid. The singing, well, I just always could."

"You could be famous with that voice."

"It's just for you." His words came out flat, disinterested.

Okay, I guess fame wasn't for everyone. "Well, I'll take every second of it I can get. Will you sing something else?"

"Anything for the prettiest girl in the world."

I blushed, and that earned me a chuckle.

"Do you take requests?"

"Try me."

"Bryan Adams—'Summer of '69.' I want to hear you sing it this time."

"Give me a minute. I've got the wrong guitar for that."

He had more than one? I poured myself another glass of wine while he disappeared, and it wasn't long before he came back with a sexy-looking black electric guitar.

"Good thing I don't have neighbours. I can't play this one quietly."

While Eli worked his magic, I gave up any pretence at decorum and danced. I even sang too, although my voice wasn't a patch on Eli's. He went through a whole repertoire—country, blues, pop, rock—and I even got to watch *those* fingers play the piano at one point.

Dinner was burnt and crispy. Neither of us cared.

CHAPTER 20

ON MONDAY MORNING, I must have stared into space for a full ten minutes before I got dressed. After retiring to bed in the early hours, I'd abandoned any attempts at being coy and mysterious and dropped into wanton and graphic. Eli had done the same.

Fuck.

What we did made the porn I may have accidentally caught my brother watching a few years back pale in comparison.

I yawned again as I wondered whether I could fit a fourth espresso into my travel mug, and then a bigger problem knocked on the door.

Cade.

Two hot men chasing after me should have been a fantasy come true, but the reality gave me brain freeze. Because no matter how much I might like Eli, Eli wasn't in New York and never would be, and Cade was right *here*.

I flung the door wide and ran to put my shoes on, and he followed me inside.

"Did you even check through the peephole?" he asked.

"Who else would it be?"

"You still need to check."

"Good morning to you too."

I felt warm breath on the back of my neck and turned to find him right behind me. He put a hand on my waist then dipped his head to kiss me on the cheek.

"Morning, tiger."

My heart fluttered. Oh, hell. Cade. Eli. Cade. Eli. What was I supposed to do about the pair of them?

Cade took me by the hand and led me out to the car. Ever the professional, he kept a polite distance from me in front of the driver, but when he turned and licked his lips, I knew exactly what he was thinking. The bulge in his trousers was a huge giveaway too.

When we arrived, I didn't know whether to run inside or climb into his lap, but luckily, Ishmael granted me a temporary reprieve.

He rushed out of the Lincoln Center to greet me wearing a shark tooth necklace, pink leggings, and a sweater with a toucan appliquéd onto it. The casual look.

"Tia, thank goodness you're here. They've delivered the wrong type of chairs and the courier bringing the toupee tape is lost somewhere in the Upper West Side."

I mouthed, "See you later," at Cade as Ishmael dragged me into the building.

Cade checked the driver wasn't looking then blew me a kiss.

Inside, I directed the lost courier using Google Maps, although why he couldn't have managed to look up directions himself was beyond me. The firm providing the chairs didn't want to admit their mistake at first, but after much cajoling, they agreed to deliver the correct ones first thing in the afternoon.

Someone had brought Ishmael's desk over from the office. I'm not sure why, because he never used it, but at least he had his paperclips. I took advantage of his printer and some clip art to print out new labels for the Ghost's bloody candles. *Vanilla with a hint of raspberry.*

Close enough.

As the day came to an end, everything had gone suspiciously smoothly. Too smoothly. What had we missed?

I found out five minutes later, when Ishmael's not-so-dulcet tones pierced the air.

"What are these?" He waved one of the skeleton masks Myrna had bought for her models.

"Masks," she replied, stating the obvious. "For the goody bag guys to wear tomorrow."

I'd never seen anyone lose it in slow motion before. Anger boiled in Ishmael's head before steam came out of his ears. He turned, fixing me with a glare that could melt steel.

"Did you pick these out?"

I quickly shook my head.

"Did you pick the models?"

"No."

He faced Myrna again. "Why didn't Tia handle the men? I specifically requested her to."

I was glad he'd asked Myrna. She could drop herself in it rather than me having to do it for her.

"Tia was new. She had no experience at all with booking models." Myrna's smug voice made me want to slap her. "I took the job on because it was more difficult and gave her the catalogue. The model booking took ages too. I had to work in the evenings."

Oh, poor her. My heart bled.

"Let me see the photos of the models."

Myrna called them up onto her screen. It was the first time I'd seen them. Well... They weren't quite what I'd been expecting.

Ishmael picked up a glass paperweight with a Lego pony embedded in the middle, hefted it, then let out a breath and set it back on the desk.

"Myrna, these are clothes models. The type of pretty boys who look good in the sample size and know how to parade along a runway. They are *not* the type of models that you send out shirtless to make the ladies sweat. I wanted pecs, abs, and taut asses." He tapped the screen with his index finger. "Not *this*."

Myrna stepped back, biting her lip, and I knew exactly what was running through her mind: *How can I pin this one on Tia?*

But Ishmael wasn't finished. "And these masks! They're something a child would wear on Halloween. They have no place in my show."

"Ishmael, it's not my fault. Tia..."

"I don't want to hear excuses. I just want it fixed."

"But it's six o'clock and everywhere's closed. Even if I start first thing tomorrow, I couldn't get new models booked in time."

"Well, then, what do you suggest? Where are we going to get a dozen hot men from at the drop of a hat?"

"I don't know," she whined. "You never said you wanted fitness models."

"I said I wanted them shirtless. That should have been clear enough."

"We'll just have to give out the bags ourselves. Tia and I can do it. Maybe we could wear some clothes from the show?"

"You won't have time, Myrna. Because tomorrow, you'll be busy looking for another job."

Ishmael stormed off in a cloud of pink sparkles, leaving Myrna speechless.

"Better update your resumé." I gave her one last grin and followed after him.

As Ishmael hopped around furiously on his pogo stick, I racked my brains. Where could I find twelve really, really hot guys with almost no notice?

The answer was all too obvious.

The next morning, I paced up and down the dressing room at the Lincoln Center where I'd been up half the night, painting. Coffee. I needed coffee, preferably by intravenous drip.

The phone call yesterday evening hadn't been as painful as I feared, but today, playing the waiting game made me fidget like nobody's business. Would my plan work?

I picked up one of the Phantom of the Opera-style masks I'd picked up at the late-night party store and tapped the centre. No longer sticky. Thank goodness.

A tap at the door a few minutes later made me jump, even though I was expecting it. Nick and Logan, two of Blackwood's finest, peered inside. Nick's friend, Ignacio, stood behind them. Ignacio didn't work for Blackwood, but it seemed he'd been in the wrong place at the right time and got shanghaied into coming. Well, he certainly had the right look.

Three. We'd got three.

"Are we in the right place?" Nick asked.

"Yes! Thanks so much for doing this."

"I'm not sure we had a choice."

Jed and Quinn came next, representing the CIA. Equal opportunities and all that. The men shook hands, bumped fists, whatever, and Jed picked up a mask.

"Not bad. You painted these?"

I nodded, smiling. The smudges of paint on my hands were a dead giveaway.

"At least someone's happy," Quinn said.

"What does Ana think of all this?"

"I've got no idea. Emmy told her what was happening, and she just shrugged then started cleaning her gun."

"Tip for you, buddy," Jed said. "Don't look at any of the women for longer than you have to."

Cade sauntered through the door, followed by four more men. He shook his head at me and blew out a breath.

"Only for you would I do this."

Guilt. Trip.

Another guy rushed in, panting, and stripped out of his leather jacket.

"Sorry I'm late. I got caught up in a car chase, and the asshole took ages to crash."

Finally, my brother walked in and poked me in the chest.

"When I have kids, you're on babysitting duty forever, you understand?

I gulped, unable to do anything but nod. What was this about kids? He'd never mentioned having children before. I blocked it out of my mind as he kicked his shoes off. I had quite enough to worry about today without the thought of baby Lukes and Macks running around.

But the men were all here. We had our dirty dozen, even if my brother being one of them was more than a little cringey.

And I had to stay and supervise as they stripped off, purely for professional reasons, although Ishmael would have taken on the task himself, I was sure. He walked in, swayed alarmingly as Nick dropped his jeans, and began fanning himself.

"Tia, I know I'm gay, but I love you. I just thought you should know that."

He smothered me in pink feathers as he hugged me, his sweater looking like a flamingo with a blowout. I was picking feathers out of my mouth when a new voice came from behind me, female this time.

"You like?"

I turned to face Emmy.

"Perfect. Thank you."

"Good. I picked them out personally."

"She did too," Logan said. "She went around the building making men take their shirts off."

Emmy shrugged. "It's a hard life."

Squeals sounded as the rest of the girls bounced in. Dan, Mack, Carmen, Lara, Georgia, Chess, and Ana. Except Ana didn't bounce, of course. She stalked like the predator she was. Bradley followed behind, rushing over to hug Ishmael before he did the same to me.

Then he turned to admire the view.

"Are we taking a vote on the most lickable?" he asked.

"Down, boy," Emmy said.

"It's actually quite difficult to decide," Dan said, scratching her chin. "What are we licking off them?"

"Daniela di Grassi, stop harassing the staff."

Logan wiggled his hips. "You can lick me any time, baby."

Emmy turned to him. "You're not helping."

Jenna rushed in next, eyes wide. "That irritating guy's just arrived. Harold Styles? He says the light bulbs in the white room aren't bright enough."

Wonderful. Just when I thought everything was sorted.

"Okay, I'm coming."

Harold was standing on a white stool when I walked in. He'd better not have left marks on that.

"These bulbs cast a yellow glow," he said. "We want white, not yellow."

"I'll see if I can find somebody to change them."

"Well, hurry up. The Ghost will be here in five minutes, and he needs the room empty. He doesn't tolerate strangers."

The click of Harold's brogues on the tile disappeared along the corridor as I reached for the radio on my belt.

"Can somebody in facilities come to the Ghost's dressing room? Urgently?"

A burst of static came back. "Fifteen minutes."

"No, not fifteen minutes. Right away! The Ghost will be arriving any second."

A soft voice spoke from behind me. "I'm here now."

I spun around to face a figure dressed in black. His hoodie was pulled forward over his head, and I glimpsed a white mask underneath it. Freaky.

"What's the problem?" he asked, almost in a whisper.

I pointed at the lights. "Apparently the bulbs aren't

white enough."

His eyes followed my finger, and he shrugged. "Look fine to me."

Really? He walked past and I caught a whiff of cologne. Hugo Boss, if my nose served correctly.

"Can I get you anything more?"

He kept his back to me as he dumped his messenger bag off his shoulder and onto the most-definitely white sofa.

"No, this is fine."

That was it? This was the diva? It was almost disappointing, but I rushed out before he could find fault with my carefully selected goodies.

The men had attracted quite a crowd by the time I got back. Every woman in the building had found an excuse to visit, it seemed. Offers of drinks, "emergency" messages, and misplaced hair accessories meant they'd all turned up in the dressing room at the same time.

"Should we oil the men up or something?" Bradley asked.

"I'll volunteer," Carmen offered.

"You're married," Dan reminded her.

"Nate's not here. It doesn't count."

"We can't have oil, not with the clothes," Ishmael said. "Perhaps I could branch out into men's swimwear next year?"

Luke glared at me. "Don't even think about it. I'll never live this down as it is."

"You do get to wear a mask."

"Oh, grow a pair," Emmy told him. "Nobody's going to be looking at your face, anyway."

Mack glanced down at his crotch. "He already has a pair."

"Lalalalala," I sang. "I don't want to hear this."

Ishmael blew a whistle, and everyone stood to attention.

"Time for the masks," he called.

They did look rather good if I said so myself. I'd roughed up the surface so the paint stuck better, and the exposed muscles were kind of creepy. Not that any of the ladies out there would care. They'd be more interested in muscles of a different kind. And Cade's artwork, which I struggled to drag my eyes away from.

"Line up, everybody," Ishmael said. "We need to get photos. Jenna!"

Dan didn't try to hide her ogling. "We've got twelve guys. I reckon we should do a Blackwood calendar."

Ignacio raised his hand. "I don't work for Blackwood."

With his Italian accent, he sounded almost as sexy as Eli and looked more than a little worried by the way Dan was squinting in his direction. Like she wanted to eat him for breakfast, lunch, and dinner.

She raised one dark eyebrow. "That's okay, honey. We'll make a special exception."

Nick covered her eyes. "He's got a girlfriend, Dan. Put your tongue back in."

"Dammit. The good ones always do." She spun on her pointy black boots and went off to flirt with her next victim.

I'd just glanced at my watch to see how long we had before kickoff when the air began to shake as bass kicked in through hidden speakers. The Ghost was earning his money, and after the amount of effort I'd gone to with his white shite, he owed us interest.

Ishmael bounced around on his pogo stick, heart-shaped earrings bobbing around. Like, actual hearts, with ventricles and a flipping aorta.

"Seats, everybody! Hot guys—go do your thing!"

The men filed out, followed by the girls, and I headed backstage to wait with Ishmael. And wait. And wait.

"Tia, Jenna, you'll have to go and round the men up or nobody'll look at the clothes."

It was like herding cats, but we eventually dragged them away from their rabid fans. One woman had scrawled her phone number across Logan's chest in lipstick, and three more tried to follow us backstage. Good grief.

The lights went down, the music went up, and one model after another walked past us along the double-width runway. Chiffon floated, sequins sparkled, and a pair of tight leather trousers with embossed skulls squeaked.

Professor Ito had set the corpses up at intervals, so the models had to weave between them as they strutted. His creations were as much the stars of the show as the clothes and their bearers, and photographers crouched, smiling, to get the best shots of all the bodies, alive and dead.

The Ghost alternated between haunting and hip-hop, and weird though he was, he sure knew how to work the decks. By the end, everyone was up and dancing at the strangest fashion show I'd ever attended. Even Professor Ito was bopping away. And the Ghost's final song? A mixed-up, rocked-out version of Maroon 5's "Sugar."

It was almost like he *knew*.

The Ghost, the corpses, the models, and the clothes

all got a standing ovation at the end, and the applause only got louder when Ishmael strode down the runway in his high heels, side-by-side with Professor Ito.

Then Ishmael sent the boys out to take a bow too, and all the heiresses, movie stars, singers, and journalists carefully selected to attend the show began whistling and throwing items of clothing. And that was putting it politely.

Backstage, the excited chatter was almost deafening. Models milled around, congratulating each other, and I got more random hugs than I could count. Finally, I retreated to the corner where Blackwood had congregated and screwed my eyes shut as Luke plucked a bra off his shoulder.

"What's this?"

Nick peered over. "I think it's from Victoria's Secret."

"Who won the phone number contest?" Quinn asked.

Logan grinned, leaning against the wall in bulging briefs. "I got forty-seven."

"Women were stuffing bits of paper in my shorts," Jed said. "If I pull them down, it'll be like confetti."

"Don't you dare!" Chess yelled from across the room. "Not until we get home."

"But it's really itchy."

"I don't care."

"Someone wrote a number on me with a Sharpie, and it won't come off," Ignacio said. "What am I going to tell my girlfriend?"

"Just say it was a dare. She'll be pissed for a couple of days, but she'll come around. You might want to pick up a box of chocolates on your way back," Jed suggested.

"You have experience of this?"

"All the damn time."

Glorious though the sight in front of me was, I couldn't help but stifle a yawn. It had been a long day. Cade ambled towards me, still wearing next to nothing, and I didn't know where to look.

Okay, I knew exactly where to look, but I tried not to be too obvious about it. After a quick glance at his oh-so-impressive package, I dragged my eyes sideways to a conveniently placed mirror that gave me a perfect view of his ass.

I thought I'd got away with my ogling until Ishmael walked past and handed me his pink fan.

"Looks as if you need this more than me."

Busted.

Luckily, Cade remained oblivious as well as tanned, toned, and totally delicious.

"Tired, tiger?" he asked.

"A bit."

Hang on—was that lipstick on his cheek? Red heat flashed through my veins at the thought of another girl getting up close and personal with him, but I cooled to a simmer when he murmured in my ear.

"I'll take you home."

"I want to speak to Emmy before I go."

"She already left with Dan and Mack. There was an emergency at the office."

An emergency? Really? Or was that just an excuse not to see me? I wasn't sure I wanted to know the answer to that. In an instant, my happy mood dissipated.

Poof.

"Okay, take me home."

And for goodness' sake, put some clothes on first.

CHAPTER 21

CADE HAD A town car waiting outside, and thankfully, he'd put on jeans, a T-shirt, and his worn leather jacket before we left the building.

I shivered as we walked over to the vehicle. I'd dressed to stand under the hot lights inside, not on the New York streets where flakes of snow were fighting their way to the ground.

Cade put his arm around my shoulders and pulled me close. I relished his warmth. And in the car, he no longer seemed to care what the driver thought as he dragged me onto his lap and wrapped me up in hot maleness.

He felt so safe, so solid, and his smouldering gaze set my insides alight. I shut my eyes for a few seconds, but that didn't help because now I could visualise what was under those clothes, every glorious, tanned inch. I wrapped my arms around his neck and snuggled against him, and as exhaustion fought with my libido, the gentle purring of the engine almost sent me to sleep.

Except then Cade was carrying me into my apartment building, straight into the lift so I could press the button for the top floor.

This was nice. Walking was so overrated.

"Key," he said as he covered the distance to my

door. I fished around in my bag and found it then managed to get it into the lock on only my fourth attempt.

Good going, Tia.

Inside, Cade finally put me down, but I didn't have time to remove my arms from his neck before he backed me into a wall.

"I've turned my phone off tonight," he whispered, right before his lips met mine.

Months had passed since I'd kissed a man, and I leaned into him, running my tongue against the seam of his lips. He yielded and slipped his tongue into my mouth. Minty fresh, with an underlying hint of coffee. Black bloody coffee.

I closed my eyes, and instead of Cade, I saw longish hair, a checked shirt, and long, slender fingers. Oh, dammit. My eyes sprang open and to my left, I saw my pyjama top, still lying where I'd flung it two nights ago when I decided it would be a good idea to cook in my bra.

In that moment, I realised what I wanted. Who I wanted.

Only one man had the power to napalm my soul with a single word, and it wasn't Cade.

Cade was one hell of a guy, a real catch, and a girl would be lucky to have him. But not this girl. Even though we'd never even touched, my body and my heart craved Eli, and whatever I could get of him, I'd take it all.

I pushed against Cade's chest, gently at first, then harder until he stepped back.

Confusion spread across his face. "What's wrong?"

"I can't. I just can't do this."

"Are things moving too quickly? We can slow down."

"No, it's not that."

"Then what?"

I took one pace back, then another, hating the hurt in Cade's eyes, hating myself for putting it there.

"There's...There's someone else."

The hurt sparked into anger, and when Cade was angry, he was scary. He turned around and put his fist through the drywall.

A sob escaped my lips, and I wrapped my arms around my chest as he faced me once more.

His expression softened a little. "Fuck. I'm not gonna hurt you. Don't look at me like that."

"I-I-I'm sorry. I'm so sorry."

"Who is it? Someone from work?"

Cade knew full well I didn't go anywhere else without him or another Blackwood minder, and his gaze lasered into me, fierce bordering on painful.

"No. I met him on the internet."

He took a step away then whirled to confront me again. "You're ditching me for some pervert you met on Facebook?"

"Not Facebook. A chat room."

"A chat room? Oh, this just gets better and better."

"I didn't mean for it to happen. I just... I can talk to him."

My cheeks heated as I recalled all the other things we'd done that weren't talking, but luckily Cade didn't seem to notice as he took a half-step forwards and cupped my cheek in his hand. Even now, I almost leaned into it, but at the last second, I remembered to stay strong.

"And you can't talk to me?" he asked.

"I barely know you. I barely know you at all."

"We could change that. I could take time off work... Spend it with you..."

Cade's voice took on an edge of desperation as he clutched at my hand, and I saw a glimmer of hope in his dark eyes.

My heart cracked as I dashed it. "We can't change." Work would always come first for Cade, and as for my heart? It had told me its darkest desires. "I'm so, so sorry."

The next sound I heard was my front door slamming as Cade stormed out of it.

Emotions got the better of me, all the pain and confusion of the past few months leaching out in tears that ran down my face unchecked. I curled up on the sofa and buried my head in a pillow. Why did affairs of the heart have to be so bloody painful? It never happened like this in fairy tales.

A soft tap made my eyes fly open, and I looked up to find a fresh box of tissues on the coffee table in front of me.

"Does this have something to do with Cade tearing past as I walked into the building?"

I nodded and wiped my nose on my sleeve. Shit.

Emmy sat beside me, cuddling me close. Where had she come from? For a brief moment, I puzzled over that question then realised I didn't care. She was here, and that was all that mattered.

"Tell me about it."

It wasn't a question or even a suggestion. It was an order. She was used to people obeying her.

"I've messed everything up."

"No, you haven't. If we were sitting here in the charred remains of your apartment with smoking bodies dotted around the place, then you'd have messed everything up."

Emmy shrugged one shoulder, and I couldn't help snorting out a laugh seeing as that had actually happened to her a couple of years back.

"I like Cade, but there's also this other guy, and I couldn't decide between them. I led Cade on. I shouldn't have done it, and now I feel awful about it."

"Have you decided now?"

I nodded.

"Then you're halfway to solving the problem."

So far, it seemed like all I'd done was create problems, not solve them.

"But what about Cade? He was so upset."

"Did he hurt you?"

"No! He just hit the wall."

"Good. I left my favourite gun at home." She rolled her eyes when she saw me tense up. "Kidding. Mostly. Cade's got a temper on him, and he needs to learn to control it better. We'll work on it."

"I'm sorry."

"Nothing for you to be sorry about, honey. So, who's this other guy?"

This was Emmy. She didn't judge, right?

"We met on the internet. In a chat room."

"Good grief. What if he's a sixty-year-old pervert?"

"He's not. We started calling each other. Then FaceTiming. He's definitely not sixty—he's twenty-two."

"Hot?"

Trust Emmy to ask that. "I'm pretty sure he is, but

I've never seen his face."

"Bloody hell. Then how do you know he's not some dodgy old man?"

"I've seen the rest of him."

Her eyes widened slightly. For Emmy, that was an expression of great surprise. "What, all of him?"

I nodded, feeling the heat as my cheeks coloured.

"Fuck, you're a grubby little minx, aren't you? So, why haven't you seen his face? He could be dog-ugly."

"He got scarred in a car accident, and he doesn't like people to see him. He hasn't left his family's ranch since it happened."

"So, what? You just call each other up and get each other off, is that it?"

"It's not like that."

Emmy just stared at me. Okay, it sounded bad, I got that. But there was so much more to the relationship, this connection I had with Eli.

"Honestly, it's not. We talk. We cook together. He sings to me."

She sighed. Underneath her abrasive exterior, she was a closet romantic. "What's his name?"

"Eli."

"Eli what? Where does he live?"

"I'm not telling you that. You'll rake over every crumb of his life."

Emmy stayed silent.

"Won't you?"

"Yes, but only because I care."

"Please, can you trust me to make my own decisions for once? And stop having your employees follow me every time I set foot out of the door. I feel like I'm constantly under a microscope."

"I worry about you."

"And I appreciate that you do, honestly. But can't I at least go to work and back without some muscle-bound robot coming along for the ride?"

"Which one's the muscle-bound robot?"

"Bernard."

"Yeah, I guess I can see that. He's good at what he does, though."

"Please? You track my phone, anyway."

She let out a deep sigh. "Fine. But if you even think you might go out drinking, you call me or you call Bradley or you call the control room direct, and they'll send someone to pick you up. Okay?"

I could live with that. "Okay. And, Emmy?"

"Yeah?"

"If you do send someone for any reason, please can it not be Cade? That would be really awkward."

"Fair enough."

"I still can't help wondering if I've made the right decision."

"What does your heart tell you?"

"That I want to spend every second I can with Eli, in whatever way he'll let me."

"Then you've made the right decision."

"It'll be difficult though, won't it?"

She fell silent for a minute, thinking. "Life with Cade wouldn't have been all roses. I've known him longer than you have, and that boy's got demons. And truthfully? I'm not sure he knows what he wants, either."

That he had his own problems didn't totally surprise me. "He wants to work with you. He told me."

"I know. And he will, in time, if he doesn't fuck up."

"So, what now?"

I was asking about more than just Cade and Eli, and she understood that.

"I've missed you," she said simply.

I burst into tears again.

"Oh, fuck, don't cry. Please?"

She shoved a wedge of tissues into my hand and I blew my nose into them.

"I thought you hated me. When Cade said you left early tonight, I figured it was because you didn't want to talk to me."

Emmy started laughing. "We left tonight because the new guy in the control room got his radio codes wrong. He meant to say 'alarm tripped on Aston Street, roving unit to attend,' and what he actually said was 'man down on Aston Street, call out the cavalry.'"

"What happened?"

"Me, Dan, and Mack went haring over there, guns drawn, only to find a couple of tourists who'd gotten confused between Bismark, Inc and The Bismark Hotel. They'd been rattling the doors and couldn't work out why no one was on reception."

I couldn't help giggling. "What did they say when they saw you?"

"There was much apologising all round, and some bowing because they were Japanese. Then we took them to the hotel in one of our patrol cars. Radio guy's been sent to the surveillance room."

Ah, yes, the surveillance room. I thought it was quite fun, spying on people, but most Blackwood employees regarded it as the ultimate punishment.

"So you didn't run off because of me?" I asked again, just to make sure.

"Of course not."

I sniffled again, and it turned out I hadn't run out of tears earlier. Emmy stiffened. She didn't handle emotion well.

"What can I do? To help?"

"I don't know. I mean, I've been such a bitch to you. Blaming you, hating you, but then Ana told me what happened wasn't your fault, and I had no idea how to talk to you, and then Cade said you were really upset and I didn't know what to do."

I paused for breath, gulping in air then hiccupping.

"It wasn't a great time," Emmy admitted.

"What happened? In Russia?"

Emmy's thousand-yard stare focused on something I couldn't see. "You don't want to know."

"But I have to. I keep dreaming about it over and over, each time worse than the last." At least, I had until Eli eased those nightmares. "Please, just tell me."

She walked to the window, staring at the city below where the snow had turned into rivulets of rain that cascaded down the glass.

"You know Isaiah got shot first?"

"Yes."

"Ryan wasn't far away, and he tried to help. There was a sniper on the roof. I'd seen him, but Ryan hadn't. I told him to stay put, and he didn't."

"Ana said you went after him. That you almost got shot."

"The bullet that killed him grazed my ear. I was a second too late. One fucking second. You don't know how many nights I've lain awake, wishing I'd started running a second sooner. Or been just that little bit faster."

I got up to stand beside her. "I wish I'd tried harder to stop him going, but Cade said he died doing what he loved."

"All those guys are on the team because they want to be there."

"And you? What about you?"

Her hollow laugh echoed off the glass.

"I'm there because it's what I was created to do. One day I'll die doing it. I know I'm on borrowed time."

No. *No, no, no.* I didn't want to talk about that or even think about it. The thought of losing Emmy tore me up inside.

"What happened to the sniper?" I asked.

"Xav dealt with him. The bastard was never going to walk away."

"And the general? Is it true...? About—"

"The general meant nothing to me. Nothing. But in his own warped way, he brought Ana up. It hit her harder than anyone."

"Ana scares me. She's not like you."

Emmy's voice dropped to a whisper. "She's exactly like me. I've just learned to hide that side of myself better." She stepped away from the glass. "Well, this has all got a bit deep for a Monday evening. I need to get some sleep and you, I assume, need to catch up with your mystery man."

"Oh, hell. What am I going to say to him?"

"Just tell him what you told me. That he's the one. If he runs screaming for the hills, at least you'll know, won't you?"

"That's not helping."

"Yeah, on second thoughts, I've had plenty of experience at fucking up relationships over the years.

Better to take what I say and do the exact opposite."

I cracked half a smile. At least she made me laugh.

"Are you still in town tomorrow? Could we have dinner?"

"I fly out for a job in the morning, but it should only last a day or two. I'll have Sloane clear my schedule after that, and we can spend some time together. How does that sound?"

"It sounds perfect."

I hugged her goodbye, squeezing hard and holding on until she pretended to suffocate.

"See you in a couple of days," she said.

"Can't wait."

What should I say to Eli? What should I say?

I wanted to tell him how I felt, but what if he did as Emmy had joked about and headed for the hills? Would he do a runner if he knew some crazy girl two states over was lusting after him like a woman possessed?

Maybe, but I still had to tell him. Emmy was right. If he freaked and changed his phone number, he wasn't the right man for me.

And neither was Cade. Find a man who put me first every time, Ryan had said. If that wasn't Cade or Eli, I'd keep looking.

Now, did I video call or do it the old-fashioned way? I spent twenty minutes fixing my hair and make-up—easier said than done when my face was all blotchy from crying—then decided to go with voice only.

I called.

No answer.

I sent a message.

Nothing.

Either he telepathically knew I was acting like a madwoman, or he'd fallen asleep. I preferred to think it was the latter.

Because what was the other option? That he'd come to his senses and realised starting a relationship so long-distance that the two participants never actually met was as insane as it sounded? I paused in front of the refrigerator and leaned my forehead against the cool metal door. What if I'd made the biggest mistake of my life and lost both Eli and Cade in the same evening?

After half an hour of pacing and hoping interspersed with two glasses of wine and most of a box of chocolates I barely tasted, I gave up, scrubbed my make-up off, and fell into a fitful sleep. All I could do was pin my hopes on the morning.

CHAPTER 22

MR. TIMBERLAKE WOKE me up, and I snatched my phone off the nightstand, almost dropping it in my haste. I juggled it from one hand to the other before finally getting it pressed against my ear.

"Eli?"

"Sugar, I fell asleep."

Oh, thank goodness!

Calm down, Tia. Deep breaths. Don't freak the hot, sexy cowboy out.

"That's okay; it makes a change. Normally it's me who falls asleep on you."

"Still, I didn't want to miss a moment of talking to you. I'll drink more coffee tonight. How was the show?"

I gave him an update on the corpses, the clothes, and the DJ, carefully avoiding any mention of the twelve hotties we'd had parading around in their underwear. Well, eleven. Clearly, my brother didn't count.

"Sounds amazing. And Ishmael fired his other assistant? For real?"

"I think so. I'll see if she turns up today."

"Do you have a lot to do?"

"We have to clear up all the mess at the Lincoln Center. I think the party may have got a bit raucous after I left."

"Raucous. You're so British."

"I can't help it."

"Don't. It's just one of the things I love about you."

Did he just say the *L* word? It was just a figure of speech, right? Like I might say I loved chocolate. Or I loved wine. No, I took that back. I most certainly did not love wine.

"Okay, I'll make sure I practise my accent. Can I call you tonight?"

The need to confess my feelings might have been bursting to get out of me, but I didn't have time for a deep and meaningful conversation before I went to work. No, I'd save that for later.

"I'd be upset if you didn't."

I smiled to myself. This guy totally had me. "Have a good day."

My smile held as I made my way to the Lincoln Center. On the subway. On my own. Emmy had kept her promise and called off the hounds, or at least, the ones I could see. I had no doubt that the red blob of my phone was being watched with eagle eyes in the control room at Blackwood.

Still, I felt free, and that was what counted.

The shambles at the Lincoln Center was every bit as bad as I'd feared. Someone had bought a bulk load of glitter and skull confetti, and the stuff had ended up everywhere. The walls, the floor, all over the chairs and the runway. How the hell did one get glitter off a plastified corpse? A dustpan and brush? A vacuum cleaner?

I was puzzling over it when Professor Ito stepped up beside me.

"Uh, I'm sorry about the, uh..." I waved at the

sparkly bits.

He cocked his head to one side and studied the mock-gymnast in front of us. "It makes her look pretty. I think we'll leave it."

Thank goodness for that.

I tiptoed off to the white room, praying the Ghost didn't like to party as much as Ishmael did. Otherwise, I'd be picking caviar off the ceiling and trying to get melted white chocolate buttons out of the pure white sheepskin rug.

I closed my eyes, opened the door, counted to three, then opened them.

What the hell?

The room was exactly as I'd left it yesterday. I opened the mini-fridge. Finding one of those with white handles and no visible logo had been a nightmare. The tins of caviar were still in there, the chocolate unopened. On the white sideboard, my carefully repackaged candles remained unlit. The white hand lotion and the bottle of white linen room fragrance sat untouched.

The only evidence anyone had been in the room at all was a crumpled water bottle in the rubbish bin.

I didn't know whether to laugh or cry. When I thought of the hassle I'd gone through trying to get those flaming candles, I felt like lining Harold bloody Styles up for target practice.

Still, it could have been worse.

I grabbed a packet of chocolate buttons out of the fridge and went to find Ishmael. He looked a little worse for wear this morning. His half-afro had collapsed, and he was wearing a huge pair of sunglasses. As I approached, he raised his head off the beanbag he'd sprawled out on.

"Good night?" I asked.

"The best. I'd forgotten how much Bradley liked to party. The cross-dressing strippers were a fabulous touch, and it was so thoughtful of him to buy the confetti in bulk."

So this was Bradley's doing? Why didn't that surprise me?

"Where's Bradley now?"

"I left him passed out in my lounge. He decided to sleep next to my giant Donald Duck model, and I couldn't budge him."

I offered Ishmael a chocolate button. He took a couple and ate them one at a time.

"Do you want me to get you some breakfast? An early lunch?"

"Could you pop to Starbucks and fetch a caramel macchiato, venti, skim, extra shot, extra-hot, extra whip, sugar-free?"

"I'll just get a pen."

Dismantling the fashion show set proved easier than putting it up, but by the end of the day, I was still exhausted. I wanted my bed. But more than that, I wanted Eli in it.

Time to talk. I dropped him a message as I dashed out of the building.

Me: Going home.

Quick as a flash, I got one back.

Eli: Ready and waiting :)

My new favourite words.

The subway started off slow then stopped completely. I sat on my coveted seat, the one I'd managed to snag when a tourist didn't move fast enough, willing the train to hurry up. What was going on? In London, the driver would have offered platitudes over the radio, but today we got nothing. After what seemed like forever, it finally rumbled off, and when it reached the platform, I sprinted up the escalator

Only to emerge into chaos.

Red and blue lights flashed everywhere. Fire engines vied for space with ambulances, and an awful lot of TV reporters milled behind the cordon. The acrid smell of smoke tinged the air.

"What's going on?" I asked the nearest policeman.

"Gas leak. A big one, judging by the bang. Heard it clear across the city."

"There was an explosion?

"Whole damn building blew up."

"I live down there. When will I be able to get home?"

"Not tonight, ma'am."

Bloody great. My plans foiled again, and now I needed somewhere to stay. But where? Emmy's apartment was a possibility, but it was across the city, and with the traffic in gridlock and the subway practically running backwards, it would take me hours to get there.

I couldn't wait that long to speak to Eli. My nerves wouldn't take it.

A flashing sign opposite caught my eye, and I came up with a new plan. A hotel room. I'd get a hotel room. I had my credit card, I had my iPad, I wasn't planning on needing clothes, and my lack of toothbrush didn't matter because Eli was two states away.

I hurried inside and smiled at the receptionist.

"Do you have a room for tonight? It doesn't matter what type."

"Sorry. Our last suite just went. It's the chaos outside—people can't get home, so they're looking for places to stay."

Dammit. Guess I wasn't the only one to think of that idea.

I tried another hotel, and another, getting further and further from my apartment. I was about to give up and call Bradley when the guy behind the counter at a grim-looking place a couple of blocks away gave me a gap-toothed grin.

"Yeah, we've got a room. Hundred bucks for the night, or twenty-five by the hour."

An hour? Who on earth would want to book a hotel room for an hour? A businessman who needed a nap?

The name on the sign said the Quality Inn, but there was nothing quality about this establishment. Wallpaper peeled at the corners, one of the chairs in the waiting area was missing a leg, and dubious stains marred the carpet.

But all I needed was a bed and an internet connection, and the dog-eared sign beside the desk advertised free Wi-Fi in every room. And at the thought of talking to Eli, a ripple of need pulsed through me.

"I'll take it."

"Name?"

The guy focused on my chest and tapped his fingers on the counter. Fat fingers with a four-letter word tattooed across the knuckles. Not a polite one.

"Ashlyn Hale."

Emmy wouldn't mind me borrowing her old identity again, right? I didn't want to give this slimeball my real name.

"Cash or card?"

"Cash."

The slimeball tapped my pretend name into his computer then rummaged in a drawer.

"Here." He handed over an old-fashioned key with a plastic tag tied on. "Check out by ten."

Believe me, I wouldn't be staying in this place a moment longer than I had to.

Room seven was at the far end of a corridor on the ground floor, and I swear I saw a mouse scuttle across in the gloom. At least I'd be next to the fire exit. I bet this place didn't meet the relevant safety standards, or hygiene ones either for that matter.

I took a deep breath and held it as I fitted the key into the lock, more in case the room smelled disgusting than anything else. Would the inside be habitable? I swung the door open and peeped inside. Okay, it was basic, very basic, but not as disgusting as I'd feared. A bed, a wobbly table, a chipped nightstand, and a chair with a questionable smear on the seat. But the sheets looked relatively clean, there were towels in the bathroom, and apart from an undertone of synthetic lemon, the place didn't smell too bad.

I'd cope for one night. After all, I'd survived being kidnapped, so I could survive this.

I set my iPad on the table and draped one of the towels over the seat of the chair. Okay, as long as I didn't think too much about where I was, this would be fine.

Breathe in, breathe out.

I'd spent the whole day considering what to say to Eli, but right now, no words seemed adequate. But this was Eli. We had a connection.

I had to believe that.

He'd said he was waiting, so I went straight for video and he answered immediately. Thank goodness. He was sitting at a table this time, and in the last of the evening light, I could almost make out his features. I caught myself leaning forward to peer at the screen and forced myself upright. *No staring, Tia. It's rude.*

"Took your time, sugar."

"My apartment's been blocked off by a gas explosion, and I had to find a hotel. It's bloody hideous." I held up my classy key with its plastic tag and waved it in front of the screen. "They don't even have key cards."

"Do you need to go somewhere else?"

"As long as I don't touch anything in here, I'll be fine."

"As long as you're okay to touch yourself." His voice dropped an octave and I almost came on the spot. "I won't kid you—I've been imagining you naked all day."

His words made heat flood through my veins like they always did, and tempting though it was to get down and dirty with him right away, I had to keep my eyes on the goal.

"Eli, we need to talk first."

"Talk?" He coughed nervously. "That sounds heavy."

"I've done a lot of thinking over the past few days, and...and..." Dammit, this was difficult. Perhaps I could send an email instead? "I don't know how to tell you."

"Sugar, what is it? You can tell me anything."

"I...I..."

"You're worrying me now."

In the end, I just blurted it out.

"I've fallen for you. I know we've never met, but I feel more of a connection with you than I ever have with another man." Yes, even Ryan. It was true. "I'm yours. And now I don't know what to do about it. I'm so scared," I finished up on a whisper.

Eli stiffened and his hands came up, tugging through his hair. *Please, don't run.*

"Sugar..." he paused long enough for my racing heart to beat ten times over. "In the last few weeks, you've made me feel things I never thought I'd feel again. Every second I've spent messaging you, talking to you, watching you—hell, especially watching you—has been a blessing. I don't know who sent you to me, but I thank them."

Myrna? Excuse me if I didn't convey his appreciation. Eli's hands dropped to the table, and I sensed a "but" coming. I was right.

"But I'm scared, too. There's so much I need to sort out in my mind, and I have to do that before we can move this forward. Can you give me some time?"

"What are you saying? That you don't want me to call anymore?"

You know what else this hotel room didn't have? Tissues. And I'd need them at this rate.

"Hell, no. Missing out on your voice every day would slay me. I just need time to work out how things can progress. I... I don't know if I can be happy with only seeing you on a screen."

Was he saying he wanted to meet me? In person?

My heart leapt.

"I can give you time. As much as you need. I don't ever want this to end."

"I hope it never does, sugar."

He reached out to touch his screen, and I did the same. The connection was there. We both felt it.

And then it was broken by a knock at the door.

Talk about bad timing. Who was it? That slob from reception? Or some poor lost tourist unlucky enough to have booked a room in this dump? I choked back a giggle at the thought of the Japanese people Emmy had rescued after the show and hoped my language skills were up to dealing with my unwanted visitor.

"Hang on. I'll get rid of whoever that is."

"Better hurry, sugar. I've got plans for you this evening."

I grinned at him. Slow or not, things were moving in the right direction. I was in for an interesting night tonight, I was sure of it.

CHAPTER 23

ELI BENNETT WATCHED as Ashlyn turned towards the door. Who was there? From the looks of the furnishings, that fine establishment didn't offer room service.

"Give me two seconds," she said.

Her iPad camera gave Eli a good view of the room, and he watched her dusky silhouette walk towards the door. He'd never get tired of those curves. His fingers itched to touch them, caress them, even for one night.

But still a fear of rejection held him back. He reached up a hand and ran his index finger along the network of scars on the left-hand side of his face. Two thick, red lines and three thinner white ones—a permanent reminder of his fucked-up teenage years.

Sure, he'd told Ashlyn about the damage. But she hadn't *seen* it.

What if she set eyes on him and couldn't stomach the sight? Even he couldn't bear to look at himself. No mirrors graced his walls, and at night, he pulled down the blinds before he could catch sight of himself in the glass. Or at least, he always used to. Since he met Ashlyn, he'd begun leaving the drapes in his bedroom open for their moonlight chats.

No, he couldn't risk losing her. She meant everything to him, more even than Delia, although that hurt to admit.

And he still hadn't told Ashlyn the whole story about the accident either. That the night he crashed his truck with Delia in the passenger seat, he'd been drinking. That when the cops had cut him free from the wreckage, still clutching at Delia's cooling hand, he'd been twice over the limit.

Everyone but his family had disowned him after the incident—their friends, his manager, his bandmates. A liberal application of money had kept Eli out of jail and the story out of the media, and he still felt sick every time he thought of the aftermath. Lying in hospital while his lawyer negotiated, attending Delia's funeral while everyone looked at him with disgust.

When he'd moved back home, his momma spent two months crying, and his daddy's words still haunted him.

"You may be my son, but I've got no pride in you anymore."

Only his little sister and her smiles as she bounced on his bed in the mornings had stopped him from ending it all.

And now he had Ashlyn. But if she found out about his past, he'd lose her too.

On screen, she clipped on the security chain and reached for the door. Snippets of conversation drifted over: "No, that's not me... You've got the wrong room."

Then, without warning, the door burst open and two men pushed inside, rushing at Ashlyn. She screamed, a horrifying screech that cut him to the core, but the noise stopped almost immediately as one of them clapped a hand over her mouth.

Eli grabbed at the screen as his heart threatened to

burst out of his ribcage. What the hell?

Was this some kind of sick joke?

The taller of the two men lifted Ashlyn clear off the ground as she struggled to get free. Her foot kicked the table and they disappeared from sight for a second, but then they came back, closer. And she sure didn't look like she was messing around.

Ashlyn bit the asshole's hand, and he uncovered her mouth for a second.

"Tell Emerson Black," she screamed.

The other man backhanded her, and she slumped forward, limp in the arms of her captor.

Then they were gone.

For a full thirty seconds, Eli stared at his iPad, gripping the sides, trying to process what just happened. As if at any moment, Ashlyn would pop up on screen, smiling, and what he just saw would be nothing but a nightmare.

But she didn't.

Now what?

What the hell was he supposed to do?

The cops. Of course, he needed to call the cops. His fingers trembled as he dialled 911.

"I need to report an abduction."

"When and where did this happen, sir?" The lady on the other end of the line sounded entirely too calm.

"Two minutes ago, in New York."

"New York's a big place, sir."

"She got taken from a hotel."

"Who got taken?"

"My, uh, friend." He'd nearly said girlfriend, but that seemed like a distant dream.

"There are a lot of hotels in New York, sir."

"It would have been in Tribeca. Or maybe just outside of it."

"I'm gonna need a name, sir."

"She's called Ashlyn Hale."

"I meant of the hotel.

"I don't have that. Look, Ashlyn lives in Tribeca. Her apartment got cordoned off because of a gas explosion tonight."

A sigh and the tapping of keys came down the line. "That cordon went on for five city blocks. What's her address?"

"I don't know that either."

"Look, if this is a prank call..."

"It's not a damn joke! I watched a girl named Ashlyn Hale get abducted from her hotel room tonight. I haven't got the name of the place, but it was downmarket. Seedy."

"And how exactly did you watch her get abducted?"

"On a webcam."

"So, you were watching a young lady in a seedy hotel, on a webcam?"

"It's not how it sounds!"

That damn woman would make a preacher cuss.

"Sir, if you don't hang up this instant, I'm going to report you for wasting police time. We have real work to do."

Eli flung the phone on the bed and paced the room. What now? He'd never felt so helpless before, not even during the crash. Delia had died instantly, but Ashlyn was still alive, and he was the only one who knew she'd even been taken.

Then he remembered her garbled yell: Tell Emerson Black.

Who the hell was he? Eli was damn sure Ashlyn had never mentioned the name in conversation.

He grabbed his laptop and typed the words into the search box. Hundreds of hits came up: The Emerson Black Box Theatre... Emerson black shoes... Emerson black office furniture. The only person he could find with that name appeared to be a YouTube rapper living in Africa.

Facebook yielded nothing more—only a couple of similar names, and none of them lived in the US.

Had he heard Ashlyn right?

Fuck, this was hopeless.

Up and down, up and down, he walked. Eli didn't even know anybody in the Big Apple, not anymore. Back when he'd had the world at his feet, a click of his fingers would have brought help running, but now? He was nobody.

And he only had one option left. He'd have to go to New York himself.

Funny how fear overrode all rational thought, wasn't it? His earlier worries seemed trivial as he grabbed a dusty duffle bag from the top of his wardrobe and flung clothes and toiletries in it. Anything else he needed, he could buy. It wasn't like he was short of cash. He'd earned enough in his teens to retire at twenty.

What should he tell his parents?

They didn't know a thing about Ashlyn, and as early risers, they'd be asleep already. No way was he waking them up for that conversation.

They were old-fashioned, and to them, a relationship began with courting and ended in marriage. He'd hurt them enough with the fallout from

Delia. No, he'd leave a note.

Momma, Daddy,

It's time I faced the world again. I'll be away for a few days—please don't worry.

Eli

He ran to the main house and left it propped up against a mixing bowl on the long trestle table where the ranch hands ate lunch. His parents would find his message in the morning.

Then it was back to his garage where two vehicles awaited. The pickup he used on the ranch every day and a black Porsche. That 911 Turbo was the last remnant of his old life, the only thing he hadn't thrown out or sold when he moved back home. He rarely drove it, but as a stickler for maintenance, he knew it still ran smoothly.

And fast.

He tapped Tribeca into the SatNav, trying to ignore the vice tightening around his chest. New York. Years had passed since he last visited the city, and his time there had been spent racing from interview to photo op to concert before collapsing into a hotel room bed for a couple of hours' sleep. He'd longed to return there one day, to see the city as it was meant to be seen, and lately, he'd wished for Ashlyn to see it with him.

He wanted to visit the Statue of Liberty with her, to walk hand-in-hand around the Met. He wanted to picnic in Central Park then take in a show on Broadway. All normal things that normal couples did.

He wanted a normal life. With her.

But fucking fate had intervened once more.

As he drove through the darkness, Ashlyn danced before his eyes. Her voice, her face, her laughter, the uninhibited way she screamed his name as she came.

He loved her.

Perhaps the revelation should have scared him, but instead it was like putting on a well-worn leather jacket. Comfortable. A perfect fit.

Six hours later, after a long journey from Augusta up the I-81 and along the I-78, Eli reached the twinkling lights of Tribeca. Dawn was breaking across the city that never sleeps, and people were already going about their business.

People.

A jaywalking jogger ran out in front of the Porsche, and Eli braked sharply. He rarely drove in town and whenever he'd been to New York, his record company had provided a chauffeur. Usually drinks and party girls too, which meant he'd never noticed how bad the traffic was. Sure, in the movies, the yellow cabs were always bumper-to-bumper with a soundtrack of honking horns, but after spending so long in the country, the smog-filled reality came as a shock. Five o'clock in the morning, and he'd be faster on his own two feet. He checked his watch for the hundredth time since he left the ranch. Six hours and five minutes. Where was Ashlyn? And more importantly, would he be in time to save her?

Back on the farm, Eli's daddy would be out in the barn, no doubt cursing his no-good son for lumbering him with all the work. Truth was, Eli would give his favourite guitar to be shovelling horseshit rather than getting lost in the Big Apple.

The British lady on his SatNav politely informed him of yet another traffic jam, and he dug his fingernails into the leather steering wheel. *Tick, tick, tick.* The second hand swept around his watch face again. He inched the car forward and saw a yellow Park Fast sign looming above. Screw this—he'd be better off on foot. In the parking garage, an attendant held out his hand for the keys, the delight in his eyes at the sight of the Porsche turning to morbid curiosity as he took in Eli's tarnished face.

"Here's your ticket, sir."

Eli snatched it off him, tugging his hood forward over his face as he steeled himself to walk the streets above.

Even before the accident, he'd hated people staring at him, and towards the end, not a day had passed without him cursing the very day he'd sent a demo track to the man who became his manager. The man who'd matched him with three other sixteen-year-olds to form Red Alert and sent them soaring to the top of the Billboard charts.

He'd dreamed of giving it all up. Of walking out on stage and announcing that tonight's show would be his last. But by then, his parents had turned from grudging chaperones to enthusiastic supporters because the money was rolling in.

So, Eli hid behind his bandmates, behind the glaring spotlights and the heavy make-up, and soldiered on until the day he nearly died.

Up on the sidewalk, he hunched over, hands in pockets as passers-by gave him lingering glances. Women, mostly. Those to his right got that gleam in their eyes—the groupie-stare, he'd always called it—

while those to his left wrinkled their noses then looked away.

Their gazes wormed under his skin like parasites in a second-rate horror movie, and he shivered even as he sweated.

Judging. They were always judging.

Eli's feet turned back the way they'd come of their own accord, his inbuilt survival instinct telling him to get back to his car and do it now. He swayed and clutched at a nearby lamp post, but as the street around him faded to black, Ashlyn's beautiful face played across his mind, front and centre.

Man up and find her, Eli. She's the only thing that matters.

He forced himself to breathe then took stock of his surroundings, doing his best to ignore the people passing on either side. Where was the damaged building Ashlyn had mentioned? He'd start there and work his way outwards.

He paused next to a homeless guy, an old drunk clutching a can of beer with shaking fingers.

"There was an explosion last night. Do you know where?"

"Left at the lights. Can't miss it."

Eli dropped twenty dollars in the man's lap and hurried on. Sure enough, he found the blackened building ahead, wisps of smoke still rising from the top. Half of the city fire department loitered behind a security cordon, and he stood on tiptoe to look past. Ashlyn's place must be in there somewhere, which meant the hotel was nearby. If he could find it, perhaps the cops would take him seriously.

He traipsed the streets, ignoring any

establishments with more than three stars. Ashlyn had said it was bloody hideous, and there sure were a lot of places fitting that description. He enquired in each and every one, with money changing hands on occasion, but the answer was always the same. No, she hadn't been there.

He was beginning to lose his grip on the thin thread of hope he had left when he reached the peeling facade of the Quality Inn. Now, that was a lie if he ever heard one.

"Nope, never heard of Ashlyn Hale," the gap-toothed man behind the counter said.

But he wouldn't meet Eli's eyes, and Eli had seen that reaction many times over the last few years. On the neighbours when they said it was good to see him. On his ex-manager when he said how sorry he was to see Eli go. On his own momma when she said how glad she was that he'd moved back home.

The asshole was lying.

What clinched it was seeing the key lying on the table next to the register—chunky metal, not a key-card, with a plastic tag just like the one Ashlyn had dangled in front of him last night. And hers had shown the number seven in thick, black script.

Yes, she'd been here.

"Thanks for your help, buddy," Eli said. "Say, you got a john I could use?"

Twenty bucks got him access to the men's room, which he bypassed as he followed the lopsided sign for rooms five to seven. Room seven was at the far end of the corridor, right next to a fire exit that hung ajar, like someone had left in a hurry and forgotten to close it.

The door to room seven was open too, only a crack,

but Eli pushed it further. Why hadn't he brought his damn pistol? It was still sitting snugly in his bureau drawer.

Inside, he found Ashlyn's iPad half under the bed, alongside her handbag and sweater. He picked the garment up and inhaled deeply. Roses and vanilla. Sweet, just like her.

He pressed the power button on the iPad, and the lock screen popped up. She'd set a cup of black coffee as her background, the same icon he used on that chat site his sister insisted on joining. Coincidence?

No, Eli didn't believe in coincidences.

How many attempts would he get to guess the password? Five? Ten? He couldn't waste any of them, but he didn't know where to start. Maybe he should give the cops another try now?

But before he could leave, a noise in the corridor caught his attention.

Soft footsteps heading in his direction, rhythmical and measured. He held his breath, waiting for them to stop, for a lock to click as somebody went into one of the other rooms.

But the click never came, and the footsteps didn't stop.

Not until they were right outside the door of room number seven.

Chapter 24

ELI SHRANK INTO the corner as the door to room seven flew open. Two people stepped inside, one from each side of the doorway, both with guns drawn.

And both barrels pointed straight at his head.

"Hands up," the woman in the tailored suit said, motioning with her head.

Eli complied.

"Who the fuck are you?" the guy alongside her demanded.

"Who are you?" Eli asked back, trying to keep the quake out of his voice.

The woman stepped forward, and her gun didn't waver. "Answer the question."

She kept her voice soft, controlled, and Eli knew instinctively that she was the more dangerous of the two. Not that the guy was soft in any way. His eyes burned with anger while the woman's stayed ice cold.

Eli kept quiet, but the man tried again.

"What are you doing here?"

"I'm looking for Ashlyn Hale." That much had to be obvious.

"Well, you've found her," the woman said, her accent English like Ashlyn's. Strange.

"What do you mean? She's not here."

"I'm Ash Hale."

"No, you're not."

She pierced him with her gaze, and he'd have backed away if he had anywhere to go.

"I mean, I guess you could be her, but I'm looking for a different Ashlyn Hale."

Another coincidence? No way. What were the chances of two women with the same name booking one hotel room?

"Describe her."

"Brown hair, nineteen years old. Beautiful."

The second Ash Hale tilted her head to the side as she peered at Eli's face. "Take your hood down."

He hesitated, and she jerked the gun.

"Now."

What choice did he have? He dropped one hand and flipped the hood away from his face, squirming inside as Ash studied him like a scientific specimen.

"You're Eli."

Not a question, but a statement.

Blood drained out of his face, leaving a chill that bit into his bones. Who the hell was this woman? Why was she here? Was this some kind of setup? A warped reality TV show that took pleasure in other people's pain? Even as he glanced around, checking for cameras, he knew he was clutching at straws. This woman was no actress. The freezing aura that surrounded her was all too real, and nobody could fake the look in her eyes. Ferocious but calm. Hard but perceptive. Those eyes saw everything but gave away nothing.

Eli swallowed the lump in his throat, forcing it down enough to speak. "How do you know?"

"Tell me why you're here."

He didn't answer. What if she was working with the kidnappers? Eli contemplated running for the door, risking a bullet to escape. But if he was dead, who would help Ashlyn? *His* Ashlyn, not this ice maiden standing in front of him.

Her expression didn't change as she tucked her gun into her waistband and pulled a folding knife from her pocket. *Snick.* Before Eli could blink, the vicious-looking black blade had embedded itself in the wall next to his ear.

"I'm waiting."

"I-I-I was talking to Ashlyn last night. On FaceTime." He flicked his head at the iPad lying on the bed. "Someone knocked on the door, and she answered it, then two men burst in and grabbed her."

The man bit out a curse and kicked the wall.

"Calm yourself," the woman snapped at him. "What else?"

"She struggled, and one of them knocked her unconscious. Then they took her."

"Did they say anything?"

"Neither of them spoke a word, but before she was knocked out, Ashlyn yelled at me to tell Emerson Black. Except I don't know what that means."

The woman blew out a breath and sank onto the edge of the bed. "Fucking hell. I honestly can't believe this is happening."

"That makes two of us."

"Oh, lower your hands. We're not gonna shoot you." She turned to the other guy. "Cade, put your gun away."

He did so, looking far from happy.

Eli itched to cover his face again, but what was the point? They'd both seen it now, and he had bigger things to worry about.

"How long has she been calling herself Ash?" the woman asked.

"I don't understand what you mean."

"When did she tell you what her name was?"

"Now you ask, I'm not sure she ever did. It was her username on the website where we met."

"What was it called?"

"SpeedChat."

The woman took out her phone and dialled.

"Nate, Tia's been taken... Yes, again... No, I can't fucking believe it either. I need you to look at a website for me. Tia signed up to it with the name Ashlyn Hale. I need to know when." A pause. "Last night. No, I didn't get the alert until a couple of hours ago. That explosion messed with communications all over the city, and then I had to fly in."

But Eli was still hung up on the first part of the conversation. "Tia? Her name's Tia? And what do you mean, taken again?"

Emmy hung up and gave Eli her attention again. "Yeah. Tia Cain. And this isn't the first time she's been kidnapped. She seems to be making rather a habit of it."

"She lied to me. I can't believe she lied to me."

The woman glanced at her friend. "Cade, wait outside."

"But—"

"Now."

He disappeared into the corridor, and the woman motioned Eli to sit next to her.

"I doubt she meant to lie."

"But when I called her Ashlyn, she never corrected

me."

"Tia's got a habit of digging herself into holes she can't climb out of. Knowing her, she wanted to stay anonymous at first, and when you got closer, she couldn't work out how to tell you the truth."

"What else did she lie about? If she couldn't come clean over something so simple..."

"Not much, I don't think. She probably didn't realise how things were going to develop between you, and I know she cares. She wants a life with you."

"She said that?"

"The night before last."

Eli's heart swelled. Ashlyn—Tia—wanted more? *She wanted more.* The warmth that spread through him was swiftly followed by liquid nitrogen, because what if they never got that more. What if he couldn't get her back?

The woman's phone buzzed, and she scrolled through a message.

"She only signed up for her chat account on the night she met you. From the transcripts, it looks like she joined to wind up a work colleague. No way would she have wanted to use her real name for that. It seems she borrowed one of mine."

"One of yours?"

"When I first met Tia, I was calling myself Ashlyn Hale. My real name is Emerson Black. Emmy. It's good to meet you. I only wish it could have been under more pleasant circumstances."

Eli pulled his hood back up as they walked out of the

hotel. Cade was leaning against a black Range Rover parked at the kerb, glowering.

"You stay here," Emmy told him. "Keep the room secure until I can get a team out to search it properly."

He didn't look happy about that, even less so when Emmy motioned Eli into the car beside her.

"Where are we going?" he asked.

"My office. I co-own a security and investigations firm."

Investigations? Eli was still floundering in the dark, but for the first time, he saw a chink of light.

"You think you can find her?"

"That's the plan."

Emmy drove like a demon, on the sidewalk at one point, and only slowed as they pulled into a car park underneath a nondescript building on the edge of the city. The elevator in the corner took them all the way to the fifth floor, and Eli kept his head down as Emmy herded him past rows of desks filled with curious eyes.

In a corner conference room with views over a nearby park, Emmy pointed at a black leather sofa.

"Get some rest."

"Are you serious?"

"You've been up all night, yes?"

"Yeah, but—"

"This isn't gonna be a five-minute job, and you're no good tired. Now, sleep or I'll have you shipped out to a hotel room."

Eli thought sleep would be impossible, but as he leaned back on the squashy sofa, the chatter building in the room disappeared. A few minutes. He'd just rest for a few minutes.

CHAPTER 25

NO, NOT AGAIN. This couldn't be happening again.

My head throbbed as the darkness faded, and a spartan room came into focus. Wow. This was even worse than room seven at the Quality Inn.

I lay on a grimy mattress, and at some point, I'd kicked free of the grey woollen blanket next to me, leaving me freezing. My clothes—where were my clothes? I'd been stripped to my underwear, and the jeans and polo neck I'd been wearing yesterday were nowhere to be seen. Light came from a single window set high in the eaves, covered with a metal grille just in case I entertained any thoughts of escape. But do you know what scared me most?

The bucket in the corner.

Surely, they didn't expect me to...? I scrambled to my knees and stumbled to the door. Locked. Dammit! I rattled the handle but nobody came, and when I peered through the keyhole, all I saw was a grubby white wall opposite.

Oh fuck, oh fuck, oh fuck. *Sorry, Luke.* He hated when I swore.

I paced the room then hopped as I got a splinter from the rough wooden floor stuck in my heel. Drops of blood spilled into the dust as I pulled it out.

"Hello?" I yelled. "Is anybody there?"

Even as the words left my mouth, I wasn't sure I wanted to know the answer.

But it didn't matter because nobody came.

I tried to jump up to the window, but the bars remained stubbornly out of reach. They hadn't even left me a glass of water, and as the hours ticked by, I grew thirsty and ever more terrified. But then again, drinking would mean using the bucket, and I didn't fancy that either.

What was happening in New York? Was I even in New York anymore? I listened carefully, but I couldn't hear any traffic outside. Occasionally, a plane flew past, a jet high in the sky rather than a light aircraft. I grimaced as I pulled the blanket tighter around myself. It smelled funny, like the week-old socks my brother was incapable of putting in the laundry basket.

Had Eli called the police? Surely he must have. Or better still, had he managed to track down Emmy? I groaned as I sank back onto the mattress. How would he have managed that? I hadn't exactly shouted her phone number, and I knew she was impossible to find online. Mack made sure of that.

No, the police were my best hope, and I hadn't even given Eli my real name. I could only imagine how that conversation went.

Dammit, why hadn't I fought harder when those men came? Emmy had taught me a whole bunch of self-defence moves, but when I actually needed them, my mind had gone blank. *Well done, Tia.*

It was getting dark by the time I heard footsteps on the stairs outside my prison, and I stiffened. Was I about to find out why I'd been brought here? A key jiggled in the lock, and the door flew open, smacking back against the wall as a dark-haired man strode in. Two others flanked him, both blond.

"Get up," he barked.

I held the blanket around myself, knuckles white where I clutched it to my chest.

"What do you want? Why am I here?"

"Get up! Lesson number one—I don't like repeating myself."

He nodded, and his henchmen grabbed my arms and pulled me to my feet. The blanket dropped to the floor, leaving me as good as naked.

The man in charge circled, studying me, then stopped in front.

"No, it's not her. This one's too young."

Was that a good thing or a bad thing?

"What are you talking about?" I asked.

"Ashlyn Hale killed my father." He stared at me, unblinking.

"I'm, uh, sorry?"

"It was an assassination." He spat the words. "And if it takes me the rest of my life, I'm going to do the same to her."

Oh. Shit.

How many assassins were there in the world who used the name Ashlyn Hale? I only knew of one. Emmy. Which meant the freak in front of me wanted to murder my sister. This got worse and worse.

"I-I-I'm not an assassin. I'm a fashion intern."

He shrugged. "Mistakes happen."

"So, you're going to let me go?"

He laughed, or rather cackled, and it made him sound even more deranged. "Of course not. You'd lead the police straight back here."

"But I don't even know where 'here' is."

"You think we'll take that chance? No, you can stay here as entertainment for the men."

"E-e-entertainment?"

"Oh, don't act so innocent, child." He reached out and stroked one cold finger down my jaw. "No woman checks into the Quality Inn alone because she wants a good night's sleep. Sluts, hookers, prostitutes. You're all the same."

"I'm not—"

"Shut up! In the words of Martin Luther, 'The words and works of God is quite clear, that women were made either to be wives or prostitutes.' You already made it quite clear which you are."

Pretty sure I didn't learn that in Sunday school.

"I was in that hotel because the police cordoned off my apartment after a gas explosion."

"You know how many excuses I've heard from women just like you? I had a problem with my heating. My landlord kicked me out. The neighbours were having a party. Liars!" He broke into a sick smile. "My men work hard. They deserve a little fun."

"You bastard!"

I tried to kick him, but he stepped back and his men nearly dislocated my shoulders.

"Calm down, child. You might even enjoy it."

They walked out, slamming the door behind them. The lock clicked, and I sank to my knees, hugging the blanket against me. This was bad. This was really, really bad.

Last time I got kidnapped, some freak with a grudge against my brother locked me in a bathroom and fed me Pop-Tarts for a few days. Okay, so he drugged me too, but at least I'd had food and a toilet even if it didn't flush. I eyed up the bucket again, crawled across the floor, and puked into it.

Emmy, where the hell are you?

CHAPTER 26

ELI CAME AROUND slowly, and at first he wasn't sure he'd woken up at all. The low hum of conversation, computers beeping, ringing phones—they had no place on the ranch. Then it came rushing back. Ashlyn—Tia—and Emerson Black.

He sat up and found the conference room transformed. Every spot at the table was occupied, a video wall flashed with pictures of men, buildings, vehicles... Worst of all was the whiteboard on one wall with Tia's picture in the centre, yesterday's date and the word *ABDUCTED* written underneath.

Bile rose in his throat. This was real.

A kind-looking woman with her grey hair fastened into a bun appeared beside him. "Would you like something to eat?"

He shook his head. "I can't."

"A drink, perhaps?"

He went to decline then realised how dry his mouth was. "You have coffee?"

"Milk? Sugar?"

"Just black."

Eli spotted Emmy on the far side of the room and walked over, withering more under every glance. None of the expressions showed hostility or disgust, more concern and curiosity, but even so, it made him painfully uncomfortable.

Emmy had changed her clothes. Gone was the suit, and in its place, she wore skintight black jeans and a T-shirt that left nothing to the imagination, including the gun at her side. Especially the gun at her side.

"Is there any news?"

"We're working on the problem."

"That's it? You're working on it? We've got to find out who took her."

"One step ahead of you there, sunshine. I knew who took her right away. It's getting her back that's gonna be the problem."

"If you know who's got her, can't you just call the cops?"

Emmy barked out a laugh. "The cops? Fuck that. They'd tie us up in red tape and stick a gift bow on Tia's body when they eventually found it."

"Then what are you planning to do?"

Emmy glanced at her gun, and Eli's eyes widened.

"You understand if anything I say goes out of this room, I'll kill you?"

She tossed out the threat casually, like she was ordering a pizza, but Eli was under no illusion about her seriousness.

"I won't talk."

Emmy took his hand and led him back to the sofa, settling into one of the seats and motioning for Eli to do the same.

"I first met Tia when I was living in England. Dating her brother, would you believe?" Emmy's eye roll suggested she didn't believe it either. "I called myself Ashlyn Hale back then. A temporary situation while I'd misplaced my damn mind. Anyhow, when I came back to the US, I didn't need that identity anymore, so I burned it for a job."

"Burned it?"

"Killed it. Ashlyn Hale was toxic. Dead and buried, never to see the light of day. She went out in style, though. Pissed a bunch of people off."

Who was this woman? *What* was she? As her words ricocheted around in Eli's skull, pieces of the jigsaw puzzle slammed into place.

"And these people tracked Tia down and thought she was you?"

"Have a gold star."

"But how did they find her if she only used that name with me? I sure didn't tell anyone about her."

"She also used it when she checked into the Quality fucking Inn, which one of them happens to own. Her name would have popped up in the booking system and rung all sorts of alarm bells."

Eli closed his eyes and groaned. *Oh, sugar.*

"Who has her? You said you knew."

"A group who call themselves the Chains of Christ."

"The who?"

"Peter chapter two, verse four. *For if God spared not the angels that sinned, but cast them down to hell, and delivered them into chains of darkness, to be reserved unto judgement.*"

"A church? She was taken by a church?"

"Not exactly. They're as Christian as I am Chinese, but they like to pick and choose Bible quotes to support their own whacked-out agenda. My particular favourite was when their founder quoted Tertullian's words at me. *Woman is a temple built over a sewe*r. That was right before I killed him."

Killed him?

"Y-y-y'all can't be serious?"

Brother or no brother, how in hell did a fashion intern get mixed up with a crazy-ass bitch like this? She was meaner than a wet panther.

"Yeah, I reckon that's why his son's so pissed at me. The irony is, until daddy died, Silas junior wasn't so interested in the whole cult thing his old man had going. I guess the opportunity to step into the power vacuum was just too good to pass up."

"You didn't think of that before you...you know."

She shrugged. "I got paid to do a job, and I did it. That's the trouble with the assholes in authority. So often, they fail to think through the consequences. I mean, look at the whole Gulf War."

A commotion near the door made both of them turn their heads, and a blond man strode in, eyes scanning the room until he spotted Emmy. He closed the distance between them pretty damn fast.

"Where the hell is my sister?"

Eli scrambled to his feet.

"Ah. Luke, meet Eli, Tia's boyfriend. Eli, this is Luke, her brother."

Eli expected scrutiny, but he got none. Luke ignored his outstretched hand and turned on Emmy instead.

"Boyfriend? You knew about this?"

"Oh, calm down. Tia's nineteen. She's hardly going to hang out in a convent in this day and age."

"Why does she tell you these things and not me?"

"Because this is how you react, and it's not the time or the place. Now, put a sock in it or get out of my conference room."

Luke gave her a death stare but stomped over to the bank of computers. A young guy slid out of his seat, vacating it for Tia's brother. Being blanked sure wasn't pleasant, but Eli understood Luke's feelings. After all, if his little sister had a secret boyfriend turn up out of the blue, he'd most likely want to lock her up in a chastity belt then stake the guy down in the midday sun until he promised to keep his hands in a different zip code.

Two more people came in, one man, one woman, and Eli fought to swallow down the lump that had clawed its way up his throat. Immersion therapy, that's what this was. He'd read about it on the internet.

But those words on the screen never conveyed how it would feel. Eli was nervous as a long-tailed cat in a roomful of rocking chairs.

"Reckon I'll get to use my new gun?" the pretty brunette asked, flinging her leather jacket onto the couch.

Rocking chairs occupied by sugar-fuelled toddlers.

"Sure. We'll need all the guns on this one. Dan, this is Eli. Eli, meet Dan."

Dan squeezed his hand with a surprisingly strong grip.

"Kinda young," she sniffed before walking off.

"And this is Nick," Emmy introduced the man. "He'll be on the rescue team too."

Nick studied Eli, taking in both sides of his face. "Don't I know you?"

Eli forced himself to look up at the man. Dark eyes, dark hair, wide shoulders. He did seem a little familiar.

"I *do* know you. You're Red Bennett. We did the security for your US tour, what, three years ago?"

Right. The memories came flooding back. Eight

weeks, forty-seven shows, sixteen cities. Interviews, meet-and-greets, TV appearances, and at the end, six days in a recovery centre while he was treated for exhaustion. Of course, the press was following his every move, and exhaustion didn't sell papers. The first evening, Eli had spent two hours on the phone convincing his momma he wasn't addicted to coke or hookers.

"Four years. But I haven't gone by that name for a long time."

"Bet there's a legion of girls who can still sing the words to every one of your songs."

"They'll have to sing them alone. I quit that life."

"After the accident?"

"You know about that?"

How could he? The local sheriff had been convinced to 'lose' the blood test results, and Delia's family accepted $500,000 in blood money. Eli had lost the respect of everyone, including himself.

Nick's smile faded. "I heard things."

Aw, hell. He knew everything, didn't he? He knew what had happened with Delia. Which meant Tia would find out as soon as she came back. *If* she came back.

Anything they might have had would be over before it started. Eli's heart stuttered, and it might as well have stopped completely for all he cared.

Dan called Nick from across the room, and he broke eye contact, leaving Eli shattered as he walked away.

Eli watched, barely seeing, as a dark-haired woman stalked in, giving Emmy a quick hug before she retired to a corner and started a silent vigil. Then the atmosphere in the room dropped a few degrees as another newcomer arrived, the king to Emmy's ice queen. Or possibly the Incredible Hulk. The guy had to be six and a half feet tall.

And he said one word. "Update."

People unfroze and scrambled around, collecting up papers and punching buttons. The big man stood impassive as minions scurried around him. Dan dropped down next to Eli on the sofa, ankles crossed.

After a minute or two, a redheaded woman stood up from next to Luke.

"Nate's about to send Rosie in."

"Who's Rosie?" Eli whispered.

"Rosie's a cockroach."

"Sorry?"

"A remote-controlled cockroach mounted with cameras. Nate flies her from his phone."

What was this? A James Bond movie?

"Who's Nate? Is he here?"

"Nah, he's our eyes on the ground in Orange County."

"Is that where Tia is?"

"Let's take a look, shall we?"

The big screen at the far end of the room cleared, and a single picture came up. A man's foot, dressed in combat boots.

"Here we go," Dan murmured as the foot grew smaller and morphed into woods then green fields. "Nate's spent hours flying her. She looks damn realistic too. One of the cleaners in our Richmond office took out a prototype when it buzzed past her ear."

Five minutes passed, then ten, and a big old farmhouse came into view. Rosie flew around the building, pausing at each window.

"Nate's looking for a way in," Dan said.

The big man spoke, to Nate, it seemed. "That window at the top. The one with the bars over it. I want to see what's in there."

Rosie flew upwards, hovering in the requested spot, and her camera zoomed in. Eli couldn't watch, but the collective gasp from the room confirmed his worst fears. They'd found Tia.

The silence was broken by the crack of a magazine slamming into place. Eli looked across to the far corner and saw the dark-haired woman holding a pistol.

For the first time, she had a smile on her face.

Chapter 27

COLD. SO COLD. No matter what I did, I couldn't get warm. I'd tried pacing, curling up under the blanket, and even aerobics, but the sheer hopelessness of the situation made me burst into tears. I didn't have the energy to move, anyway. All they'd brought me was a jug of water and a single cheese sandwich. They didn't even use butter.

The moon was dropping, and I watched the shadows creeping across the floor, the dawn of another day in hell.

Then footsteps sounded on the stairs again.

Please, don't let it be that weird freak from yesterday, the one who told me I must be a prostitute because I'd happened to have really bad taste in hotels.

It wasn't.

It was worse.

The door swung open and a ferrety man swaggered in. He rested his hands on his knees as he crouched in front of me.

"Good morning, Ashlyn."

The corner of his lip twitched up in a nervous tic, once, twice, three times.

"What do you want?"

"You. Silas has given you to me to do as I please."

He patted his crotch, and the remains of the

sandwich rose up my throat. No, no, no. Tell me this wasn't happening. It couldn't be happening. This was all a nightmare, and I'd wake up soon.

In my nightmare, I shoved Ferret-Features backwards and ran for the door, but before I could get it open, he grabbed my arm and flung me across the room with a wiry strength I hadn't suspected.

"Tsk, tsk, tsk. Good thing I like my girls feisty."

"Get the hell away from me."

"You know how long it's been since I had a woman? Eight months."

He thought that was something to brag about?

"Well, you're not having this one."

"Beg to differ, little lady. You were a gift."

"Fuck you. It's my body."

"In this house, everything belongs to Silas."

I shoved at his hands as he grabbed my bra strap, and his answering backhand made me see stars. *Think, Tia, think.* Emmy had drilled all that self-defence training into me, but a real emergency was nothing like the gym. I jabbed at Ferret's eyes as he straddled me, but he batted my hand away. My efforts were a minor irritation, nothing more.

I tried to struggle as Ferret-Features pinned me to the floor, but all I got was more splinters. He fumbled with his belt, holding my hands above my head with one hand. Those beady eyes glittered in the moonlight, and I longed to poke them out.

His cock pressed against my stomach, already hard, and I leaned to the side and retched. This wasn't happening. I closed my eyes, trying to take myself someplace else. Back to my apartment, Riverley, my childhood home in Lower Foxford. Anywhere.

Then his weight disappeared, and I heard a quiet grunt.

What the...?

My eyes popped open and through blurry vision, I came face to face with Ferret, only now he had a knife handle sticking out of his left eyeball.

A different kind of fear clutched at my stomach, and this time I really did puke. My stomach contents splashed on the floor, landing beside drops of Ferret's blood. I looked up in time to see Ana wipe the knife blade on Ferret's jeans and tuck it back into her waistband.

Her face was a hard mask, and she made a cutting motion against her own throat. The message was clear: Make a sound and die.

My muscles refused to cooperate as Ana wrapped the blanket around me, grabbed my hand, and tugged me towards the door. Before we went through it, she put a finger to her lips in one last warning.

I got it.

I'd always known Ana was dangerous, but until today, I'd never seen her in action. She moved quickly on silent feet, gun ready, hurrying through the maze of passages with a familiarity I didn't understand. How the hell did she stay so calm? She'd just killed a man, for crying out loud. The picture of the knife in Ferret's eye popped into my head again, and I heaved, but Ana gave me a scathing look and I swallowed the bile back down.

Voices sounded up ahead, and Ana pulled me into a doorway, tucking me behind her as she waited with the gun in one hand and her knife in the other. My wheezing sounded like a hurricane in my ears, and I tried to stay quiet, all too aware that Ana wasn't even breathing hard. At that moment, she seemed more like a robot than a human being.

Then the men passed, and we were out in the corridor again and heading for the stairs. Almost there... Almost there.

Except when we reached the landing, I saw a horror scene unfolding outside the window.

Emmy stood in the middle of the driveway, hands in the air as, well, there had to be forty men out there with guns aimed at her. Her lips moved, but I couldn't make out the words. And as I watched, frozen, one gun barked, and a red stain spread out on her chest as she collapsed to the ground.

No, no, no, no, no.

I opened my mouth to scream but Ana clamped her hand over the top of it, the other arm snaking around my chest like a metal band. She half carried, half dragged me down the rest of the stairs and pushed me in front of her through the house.

"Hurry the fuck up," she snapped, her harsh Russian accent coming to the fore rather than the American drawl she usually made the effort to speak with.

I tried, but my feet tripped over each other as messages from my brain got confused between terror and panic. Darkness, the stench of fear, and then blood as Ana killed another man without breaking a sweat, her knife inserted into his chest and twisted with clinical efficiency.

A door appeared in front of us, old and heavy. I blinked in the daylight as we burst outside, then we were running across a garden, frost twinkling in the early light.

"Clear," Ana said, and she must have been speaking into a headset.

Gravel on an overgrown path bit into my feet as a missile streaked through the sky, past the spot where Emmy lay motionless, and hit the front of the house dead centre. The screams of dying men filled the air, accompanied by the chatter of automatic weapons from all directions as the Blackwood team opened up from the tree line.

Ana shoved me behind a low wall and leaned over, firing at anything that moved. I heard her counting calmly as she took men down. *One, two, three.*

I was shaking all over, and somewhere along the way, I'd lost the blanket. But my shivers didn't come from the cold. No, I trembled because Emmy had just given up her life for me. I didn't deserve it. I didn't deserve her, or Luke, or Mack, or Eli, or even Ana. Because of my stupidity, I'd lost the closest thing to a sister I'd ever had.

First Ryan, now Emmy.

And this time, it was all my fault.

"*Blyad*," Ana cursed as heat flashed over us, followed by the roar of another explosion. "What the fuck were they keeping in there?"

I didn't know.

I didn't find out either, because everything went pitch black.

Chapter 28

A HAND GRIPPED mine as I tried to work up the energy to open my eyes. I was in hospital, right? The machine that measured my pulse was beeping away, sounding far calmer than I felt. For ten minutes, maybe twenty, I'd been trying to sort out the jumbled thoughts in my head with limited success. The hotel, my prison, Ferret-Features. Then Ana, dragging me through the house. Emmy, falling to the ground, a red Rorschach spreading out on her chest.

Tell me, Tia, what do you see?

Death. I see death.

Now I knew how Emmy felt when she saw Ryan die. The utter despair of watching the inevitable without being able to do a damn thing about it.

If only I could have turned back the clock and called myself anything but Ashlyn. Because I was the one who'd landed us in this mess, wasn't I? Me and my stupid need to get back at Myrna.

But if I hadn't been in the chat room that night, I wouldn't have met Eli. Even in the darkness, he reached out to me, past Emmy, past my guilt and my regret, his face fuzzy but his fingers clear. Oh, hell. With the way I'd disappeared, he must be going out of his mind. I needed to call him. Message him. Something.

I forced my eyes open, only to find a stranger sitting next to my bed. An undeniably handsome stranger, with tousled brown hair and muscular arms, but a stranger nonetheless.

"Who are you?"

He turned to face me head on, and now I caught sight of the scars on his other cheek. No... No, it couldn't be...

"Eli?"

"It's me, sugar."

"You came. I can't believe you came."

"Being kidnapped was kinda drastic, don't you think? We both know I'd have come anyway."

I tried to sit up, but my muscles did their own thing and I flopped over sideways. Eli helped me out, and I flung my arms around him.

"I still can't believe you came."

Emotions got the better of me as I sobbed against his shoulder. What a way to meet the man I wanted to spend my life with for the first time, eh?

"I thought I'd lost you," he whispered.

"Never." I clung on tighter and blew his hair out of my mouth. "You'll never lose me." But then I thought of who I'd lost and began shuddering. "Emmy got shot."

"I heard about that."

"You met her?"

"She's one scary lady."

"But a good person. The best."

"We got on okay once she stopped pointing her gun at me."

I choked out a laugh. "She threatened to shoot you?"

"It was no joke."

"I-I-I can't believe she's gone."

"Not for long. She said she'd be back in a couple of hours."

Hold on. What? A couple of hours? Not all eternity?

"Emmy's alive?"

"Sure is."

"But she got shot. I saw her get shot."

I pulled back to look at Eli. He shrank away, on instinct it seemed, and I didn't know whether to avert my gaze or hug him or hold my ground because I didn't care about those scars he hated so much. I snuck another glance. They weren't that bad, anyway.

He swallowed hard, and this time, he didn't flinch when I looked into his dark brown eyes. Flecks of bronze ringed his irises, sparkling under the harsh strip lights. Yes, I could get lost in those deep pools.

"She's been bitching to no end about that bullet," Eli said. "Her vest took the force, but I hear it left one hell of a bruise."

A bruise? "But there was blood everywhere."

"Don't know anything about that, sugar, but I swear she was right here earlier and she sure looked sprightly."

Emmy wasn't dead. *She wasn't dead.* The vice around my chest loosened enough for me to breathe properly.

"That's what I wanted to see," Eli said. "A smile."

He gave me one of his own in return, a perfect row of white teeth, and...oh, sweet Mary Jane, he had dimples. I'd never dared to imagine his face too clearly, but he was everything I could have dreamed of and more. That grin made my heart hop, skip, and jump so hard it could have won Olympic gold.

"Where is Emmy?" I made a concerted effort to pull my wandering mind back to the task at hand. "Can I see her?"

"She had to go do paperwork. Apparently, if you blow up a house in the good state of New York and leave forty men filled with bullet holes, there are a lot of forms to fill in."

"Are we still in New York?"

"No, Richmond. She had you airlifted back."

"I don't remember that."

"You've been unconscious for two days. Seemed whoever was in that house had been stockpiling explosives, and when it went up, you got hit by falling masonry."

That explained the headache. "Two days? I'm still so tired."

"Why don't you go back to sleep? It'll help you feel better."

"Will you stay?"

He scooted his chair closer to the bed and squeezed my hand. "A herd of mustangs couldn't drag me away."

The sound of low voices woke me, and right away, I recognised one of them as Emmy's.

"Have you told her yet?"

"No." That was Eli.

"Well, you should. Might as well get it over with."

"Tell me what?" I mumbled.

"Hey, you're awake," Emmy said.

The bed dipped as she sat on the edge, and I blinked to clear my blurred vision. Why did my eyelids feel so heavy today? Oh, shit. I took in her arm, trussed up in a heavy sling at odds with the tailored suit she wore. Calvin Klein. The suit, not the sling.

"What happened to your arm? Is it broken?"

"This?" She pulled off the sling and dropped it on the bed. "Nothing's wrong. I just got Dr. Beech to put it on so the bean counters couldn't make me fill out endless forms. How's the head?"

Oh, Emmy. Welcome back.

"Sore."

"You want me to call the nurse? Get you more painkillers?"

I tried to shake my head then realised the error of my ways. "No, thank you. I still don't understand how you're even alive. I saw you bleeding."

"That was Bradley's doing. He stuck little packets of fake blood all over my bulletproof vest. It's so much more fun to get up and shoot someone when they think you're already dead."

"But what if they'd shot you in the head?"

Her expression grew serious. "Well, we wouldn't be having this conversation, would we?"

Bloody hell. She really had put her life on the line. "You're crazy. Uh, in a good way?"

"It was a calculated gamble."

"With terrible odds."

"Silas junior is a big fan of quoting scripture. Matthew, chapter five, verse thirty-eight: 'Ye have heard that it hath been said, an eye for an eye, and a tooth for a tooth.' When I killed Silas's father, I stabbed him through the heart." She nodded to herself. "Silas was always gonna go for the chest. I'm just lucky he was a decent shot."

"Why were you out there at all? I mean, why not sneak in?"

"Because that place was teeming with armed-to-the-teeth motherfuckers. One wrong move, and we'd have had all-out war, and the risk of casualties on our side was too high. We didn't have time to finesse a plan, so we opted for distraction while Ana did her thing. And judging by the way she found you, we were right not to wait."

I owed thanks to Ana too, even if the vision of Ferret-Features with that knife sticking out of his eye was sure to give me nightmares for years ahead. But none of that changed what Emmy had done.

"How could you stand there, knowing it was coming?"

"It's my job."

"I still don't understand why you do it. It's not like you need the money."

"No, I need the rush." Her voice dropped to a whisper. "It drives me."

"But—"

"And I had Black in my ear, telling me to stand fucking fast. He gives me the strength I need."

Even though I'd known Black a while now, and he'd been nothing but kind, he still scared the crap out of me. Like everyone at Riverley, I saw the Blacks' semi-private personality, where Emmy laughed and joked around and Black put up with it. But this new side? The one where she did his bidding? This was new to me and it left me cold. I shivered, and Eli squeezed my shoulder.

"You want an extra blanket, sugar?"

"Yes, please."

He got up and headed for the door, and I couldn't help watching him go. That ass. Emmy laughed when she saw where my gaze was directed.

"How did the house get blown up?" I asked in an attempt to change the subject. "Did I see a missile?"

"Ah, yes. We brought it back from Russia, and Black's been dying to try it out." She sighed. "Good to know General Zacharov served some useful purpose."

"Will you get into trouble after this?"

"Hell, no. That secondary explosion? They had a whole bunch of goodies in the cellar. Fuck only knows what they planned to do with them. We've done some negotiation, and the whole thing's been written off as an accident. Just some poor, dumb extremist schmuck getting his wires crossed."

"How did you find me?"

"Cade was in the control room the morning after you got abducted, and when he saw your phone signal coming from the Quality Inn, he tried to call to tell you the place was bad news. When you didn't answer, he phoned me, and we went to find you."

Seemed like I owed Cade a debt of gratitude too.

"I'm sorry you missed your meeting."

"I'm not. Meetings are boring."

"And Eli? How did he get here?"

"He drove through the night and made it to the hotel just before we did." Emmy stroked my hair back from my forehead. "He's the real deal, honey. You're lucky you found him."

"What were you saying about him needing to tell me something?"

"Eli's got a few secrets."

I stiffened. Secrets? I hated secrets. At least, when

they weren't mine, I hated secrets. "Are they bad?"

"Not my place to tell. Just remember, keep an open mind. Everyone makes mistakes. You, me, everyone. It's what you learn from those mistakes that matters."

"I'll remember that. I promise."

"And like I said, Eli's good for you. Believe me, if I thought he wasn't, he'd be back in West Virginia by now."

Oh, I did believe her. "I know that."

"Nick knew him already, by the way. He's worked for Eli in the past."

"Nick worked for Eli?"

Emmy just smiled. "I'll see you later. Be good, and don't eat all the chocolates Bradley brought or you'll be sick."

"Wait, what?"

She picked up the sling and sauntered out, leaving me grinding my teeth in frustration. Sometimes, I didn't like her very much.

How had Nick worked for Eli? Nick headed up the executive protection division, bodyguards. Why did Eli need a bodyguard?

"I got your blanket and an extra pillow, just in case," Eli said, smiling as he came back in.

I pointed at the chair. "Okay, pal. Time to spill."

Chapter 29

OH, HELL. WHAT had Emmy said to Tia?

Eli spread the blanket over her and adjusted her pillows, playing for time before he made his confession. Would she want to know him afterwards?

Finally, he took a seat, his mouth suddenly dry.

"There are a couple of things I need to tell you."

Tia smiled, and he couldn't resist reaching a finger out to trace her lips, maybe for the last time.

"You might not like me so much when I'm done."

"I'm not sure that's possible."

Best to get the worst over with first. "I told you about my accident."

Eli brought his hand up to trace the scars without thinking then forced it back into his lap when he realised.

"Yes."

"I was the one driving that night, and I'd been drinking." He buried his head in his hands. "I don't even remember what happened. We were laughing, then a tree..." A tear rolled down his cheek, and he swiped at it, embarrassed. "It was my fault. I shouldn't have got behind the wheel."

He waited for the shock. The disgust. The anger. All valid reactions he'd seen over the years.

"But it was still an accident, right? It wasn't like you

meant to hurt your girlfriend."

"Of course not! I-I-I loved her."

"Do you still drink and drive?"

"I don't drink at all."

A pause. A long pause. Eli closed his eyes, waiting for the inevitable rejection.

"Then it's in the past."

What? He looked at Tia and saw her smiling.

"You're not upset?"

"I'm sorry it happened, for both of you. But you shouldn't have to spend forever paying for your mistakes."

"That wasn't quite the reaction I expected."

But it was better than he could ever have hoped for.

"I've spent the last year living with Emmy, and if nothing else, it's taught me to see things from a different perspective. That I shouldn't be so quick to judge people. Every story has two sides."

The worst of the tension that had been building inside Eli since that memorable day on SpeedChat seeped away. Tia knew his darkest secret, and she still wanted him. And as for his scars? She barely seemed to look at them.

He bent to hug her, gently as she was still covered in bruises. "You've just made me the happiest man alive."

"Uh, what's the other thing?"

"Other thing?" Eli couldn't think straight.

"Secrets, plural?"

Oh. He gave a nervous cough. "I used to be a singer."

"You still are a singer. Your voice is amazing."

"I mean a professional singer. A band, touring, the

whole works."

"Which band?"

"Red Alert."

Her eyes widened. "I knew I'd heard your voice somewhere!" Another pause as the wheels turned. "You're...uh, you must be Red Bennett?"

"I'm Elijah Bennett."

"I used to listen to your songs."

She hummed a few bars of one of the band's old hits, and Eli laughed.

"All in the past."

"You just disappeared. Was that because of the accident?"

He nodded. "Our manager wanted to replace me, but the other guys vetoed that idea. We'd all had enough."

"Fame wasn't everything it's cracked up to be?"

"The first year was okay, but the novelty soon wore off. We didn't know each other before the record company put us together, and we had nothing in common. Nothing. Imagine spending every hour of every day away from home with a bunch of virtual strangers."

"When you put it like that... Do you see any of them anymore?"

No, never. His bandmates had abandoned him in favour of their own ambitions. One had a solo career now, and while he hadn't exactly set the world alight, his songs still popped up on the radio. The other two? Eli didn't know and he didn't much care. In fact, the only contact he'd had with anyone from his past came less than a week ago, when he'd dug the Ghost's email address out from the depths of his computer and written a long and rambling message begging the man to play a song for Tia at the fashion show. Something with the word sugar in the title. A single line had come back from his old acquaintance: *I'll do it.* But Tia didn't need to know all of those details.

"No, we don't keep in touch. My girlfriend—Delia— was one of our backup dancers, and she was the only thing that kept me sane in that world."

"I'm so sorry you lost her."

"And I'm sorry you lost your boyfriend."

Eli brought Tia's hand to his lips, kissing her knuckles, and she used that same hand to tug him closer. Their eyes met and copper flecks sparkled in hers, dancing fire that matched her spirit. In the flesh, she was even more beautiful than Eli had imagined. She leaned up, closing the distance until her lips met his. Nerves suddenly hit him. How long had it been since he'd been this close to a woman? Stripped of fame, the only thing he had to offer was himself, and he was terrified she'd find him wanting.

But she nibbled his bottom lip, and he couldn't help but yield. Seemed like that frantic trip from West Virginia had landed him up in heaven.

That little sigh she gave made his cock twitch, and he threw a mental bucket of water over himself. *Take things slow, Eli.*

He tangled his fingers in her hair, just as he'd always longed to do, silken strands that still smelled of vanilla even after all she'd been through. Or maybe that was just her.

A cough at the door made them both turn their heads guiltily, and the doctor smiled as they sprang apart.

"Good to see you're feeling better, Tia."

She glanced at Eli and smiled. "Yes, much better. Can I go home?"

"Not yet, I'm afraid. You've had a nasty head injury, and we need to keep you in at least one more night for observation."

"But I feel fine. Better than fine."

"Can you imagine the grief Mrs. Black would give me if I sent you home early?"

Tia sagged back against the pillow and huffed. Clearly, she could.

"I just need to take a blood sample and check on your stitches," the doctor continued.

"What stitches?"

Dr. Beech, according to his badge, tapped his forehead, and Tia reached up to her own, feeling the white bandage taped over it. Seemed she hadn't noticed that before.

"Ouch. How many?"

"Sixteen. I'll change the dressing and put on some antibiotic ointment. We'll try to keep the scarring to a minimum."

As he spoke, he glanced at Eli, who resisted the urge to turn away as his heart thumped against his ribcage.

Tia had offered him a new chance at love, and he needed to learn to cope with those looks because they'd never stop. No more hiding away on the ranch. No more wasting his life. He concentrated on his breathing as the doctor did his job, in and out on a mantra.

New love. New life. New love. New life.

"What now?" Tia asked when Dr. Beech had left.

"It'll heal," Eli said, more to himself than to Tia.

"Even if it doesn't, you'll always be beautiful."

"Don't think of it as a scar. Think of it as a story. Our story, and it's just the beginning." She shrugged, nonchalant. "But that wasn't what I was talking about. Where are you staying?"

Eli pointed to the cot at the foot of the bed. Emmy had got one of the orderlies to bring it in that first night at the hospital when he'd refused to leave. *A story.* Chapter one of Tia and Eli, and he couldn't wait to write the whole book.

"You've been here the whole time?" she asked.

"I only just found you. I wasn't going to leave you."

A tear trickled down Tia's cheek, and he reached out to wipe it away. "Don't cry."

"It's okay. It's a happy tear."

He pressed a kiss to her forehead, carefully avoiding her wound. "Then cry away."

She pulled him onto the bed next to her, and he wrapped her up in his arms. Right where she belonged.

"But seriously," she said. "What now? Are you going back to West Virginia?"

"Not if you'll have me here."

"I'll have you anywhere."

"I could rent a house near yours. I've still got money."

"Or you could stay at Riverley, for now at least."

"What's Riverley?"

"Emmy's house. Well, estate."

"I can't just invite myself to stay in somebody else's home."

"She won't mind, honestly. Everyone else stays there. It's got, like, thirty bedrooms over two houses—she probably won't even notice."

"I'm still not sure..."

The thought of moving in with strangers made his stomach clench, like the fist of his past had closed over it and squeezed.

"Please? If I ask her and she tells you it's okay?"

How could Eli turn Tia down? He'd sleep in his car if it meant staying close to her, and the Porsche had really tiny seats.

"All right, sugar. I'll stay."

CHAPTER 30

"YOU DRIVE A Porsche?" I asked, stopping short as Eli bleeped his car open. He'd even managed to get a parking spot right outside the front door of the hospital.

"A leftover from my previous life."

He opened the passenger door and helped me inside, always the gentleman, and I shivered as his hand brushed against my waist. He may have called me sugar, but he was definitely the sweeter one.

For all my bluster about Riverley's open-door policy, I'd still been nervous yesterday when I asked Emmy if we could stay. After all, I'd left under a dark cloud and barely set foot on the estate since.

But she'd only grinned. "You want the good news or the bad news?"

"The bad news first."

"Well, they're kind of the same. Bradley's redone your room. Whether it's good news or bad news depends on how much you like bronze."

"Bronze?"

"He heard about Eli and decided you needed something more manly. I got him to move the plastified hamster into the gallery. You can thank me later."

"The what?"

"Professor Ito sent it as a gift. It came in a little

display case and everything. Ishmael sent you dresses, and they're in the wardrobe."

"I need to thank him. And apologise for disappearing."

"Don't worry—he understands. At least you waited until after the show to get kidnapped again."

There had been a small glitch shortly after that when my brother turned up at my bedside. It seemed he'd been busy in the time I was unconscious. After practically ignoring Eli, Luke had perched on the side of the bed the instant Eli left the room to fetch me a drink.

"Tia, tell me you don't plan to keep seeing that guy."

"He's coming to stay with me at Riverley."

"You're not staying at the apartment with Mack and me?"

"Emmy and I cleared the air."

Luke blew out a breath. "Fine. But Eli Bennett isn't going with you."

"Yes, he is. It's already agreed."

"Over my dead body."

Emmy and Dan walked in behind Luke, and I breathed a sigh of relief. Reinforcements had arrived.

"That can be arranged," Emmy said. "What's the problem?"

"My sister wants to shack up with a guy who spends his evenings talking to fourteen-year-old girls in an online chat room. I looked through his transcripts."

Eli came back right at that moment. "That's my sister and her friends. I only joined to keep an eye on how many weirdos are on there. She's at the stage where she wants to hide everything from me and our parents."

"Is nothing bloody sacred?" I asked Luke.

"I worry about you."

"As do I," Emmy said. "And believe me, my background checks were more comprehensive."

"Emmy! Perhaps I should move back to New York to get some privacy. With Eli."

Eli wrapped an arm around my waist and faced up to them, even though I could feel him shaking.

"I care about Tia very much, and I'd never do anything to hurt her. Sugar, I don't mind them checking my background. I've got nothing to hide anymore, and it only means they care."

Luke deflated a bit, and Emmy smiled. "See? We're all good. I'll get things ready at Riverley."

So, now we were on our way to the Riverley estate, and Eli gave me a shaky smile as he started the engine. This was a huge step for him. He'd told me more about his parents and his strained relationship with them, a relationship that had become almost unbearable after Delia died.

"You okay?" I asked him.

"Scared as hell."

His hand came up to his face in an unconscious gesture, and I gently pulled it away.

"Nobody'll care about that."

"It's weird. My whole singing career, I got taught that my looks mattered as much as my voice, and my manager said the only way people would buy my records with me looking like this was out of sympathy. I didn't want sympathy."

"Well, I think you're hot." The way his eyes cut in my direction and held for a beat too long told me he thought I was fibbing, but I knew the truth. "You light me up from the inside out, you and your filthy mouth."

And filthy hands, I hoped. My eyes closed of their own accord as I imagined those long, slender fingers trailing over my bare skin. This time, my mind had skipped the gutter and headed straight for a storm drain.

Good grief.

But I needn't have worried, because Eli was right alongside me in the rushing water, doing the breast stroke.

"Don't know what I did to deserve you."

"I do. You're the kindest man I've ever met, Eli Bennett."

"Hope you taste as sweet as you look, sugar."

Freaking heck! I was saved from doing something stupidly un-PG in the car park by a slightly dented Ford Taurus that pulled up two inches from the Porsche's bonnet, the driver motioning to ask if we were vacating the space.

"Guess we'd better get going," Eli said.

I twined his fingers through mine and brought them to my lips. "Guess we better had."

Back at Little Riverley, Emmy's modern home that stood next to her husband's gothic mansion, Bradley rushed out to meet us, arms wide.

"You're back! I can't believe everything that happened. I mean, the show was wonderful, but then you got kidnapped and Emmy blew everything up again."

Emmy appeared behind him. "Not guilty. I didn't blow anything up."

"You. Black. Same difference. You're joined at the hip."

"Not the hip, Bradley."

"Ugh!" He flicked non-existent hair. "I don't even want to think about that." He took my hand and pulled me towards the steps. "Come look at your room. I didn't know whether you'd want to share with your new man yet so I redecorated the one next door too. Like a joint theme."

Eli smiled, but his eyes said *what the hell have I got into?*

"It's okay," I whispered. "He's always like this."

When we got up to my old room, I barely recognised it. Bradley had stripped everything out and started from scratch. I almost choked when I saw my new bath—a twin of the one in New York. That wasn't lost on Eli either.

"Reckon I should FaceTime you later," he whispered as Bradley explained the settings in my new shower.

"What, from three feet away?"

"That far?"

Oh, I needed to get rid of Bradley right now. "You know what it needs?" I asked him.

"What?"

"Room fragrance. White linen, perhaps?"

He snapped his fingers. "You're absolutely right. I'll get on it."

I kicked the door shut behind him and backed Eli

over to the bed. He grabbed my waist, and we both tumbled onto the shiny bronze quilt.

"I've got you right where I want you, Mr. Bennett. Red. Where did you get that nickname, anyway? I always figured Red Bennett would have ginger hair."

"You didn't know what I looked like?"

"I liked listening to your songs, but I was never into the whole groupie thing. The posters on my bedroom wall at that age were all horses. So, Red?"

"I was the only one in the band from a Southern state. The other guys called me redneck as a joke, and it stuck."

"And you used it on the internet? WellRed?"

"A play on words. My sister never realised."

"Well, you'll always be Eli to me."

"I'm having a hard time thinking of you as Tia."

My cheeks heated. "Sorry about that."

"Doesn't matter. You'll always be my sugar."

His. I liked the sound of that. No, I loved it. I bent forwards to kiss him, and as our lips met, I got my first proper feel of his cock, hardening against my stomach. Pleasure rushed through me, but when he rolled us so I was underneath him, fear overrode everything as I went back to my prison. Darkness closed in as the weight of Ferret-Features pressed down on me, and I gasped for breath.

"Off. Get off. Please."

Eli sprang back, eyes the size of dinner plates. "What's wrong? What did I do?"

"Nothing. It's... It's just a memory came back. Of being in that house right before Ana rescued me." I scrambled onto unsteady feet and rested my head against his chest. "When I felt you on top of me..."

"If that man wasn't already dead, I swear I'd kill him myself."

"I love you." Shit! The words just popped out. I clapped a hand over my mouth as Eli stared at me. "Oops. Too soon?"

His head dipped as he chuckled, and when it came back up, he smiled. "I love a woman who doesn't get all cryptic, so I guess that means I love you too, sugar."

A little squeak escaped as I buried my face in his shoulder.

"And I'll tell you something else," he continued. "We'll take this as slow as you need to feel comfortable. We've got the future ahead of us. There's no rush."

"Thank you."

"You hungry, sugar? One thing I really want to do with you is cook in the same kitchen."

"I can't actually cook."

"Then you can watch while I make us dinner."

Downstairs in the kitchen, Eli sang softly as he cut chicken into strips and chopped peppers and onions. Tonight, I didn't need wine. With Eli teetotal, I really should try to cut back, although I did have to thank alcohol for bringing us together in the first place.

"What are you making?" I asked.

"Fajitas. On one tour, we had a Mexican chef, and he showed me how to get the spices right."

"No habaneros, okay?"

Eli put the knife down and gave me a quick kiss. "No habaneros."

Unsurprisingly, the meal tasted delicious. We ate together in the dining room, which rarely got used as everyone tended to congregate in the kitchen. I'd never found a ladylike way to eat fajitas, but with Eli, it didn't matter. We could laugh as well as love.

Then he discovered the music room and played soppy songs on the piano with me squashed on the stool next to him until I fell asleep and keeled off sideways.

Oh my gosh. Embarrassment didn't even begin to cover it.

But Eli only grinned. "Time for bed, sugar."

And time to broach the big question.

"Which bed?"

"I'll sleep in the room next to yours. Taking things slow, remember?"

I did, but my body wasn't entirely happy with that decision as I crawled under the quilt alone.

Sweat dripped off me as I woke in the early hours, and I sat bolt upright in bed, screwing my eyes shut in an attempt to block the vision of Ferret. I kind of wished I hadn't eaten so many fajitas because now I felt quite sick.

I stumbled to the bathroom and brushed my teeth, but even the minty fresh toothpaste couldn't take the bad taste in my mouth away. In the bedroom, I stared at my twisted sheets, at the dampness caused by perspiration and tears. No, I didn't want to get back into bed. Not mine, anyway.

I wanted Eli.

Screw slow.

The lights were on in the hallway as I slipped out of my bedroom door. I paused. Should I go back and change into something...I don't know...slinkier? I mean, Wonder Woman pyjamas hardly screamed sexy, did they?

Eli never seemed bothered by what I wore, but even so...

I never finished the thought. Emmy walked around the corner, except it wasn't Emmy. Her eyes were open and vacant, and as she took another step forwards, I noticed the glint in her hand. Shit! She had a knife.

I'd heard about her sleepwalking, and I'd also heard about the damage she'd done in the process. But until now, I'd never seen it for myself.

"Emmy?"

Nothing.

"Emmy, wake up!"

She never blinked, just took another step towards me. At least she was past Eli's room now.

I backed away, almost tripping over my own feet. Where was her husband? Oh, that's right, New York. She'd mentioned it earlier. I turned and ran along the corridor, racking my brains. Who else was in the house? I recalled the sound of a car earlier, the loud rumble of a Dodge Viper. Not Emmy's. Ana's. Was she still here?

I skidded to a halt in front of her door and knocked. Simply walking in would be suicide.

"Who is it?"

Oh, thank goodness. "Tia. Emmy's sleepwalking and she's got a knife."

The door opened a second later, and Ana stepped out, dressed in black sportswear. Did she ever go off-duty?

No, it seemed, because after a brief scuffle—quick precise, and lethally efficient—Emmy's knife dropped to the floor and Ana slapped her hard.

"*Prosnees!*"

Presumably, that meant "wake up" in Russian. I winced at the sound, but Emmy blinked a couple of times then sagged back against Ana, both of them sitting on the thick carpet.

"What did I do?"

"Scared Tia. Nothing else."

"Shit." She looked up at me. "I'm sorry."

"The nightmares are back?" I asked.

"They rarely leave nowadays."

And I'd only added to them. The first kidnapping had been bad enough, but now I'd seen firsthand the death and destruction she lived with on a daily basis, I understood a tiny bit about what must go through her head at night. I only wished I could help.

"Can I get you anything? A cup of tea?"

"Handcuffs."

Ana hoisted Emmy to her feet. "I'll take care of her."

"Uh..." My tongue felt all fat. "I need to thank you. For...you know...and now again."

Before I could think the better of it, I wrapped my arms around Ana, and she hugged me back, a little awkwardly, a little stiffly, but still a hug.

"It's my job."

Exactly what Emmy always said.

"I'm glad you're here."

She broke into a smile, just for a second. "And I'm glad to be here. Now, go and finish sneaking into your boyfriend's room. That's what you were doing, no?"

"Uh, yeah. Thanks again."

I scuttled off before she could guess any more of my

secrets and tiptoed into Eli's room.

"Sugar?"

I didn't bother to answer, just lifted his quilt and crawled underneath it.

"Sugar, are you okay?"

"Please, just cuddle me."

"With pleasure."

CHAPTER 31

THE NEXT MORNING, I cracked an eyelid open and found myself draped over a golden chest with a smattering of brown hair. Eli.

That was it. I was staying in bed for the entire day.

Eli stirred as I snuggled against him, and I couldn't help smiling as he kissed my hair.

"Comfortable?" he asked.

"I'm never moving again."

My stomach chose that moment to let out a massive grumble, and Eli chuckled.

"Want me to get up and make you some breakfast?"

Yes, this man put me first. He'd always put me first. And while I still missed Ryan like crazy, every day the ache in my chest got a little fainter as love filled me up from the outside in.

Sure, Eli and I still had to work out plans for the future, but the important thing was that we had a future. Maybe we'd get our own place one day. Perhaps I'd get another job. Who knew? But whatever we did, we'd do it together.

"I guess we should eat something."

"What do y'all want?" He let his drawl come to the fore. "Fashionista's breakfast—chopped fruit and low-fat yogurt? Danish pastries? Full English? Pancakes? Or do you want me to get all Southern with grits and biscuits?"

"I never really got the whole biscuits thing. I mean, you serve them with gravy? In England, we call them scones and eat them for afternoon tea with strawberry jam and clotted cream."

"And your biscuits are cookies, right?"

"Yes. And our cookies are biscuits that come with chocolate chips or occasionally raisins. Don't even get me started on the whole crisps versus chips versus French fries thing."

"I'll do jacket potatoes for dinner."

Eli sat up, lifting me with him, and as the quilt fell down, I got a better look at the body I'd only ever seen in shadows. Whatever he did on that ranch, he needed to keep doing it, because hot damn...

His whispered, "Beautiful," snapped me out of my daze, and I found him looking at me in the same way. I twisted around to stare at both of us in the mirror at the end of his bed, smiling wider than I thought possible at the picture we made. Scars or no scars, Eli was undeniably handsome.

"Been a long while since I looked at myself in the mirror," he murmured. "I threw all of mine out."

I pulled his arms around my shoulders. "You look good on me. Perfect."

"You're the perfect one. And I'm making you pancakes."

I lingered for a few seconds to watch Eli's arse as he headed for his bathroom then scuttled back next door. Even that small distance was too far, but I comforted myself with the thought that it was only temporary—he'd be sleeping in my room tonight.

Down in the kitchen, Eli ended up cooking

pancakes for a subdued Emmy and a back-to-her-usual-icy-self Ana too. Mrs. Fairfax, Emmy's housekeeper, watched him work for five minutes then declared the kitchen was his for the morning.

"You'll be having my job next," she chuckled as she headed for the laundry room.

"Do you have plans today?" Emmy asked.

Besides going back to bed? "Uh, I thought I'd give Eli a tour of the estate."

Out of the window, I spotted Dustin, Emmy's groom, walking across the pasture with Lucy and Kitty in tow. Only Emmy would have a pet Doberman whose best friend was a jaguar.

"Why don't we do that on horseback?" I suggested.

After all, Eli was part cowboy.

"If you're riding, you're on Dustin's mare," Emmy said. "No way are you going near Stan when you're getting over a head injury."

"What's wrong with Stan?" Eli asked. "That short for Stanley? I have an uncle named Stanley."

"No, it's short for Satan. Stan's a Spanish stallion with the soul of a rodeo pony." Emmy smiled sweetly. "But if you enjoy a challenge, you're welcome to borrow him."

Eli tipped an imaginary hat. "I'll take you up on that offer. My old pony spent half her life trying to dump me into the dirt. Kind of miss her."

"Just don't fall off. We've all spent enough time at the hospital this week."

"Don't you worry about me, ma'am."

I didn't know whether to laugh or gasp when Stan took off across the field beside the stables with Eli hanging onto his mane. That horse sure was living up to his namesake this morning. After one fast circuit and too many handstands to count, Eli finally circled him back. At least he was laughing. That meant I could too.

"Emmy wasn't kidding," he said

"Nope. But now he's tested you out, he'll settle. Fancy a ride through the woods?"

"Why not?"

Because Dustin had bought his mare a new saddle, that was why not. Some elaborate western job with a high pommel that rubbed me *right there* every time she took a step. By the time I slithered off back at the barn, having listened to Eli's honeyed tones for almost two hours, I had to clench my thighs together to stop from coming on the spot.

"You okay, sugar?"

"No, I'm not okay. I'm horny as hell and your voice is driving me crazy."

Shit. All that lust had broken my brain-to-mouth filter again.

"Give me one minute."

Eli turfed the horses out into their respective paddocks, put their saddles and bridles away, then returned, wrapping his arms around my waist as he backed me into the hay store next to Stan's stable.

"It's getting hot in here," he muttered.

"Oh, that's the central heating in Stan's stable."

"Are you shitting me? The horse has heating?"

"Bradley."

I didn't need to say more than that. Eli had known Bradley for less than a week, and he already understood him, as evidenced by his eye-roll.

But his face straightened again as he leaned in to kiss me, slipping his hands first inside my jacket then under my jumper too. His thumbs grazed my nipples, and I shuddered against him.

"Fancy a roll in the hay, Mr. Bennett?"

He pressed his hips against mine, and the feel of his hard cock against me did nothing to cool my raging hormones.

"Might be a little prickly, Miss Cain."

"I don't care."

"What happened to taking things slow?"

"My body didn't read the memo."

I reached down and palmed his cock through his jeans, and he let out a low groan.

"You want to go back to bed?" he whispered.

I nodded, throat thick with... Lust? Nerves? Love? All of the above?

We practically ran for Little Riverley, and luckily, nobody saw our mad dash up the stairs. I was tearing at Eli's top before we got my bedroom door shut. If I'd got hot and bothered during our video calls, now I was about to detonate.

I threw my jumper across the room and almost fell over trying to get out of my jodhpurs. Eli shucked his jeans then hesitated when it came to his boxers.

I paused, hand on my bra catch. "What is it? What's wrong?"

"Are you sure this is a good idea?"

"Uh, yes?" I plopped onto the end of the bed. "Why? Aren't you?"

"It's been a long time since I was with a woman," he whispered.

I ran my hands down his arms and wrapped them around my waist. Then I had a rethink and repositioned his hands on my ass. Better.

"Red, you can give me an orgasm with your voice alone. Having your fingers and your cock in the mix is an added bonus."

I shoved him down onto the bed and straddled him. The Ferret incident still lurked at the back of my mind, but Eli knew that, and he made no attempt to switch places. I ground against his erection, hitting the sweet spot before I leaned forward to kiss him. Oh, I wanted to touch him, lick him, ride him, suck him—call me a kid in a candy store—but I couldn't do it all at once.

"Shit!" Eli bit out, turning his head to the side.

"What?"

"I don't have protection. I mean, this was the last place I thought I'd end up when I left home."

"Nightstand. Top drawer. Bradley stocks every bedroom in this house."

Eli rolled over and pulled out a handful of condoms. "Pick your flavour, sugar."

I grabbed the nearest one and tore into it with my teeth. Synthetic strawberry. Yum. Sod the foreplay—we could do that later. I just wanted to get acquainted with what he kept in his underwear. A touch of giddiness came over me when he pushed his boxers to his knees and flexed his hips, probably because all my blood rushed south. I felt it pulsing through my pussy, dancing to Eli's tune.

He gripped my hands as I eased down onto him, relishing the fullness as the evidence of what he did to me dripped onto his thighs. Oops. Sorry, not sorry.

"I won't hold out for long, sugar."

"Doesn't matter. I won't either, so we'll just have to go again."

Oh, the hardship.

From one kind of riding to another, and I had a new favourite position. My orgasm tingled from my fingers to my toes, followed by a rush of heat as Eli came too. I collapsed over him, and he peppered every inch of me he could reach with kisses.

"I love you," I mumbled into his neck.

"Love you too, sugar."

"Sing me a song."

"A song? Okay, I know the perfect one."

As I lay by his side, one leg draped over him and our arms around each other, he sang me Etta James again, "I just want to make love to you."

Yes, he was right about the "perfect" part.

Chapter 32

IN THE MORNING, Emmy and Eli both offered to drive me to the hospital to have my stitches taken out.

"I'm going anyway," Emmy said.

"Why?"

"You're not the only one who got hit by flying shrapnel."

She rolled up her sleeve to reveal a cut on her forearm, not as long as mine, but it still had at least half a dozen stitches.

"You did that rescuing me?"

"Occupational hazard. I need to get the stitches taken out then have a quick consult with my plastic surgeon."

"You have a plastic surgeon?"

"If I didn't, I'd look like Freddy Krueger by now. I've had that many scrapes over the years."

Eli's hand tightened around mine.

"Do you think I could talk to your surgeon?" he asked.

"You want to get your face done?"

"I've never really thought about having it smoothed out before. But now..." He glanced at me. "Is your surgeon good?"

"My surgeon could make Jabba the Hutt look like Brad Pitt." Emmy stepped closer, eyes fixed on Eli's.

Eyes that saw too much. "You wanted to stay like that, didn't you? You thought you deserved it."

His expression said she'd hit the nail on the head.

"I'll make you an appointment, yeah?"

He swallowed hard and nodded.

Moving on. We were moving on. Perhaps I could get the surgeon to fix up my forehead too? Did he offer a bulk discount?

When we got to the hospital, it turned out that the surgeon could fit Eli in for a consultation right away, and better still, he thought there was a good chance of removing the scars, or at least improving them significantly. Not that I cared what Eli looked like, but I wanted him to feel confident facing the world again.

Today was a good day.

Or so I thought until we got out to the car park and found Emmy pacing in front of the Porsche Cayenne she'd borrowed from Black, scowling as she held her phone to her ear.

"No, no, no, no, no. No party... Not even a small one... I do not need to lighten up... Look, James is coming over tonight... No, he doesn't need to chill out either."

She jabbed at the phone and threw it onto the car seat. It bounced off, landed on the asphalt, and the screen broke.

"Fuck it."

"What's up?"

"Bradley's throwing a party this evening. The little shit waited until he knew I'd be out for a couple of hours to move the heavy artillery in."

"What's the occasion?"

"Ishmael's show was a success. You escaped from a

bunch of armed extremists. Eli's moved in. It's Thursday. Take your pick."

"I love Bradley's parties."

"Good grief."

Eli spoke up. "I haven't been to a party for years."

"Then you're in for a treat," I said, squealing a little by accident.

Emmy climbed into the driver's seat with the reluctance of a condemned woman. "A treat. Right."

"How bad can a party be?" Eli asked.

"On a scale of zero to Nagasaki, we're talking Hiroshima."

Music was already belting out of the Riverley Hall when we got back. I heard it halfway down the driveway, even with the car windows closed. It wasn't as good as the Ghost's efforts, but it more than made up for it in volume.

Eli's earlier laissez-faire attitude had disappeared, replaced with a lip chewed ragged by the time Emmy parked the car.

"How am I going to get through this?" he asked.

Emmy turned in her seat. "Remember, most people have scars. They just wear them on the inside."

Wasn't that the truth?

I took Eli's hand, and he hung on in a death grip as I led him into the madhouse. Until now, we'd stayed on Emmy's part of the estate, and Eli did a double-take at the suits of armour flanking the front door of the older mansion. And choked out a laugh when Ishmael and Bradley ran up wearing matching rainbow-coloured tutus.

"You're okay!" Ishmael squeaked, wiping a tear from his eye. "You had us all worried."

"Uh, I think so."

"And this is your new man?" I didn't get a chance to answer before Ishmael grabbed Eli's free hand, kissing it before stepping back to appraise him critically. "The country look. Not bad, but you'd be hotter with a man-bun. Are those boots genuinely worn or did you pay extra for the scuff marks?"

Eli gave a strangled cough, and I had to unpeel his fingers from mine because my circulation was in danger of being cut off.

"Yes, this is Eli. He's a proper cowboy, and I like his hair the way it is."

"I suppose with that body he can get away with anything." Ishmael gave Eli's biceps a reverent squeeze. "I brought presents for everyone. Look!"

I looked. Believe me, I looked. Lottie and Nigel hopped past on pogo sticks while Jed and Quinn tried to out-hula each other. Even my brother had glitter in his hair. Oh shit—was that Dan attempting to pole dance?

I stopped to watch, along with half the men in the room. Did that bikini even count as clothing? It barely held anything in, but as she leapt into a spin, I had to concede she'd got the moves.

At least, until she spun down the pole and landed on her ass.

"Is it always like this?" Eli whispered.

"Pretty much. Yes. It's easiest just to go with it."

"It makes my old world look almost normal."

Half a dozen guys sprang forward to help Dan up,

and she teetered over to us on a pair of perspex wedges.

"What's with the slutty stripper shoes?" I asked her. Bradley would have a heart attack.

She accepted a cocktail from a waitress on roller skates and shrugged. "I found them in Emmy's wardrobe."

I looked around and saw Emmy turn pink. Black was standing behind her by then, one arm around her waist, and his lips curved up in a barely there smirk. A rare display of emotion from him.

Yes, there was totally a pole hidden away somewhere in this house.

Emmy quickly changed the subject, grabbing Bradley by the arm as he tried to hurry past.

"What's with all the manga waitresses?"

"They were Kamiko's idea. She's into cosplay."

"Dare I ask who Kamiko is?"

"Professor Ito's daughter. She's going to be Ishmael's new assistant."

Ishmael materialised beside Bradley. "I needed someone after Myrna left us, but if you want to come back too, I'll always have a job for you."

"I loved working for you, really I did, but I'm moving back to Virginia. I need to be near my family."

Ishmael nodded sagely. "I thought as much. Maybe you could visit for the shows?"

I stepped forward and hugged him. "I'll definitely do that."

"So, where are all the half-naked men?" Dan asked. "I hoped you'd have them giving out more goody bags."

"Most of the men are here," Emmy said. "Perhaps after a few drinks..."

"No way," Nick said. "We're keeping our clothes on

tonight."

He'd appeared with a guy I didn't recognise in tow. Hot, but slightly grumpy looking. Dan didn't miss the arrival of the newcomer either.

She tossed her hair, put a hand on one hip and asked, "Who's this?"

"Ignacio's brother, Cristiano. Ignacio couldn't make it. Apparently, he's not allowed out after the Sharpie-phone-number incident."

Dan glanced down at Cristiano's left hand. No ring. Her eyes took on a predatory gleam.

"You haven't been here before, right? Let me show you around."

Dan stroked his arm, and he gave her a good look up and down before smiling.

"It certainly looks interesting."

Dan's nipples went pointy at the sound of his voice. Husky Italian, very hot.

"Oh, it is. You can't leave without seeing Emmy's car collection."

"Don't you dare," Emmy said. "Last time you 'showed someone my car collection,' you dented the bonnet on the Viper."

"It wasn't my fault. The alarm went off and nearly gave us a heart attack."

Emmy's eyes narrowed.

"Okay, okay. Cristiano, let me show you the boathouse. It's spectacular at this time of night."

They walked off arm in arm, and I had the feeling it would be the start of a beautiful, but brief, friendship.

The party got wilder, with the waiters serving pretzels out of tambourines and carrying guitar-shaped cookies on cymbals, but Eli relaxed beside me as he realised people were treating him like a person and not a freak show or an ex-boy band star. And yes, when Bradley set up a karaoke kit in the middle of the night, Eli climbed onto the makeshift stage and belted out songs with everyone else. The only difference was, when he sang, every head in the room turned to listen.

Including one of the roller-skating waitresses, unfortunately. She got distracted and rolled right into a table of cupcakes, ending up a little multicoloured. Slater, another of the Blackwood boys, helped her to her feet and offered to lick it off. She swooned into his arms, and he wheeled her carefully out of the room.

Even Cade turned up. That had the potential to be awkward, especially when he beckoned me into an empty room.

"Do you mind if I go?" I asked Eli. Uncomfortable or not, I needed to thank Cade for his part in my rescue. "Will you be okay?"

Eli swallowed, his Adam's apple bobbing. "I'll be fine."

Really? Then why was his voice shaking? "Don't worry, I'll stay. I can speak to Cade another day."

Eli tugged his hand away from mine. "Sugar, I'll be fine. I have to learn to deal with this."

Those bottomless eyes shone with determination, and I realised I had to let him tackle a demon or two.

"I won't be long. Promise."

"Not going anywhere."

I scurried off behind Cade, catching up as he held the door to the music room open for me.

"I need to apologise," he said once we got inside.

"Why?"

"For being angry when, you know..."

"It doesn't matter. It wasn't a good time for either of us."

"But if I hadn't reacted like that, maybe you wouldn't have sent me away and you wouldn't have been taken."

Aw, hell. He sounded freaking devastated.

"It wouldn't have made a difference. Having a bodyguard around all the time made me feel suffocated. I'd already had a heart-to-heart with Emmy and told her I wanted to travel to and from work alone. I'd have done that however things were between us."

"Really?"

"Really."

His shoulders dropped a notch. "Can we stay friends?"

"I'd like that."

By the time I got back to the ballroom, Emmy and Black had disappeared, and Bradley had found a video of Red Alert.

"Eli." The microphone went flying in his direction. "Time to sing again."

I was ready to make an excuse and get us out of there, but Eli surprised me by shrugging.

"You're okay with this?" I whispered.

"These folks are growing on me."

Thank goodness. I could hardly contain my smile, because this crazy bunch was my family and, I hoped that one day Eli would be too.

And right now, he hopped up on stage beside Bradley and blessed our ears with his superstar singing voice. At least, until Bradley cued up another clip, this time with Eli in a pair of super-dodgy dungarees.

"Think it's time we called it a night, sugar." He

dropped the mic, grabbed my hand, and led me towards the door. "I never want to see those outfits again."

"Aw, the pink shirts were cute."

"We nearly quit the day the stylist brought those in."

"Well, I think you still looked hot."

He leaned down and kissed the end of my nose. "That's all that matters."

"Shall we go to bed, Mr. Bennett?"

"That sounds like a great idea, Miss Cain."

Eli draped an arm over my shoulders as we walked along the gravel drive that connected the two main Riverley houses. Now the moon was high in the sky, the cold air nipped at my exposed skin, but the blood running hot in my veins kept me warm. Would we have a repeat of last night? We were both kind of tired, but the thought of Eli's cock pressing into me again was like a shot of caffeine to my libido.

Until he stopped short, staring.

"Is that...?"

Oh. A green and white helicopter was parked on the lawn with two more identical choppers parked behind it. The decoys.

James had arrived.

"Marine One? Yes."

"The *president* is here?"

"He stops by from time to time. I think it's the only place he gets to relax and be himself."

A gaggle of Secret Service agents stopped us at the door, but Emmy popped out of a side room with Ana and waved us through.

"Are you joining us for drinks?" Emmy asked. "The

night's still...well, not young, but it's not over."

I looked at Eli, who shrugged.

"Why not?"

"We're in the music room."

We were walking along the corridor when the first chords from an electric guitar sounded. Eli and I looked at each other.

"It's James," Emmy said. "Did you know he and Black were in a band together at school?"

"Seriously?" I asked.

"Yeah. They used to get on better than they do now. I kind of got in the way of things." A smile flickered across her lips. "But they haven't got into a pissing match yet tonight, which is a good thing." She took Eli's hand. "Come on, you can show them how it's done. James'll switch to drums."

Of all the ways I'd imagined tonight ending, drinking apple juice while squashed between an assassin and the first lady, watching my boyfriend, the leader of the free world, and the president of the United States playing a pretty decent cover of "Born in the USA" wasn't top of the list.

Who needed Ishmael's brand of crazy?

I had it all right here at home.

WHAT'S NEXT?

The Blackwood Security series continues...

White Hot

When private investigator Daniela di Grassi is given a new case, the evidence is so compelling that even her client himself thinks he did it.

Ethan White was one of the world's top music producers, at least until last week, when his spectacular fall from grace began with the discovery of a mutilated college student in his bed.

A dead girl nobody cares about, cops with one agenda, and a prosecutor with another—nothing about this case is simple. And when Dan digs deeper into the mystery, the conflicting clues aren't the only thing she finds intriguing. Ethan's got his own secrets too.

As the worlds of black and white collide, who will come out on top?

Find out more here: www.elise-noble.com/white

If you enjoyed Red Alert, please consider leaving a review.

For an author, every review is incredibly important. Not only do they make us feel warm and fuzzy inside, readers consider them when making their decision whether or not to buy a book. Even a line saying you enjoyed the book or what your favourite part was helps a lot.

Want to stalk me?

For updates on my new releases, giveaways, and other random stuff, you can sign up for my newsletter on my website:
www.elise-noble.com

Facebook:
www.facebook.com/EliseNobleAuthor

Twitter: @EliseANoble

Instagram: @elise_noble

I also have a group on Facebook for my fans to hang out. They love the characters from my Blackwood and Trouble books almost as much as I do, and they're the first to find out about my new stories as well as throwing in their own ideas that sometimes make it into print!

And if you'd like to read my books for FREE, you can also find details of how to join my review team.

Would you like to join Team Blackwood?

www.elise-noble.com/team-blackwood

END OF BOOK STUFF

I felt a little guilty for what I did to Ryan in Ultraviolet, so I figured I'd better make it up to Tia and give her a story. I knew from the start that it would be a little different to other Blackwood books due to Tia's age and background. No way was I going to give that girl a gun (although in the dim and distant past when I was writing Pitch Black, I did consider turning her in to Emmy's sidekick—no, that would never have worked).

Mostly, I write in silence or with white noise in the background, but for Red, I played the tracks from the story instead. I must have listened to "Summer of '69" a hundred times, but my darling boyfriend finally took the hint and took me to see Bryan live, so it was all good.

The first part of the story turned out lighter, especially after Ultraviolet, which was pretty dark. I actually wrote the first draft of Red in 2014, right after I wrote Trouble in Paradise, and I think some of the feels from that book carried over. In my outline, there was never going to be a love triangle, but Cade wrote himself into the story out of nowhere and I'm quite pleased with the way it turned out.

So, will we hear more from Cade? I think so, yes. Maybe one of the other characters too...

In the meantime, I've spent the last three months

working on a little Emmy/Black project. Something I've wanted to do for a long time and finally, finally got done. There's a little creativity on Emmy's part, and there may or may not be a trip to Las Vegas at the end. More about that soon :)

Thanks as always to my awesome team. Firstly, my beta readers for this book: Jeff, Terri, Lina, Musi, Stacia, Jessica, Nikita, and Quenby. My editor/genius Amanda for correcting all my mistakes, and Abi for drawing Tia on the cover. And lastly to my proofreaders: John, Lizbeth, and Dominique.

OTHER BOOKS BY ELISE NOBLE

The Blackwood Security Series
Pitch Black
Into the Black
Forever Black
Gold Rush
Gray is my Heart
Neon (novella)
Out of the Blue
Ultraviolet
Red Alert
White Hot
The Scarlet Affair (2018)

The Blackwood Elements Series
Oxygen
Lithium
Carbon
Rhodium (2018)

The Blackwood UK Series
Joker in the Pack
Cherry on Top (novella)
Roses are Dead
Shallow Graves (2018)

The Trouble Series
Trouble in Paradise
Nothing but Trouble
24 Hours of Trouble

Standalone
Life
A Very Happy Christmas
Twisted

Printed in Great Britain
by Amazon